It has often been said that truth is merely the point of view we grasp onto for any one specific situation—to provide clarity and solidity. Consider the situation you are about to read in this book.

While much of this story is based on truth and actual events, so much remains unknown. For entertainment purposes, the authors have taken the liberty to embellish events and create a complete story.

Because of this, the authors, publishers, and all other parties involved make no claim of authenticity and, in actuality, offer this work as a fictional story. It has been clearly stated that Carl Begovich is Frank Mattich. Other than that, no references within should be taken to represent someone alive or dead .

Further, any similarities should be viewed as purely circumstantial and coincidental.

Published!
An Affiliate of Village Voices Gallery
1010 10 Avenue West, Bradenton, FL 34205

ISBN-13: 978-0-9846827-3-7
ISBN-10: 0984682732

Cover illustrations by Al Musitano

Manufactured in the United States

Carl Begovich, now retired, lives in Florida with his wife and three
daughters. He wrote the original screenplay based on events in his
life and co-wrote this novel. He is currently in negotiations through
his agent regarding the movie rights.

Al Musitano has written a number of published short stories,
including a story in an anthology. A columnist for the Bradenton
Herald's Accent section, and more recently for Creative Loafing, he
has written a dozen novels. He regularly attends critique meetings
with Sarasota Fiction Writer's, as well as co-chairing as group
leader for Florida Writers Association Manatee.

Steel Mill Mafia

The Pittsburgh Connection

By

Carl Begovich

&

Al Musitano

Acknowledgements:

We would like to personally thank our agent and publisher. A special thanks goes out to Dona Lee for her diligence in editing this work.

We cannot offer enough appreciation to our family members who put up with our working nearly twenty-four hours a day for just over two months. Thank you for your patience.

One special note. Our sincerest thanks goes to Mr. Martin Scorsese, director of Goodfellas. Although his schedule did not allow him the time to write a forward for us, he offered his best wishes for this endeavor.

Chapter 1

Raindrops sounding like hardened steel, as if made at a local factory, roared against the ground drowning out all other sound. The Ford Galaxy rolled to the curb smoothly, barely avoiding hopping over the top, its gentle engine noise smothered by Mother Nature. The car pulled to a stop in front of an abandoned warehouse. The engine went dead. The headlights winked out—fading away into the night without so much as a goodbye. No one got out.

A few trees stood majestically along the sidewalk. Standing like wooden pillars, they looked out of place in this part of town. In truth, most of this area had been wooded a hundred or so years before. Slowly, methodically, they'd been cleared away to make room for civilization. A few, like these fine specimens, remained as testament to an Earth almost completely abandoned to concrete.

Further along this same access road, several larger buildings lined up like a troop of Army trainees. They towered along the road only slightly askew in random, patternless fashion, suggesting they had been erected in an age when surveying was immature and inaccurate, but construction was strong and lasting. The buildings would be here in another hundred years—and probably still unused.

The rain struck hard at the car, forcing the metal to cool much quicker than normal. The continuous thrumming accented the ticking from under the hood. The now almost-quiet engine joined the dull roar of the night storm, transformed into a symphony of man and nature, threatening to drown out any random thoughts going through Frank's head. The windows, made translucent by the unbroken stream of water, began to fog. Heavy water continued to fall from clouds that hadn't looked so imposing earlier, though some rain seemed imminent even then.

Frank sat silently in the car, trying to get comfortable, his six foot-four stature crammed tight. Even a large sedan barely accommodated him. He sat with another man, a smaller man. The storm had settled over the town with anger. Frank wondered if it might be trying to tell them to forget this crazy idea and go home.

Nights in Pittsburgh, Pennsylvania could become extremely cold, but none were worse than when almost-freezing rain fell in opaque sheets, blinding even the sharpest vision. Water pounded mercilessly at the pavement, then ran off in tiny rivers seeking drainage ditches for release. Once underground, it would become part of whatever recycling system nature and man had devised for it. Someday, Frank thought, he'd be drinking some of this deluge. Irrationally, he decided to be extra careful where he stepped or what he dropped into the water, even though he had no intention of getting out of the car.

Despite the deafening rain and gun-shot thunder, roaring above it all was the silence that had fallen between the two men in the car. No words could pierce it. The radio had been broken for weeks. Frank looked to his right.

His friend from childhood, Eddie Schultz, sat beside him, listening to the music of the falling water droplets. The look on his too-attractive-for-a-man face suggested he enjoyed the rain. His eyes remained closed and his lips slightly curled up at the corners. Two years younger than Frank, 'Schultzie'—as his friends called him—looked peaceful and happy, like he'd just eaten a big meal.

Schultzie had always been a good friend. He stood with Frank through many of life's little tests and could always be counted on. Frank felt the same way toward Schultzie, and often proved it, like now. Schultzie had a knack for getting into trouble, even when he hadn't done anything wrong. But he was no angel.

"Frank, what are you worried about?" Schultzie asked, pulling Frank out of his thoughts.

Frank wasn't the type to back out of anything, especially when it involved money. Lots of money. But something about this felt wrong and the rain did nothing but amplify his ominous mood. Schultzie carried his own brand of trouble around with him like a second set of car keys. Frank couldn't shake the feeling no matter how much his friend assured him. Nevertheless Schultzie sounded quite sure of himself as he spoke.

"I don't like it," Frank spat out for at least the tenth time.

"Aw, what's not to like, buddy?"

"It's not how we do business, that's all," Frank explained.

As soon as the words left Frank's mouth, a clap of thunder held them both in a moment of terror, as if a gun had been shot off right between them. *Christ, I feel like I'm at the movies,* Frank thought.

"Relax. It's not like it's your money, Frankie" Schultzie said, waving his hand in front like he was swatting at a bug. Schultzie was the only person alive that still called him that.

Friend or not, Frank always thought Schultzie had a way of dismissing any real cause for concern. He acted far too casual during moments of intensity when he should be at the height of his attention. The habit aggravated Frank.

Frank planned his deals so carefully, and taking them lightly seemed too much like a slap in the face. He reminded himself that it wouldn't be any better if the deals went sour all the time, either.

He shifted in his seat and glared at Schultzie. He felt anger at being kept from what he'd rather be doing on such a fine evening. And stubbornness was never attractive. But the other man had no intention of changing his mind about this deal.

9

"You're right," Frank insisted over the rain. "It's *not* my money. That was two-hundred 'G's of Mike Riley's money. Now it's two-hundred 'G's of coke. And it's my ass if this doesn't go down right." Frank poked his finger firmly into his own chest. "Mine!"

"Hey, Frankie. Come on. We got two-hundred grand worth of coke there. We can sell it for three. Then we give Mike Riley back his money and we're each fifty-grand richer. I'm a genius."

"I don't know why I let you talk me into these bullshit crazy schemes."

"Because you know that I'm the brains of the outfit."

"Yeah right, Einstein."

A gentle uneasiness within Frank, far greater than butterflies, grew into the size of a small lizard running up the walls of his stomach and falling back down. Running up and falling down. Frank wasn't used to being afraid, he normally controlled the lizard. But not this night.

Tonight the lizard raced chaotically out of control. Tonight Frank's stomach churned. Schultzie, his life-long friend, best of all friends, could be hurt. In fact some sixth sense of Frank's told him something would for sure go terribly wrong. His instincts were rarely wrong. He just wanted to protect his friend.

"Why don't I tag along with you, just in case?" Frank asked.

"You can't do that."

"Why not?"

"The deal was, *just* me, Frankie. They see someone else and it'll be blown. Besides, look at you."

"What?" Frank felt like he'd grown a third eye.

"All clean shaven and sharp haircut. You look like a fucking narc."

Frank chuckled nervously. All he wanted was a simple life with his wife and kids.

10

Maybe open a store or a night club. It didn't matter, as long as he made a clean start. Maybe, if Schultzie pulled this off, he'd be fifty thousand closer. Eddie walked away from a number of situations with barely a scrape in the past.

Even though he had the poor luck to get into awkward positions—he also did fairly well falling out of them. Perhaps it would be okay, after all. *My nerves are spasming all over the place. Maybe I'm getting just a little too old for this shit.* Frank tried to relax, ignoring the aches in his body that confirmed his last thought about age. *Probably just all this freezing God damned rain.* He rotated his shoulder. After a few moments, he managed to relax…a little.

"How much longer?" he asked Schultzie.

The younger man looked at his watch. He brought his arm closer to his face to better see in the dark. "Another couple minutes, now. Eleven sharp, remember?" He reached into the back seat and lifted out the duffel bag, straining to get it over the headrests.

"Jeez, I wish this would just be over. You're always coming up with these get rich quick schemes."

"Christ, Frankie. You sound like Ralph Kramden."

"Yeah well, you look like Ed Norton."

"Fuck you."

"Hey, Norton!" Frank called in a reasonable imitation of the old Honeymooners character. "Come on down here, I've got something to show you. Ha, ha!"

"Hey there, Ralphy boy. How's it goin' there, pal-o-mine?" Schultzie shot back in an attempt to do his part, as if he too were in the show. Neither man had the right to consider quitting their day jobs, but both laughed at their own boundless talent.

"Get outta here, ya bum," Frank said in a more natural voice. Then he added with increased sincerity, "Please be careful, Eddie."

"Damn, Frank. It's like riding with my mother. I'm only two years younger than you."

"I'm *not* your mother."

"If you wash my undershorts, I won't be able to tell the difference."

Frank shook his head fervently from one side to the other, but said nothing. He found it difficult even to speak. Schultzie smiled wanly and opened his door, staring at the sheets of water he had to run through. It showed no signs of slowing for him or anyone else. Frank took a deep breath and grabbed Eddie's arm.

"You sure about this guy?"

"Yeah, I'm sure. He's good."

Frank let go of his friend. *Good for what?* "I'm serious, buddy. Be careful."

"I will. Just wait here. I won't be long," Schultzie reassured.

"It'll take a while to test it," Frank retorted.

"They tested it last night to be sure. They were amazed at the quality."

"So the deal is set? What about the money?"

"I told them to bring me large bills. I'll count it quick and get the hell out of there."

"Yeah," Frank responded without conviction. "I'll wait *ten* minutes. No more. Then I'm coming in."

"Hey, have a little faith in me, man. I haven't got you killed…yet," Schultzie added, stepping out of the car.

The door slammed shut, jolting Frank more than the thunder had. He sat back and watched the shadowy figure holding his coat over his head with one hand and carrying the duffel bag with the other, as he disappeared into the door big enough for an aircraft hangar. No one else went in or out from where Frank could see.

He sat in the car staring, once again, at the tiny stream that flowed under the car. It had now grown into a river he could submerge his entire hand in. An occasional leaf floated along like a life raft for a bug. They would all flow under the car and through the grate covering the sewer below.

A long while later, when Frank looked at his watch, he noticed only eight minutes had passed. He sat nervously, gripping the steering wheel, then wringing his hands, then looking at his watch again. *Where the hell is he? How much longer could it take?* The storm raged on without mercy, just a thin pane of glass away. Frank tried to see or hear anything from the warehouse.

"Aw, hell." Frank looked at his watch again. 11:09. He blinked in surprise. It felt like an hour.

He reached for his own door handle, wrapping his fingers around the chilled metal. Thunder, suddenly less expected than before, boomed again. The hairs on Frank's neck stood on end. He felt goose bumps on his arms. This clap sounded different, echoing as if in a tin can. It didn't *roll* like thunder.

Frank began to feel the worst may have happened. His hand, still resting on the handle, faltered. He searched his field of vision for any sign of his friend exiting the building and returning. Several long seconds went by, but in the end, Frank pulled the handle up and shouldered the door open, letting the storm in.

He stepped into the rain and headed, apprehensively, toward the large, open doorway, oblivious to the water pouring down the collar of his jacket. Frank hadn't even bothered to turn it up for protection. Dim, orange light, from a street lamp, washed only a few feet past the entrance, then died quickly, giving way to a heavier darkness inside. He neared the edge and turned, backing against the wall. At times like these, he wished he carried a gun. He felt sure he wouldn't find anything good inside.

He rushed in. The faint light from outside reflected off several utility fluorescents mounted overhead, no longer any real help in the darkness. After a few moments, Frank could see in all directions. He spun quickly, trying to appear armed and ready. He turned to face each man, convinced of their formidability.

But no one occupied the building. No signs of a struggle. No empty bullet shells. No money. No coke. No Schultzie. The rain sang its song even louder against the tin roof, echoing throughout the almost empty warehouse. A few crates and one rusted piece of old machinery Frank didn't recognize occupied one corner, guarding over the emptiness that filled the rest of the building.

Tears fell down Frank's cheeks, joining with the rain. He ran to the opposite door, as large as the first, which allowed a strong breeze through the building. He stared into the impossible-to-pierce darkness, clouded by rain. Frank blinked away the water. Did a shadow move or did he just *wish* he saw something? Trying to force his eyes to adjust quickly, he shouted into the emptiness.

"Eddie! Are you there?" He yelled again. "Eddie!"

Chapter 2

Frankie's dad worked sometimes sixteen hours a day at the steel mill and his mother cleaned at the school until late dinner time. Emigrating from Yugoslavia at the ripe old age of fifteen, Joseph Mattich wanted the *all-American* life. He wanted to keep his family safe and happy, with all their needs met. To Frankie—now at the edge of twelve, looking up at his father—it all seemed so elusive. *If my dad can't do it, how can I?*

Frank looked down the row of houses all connected, facing the river and the Duquesne railroad track, sitting peacefully with their backs to a hill. Behind the houses, before the hill, sat a dirt alleyway and every Monday the garbage truck would glide through as easy as you please. They stopped only to pick up and empty the cans, then they'd move right on through without so much as a wave.

Joseph spent only a few hours at home, mostly to sleep. But when he was awake, he sat in his chair watching the old black and white T.V., reading the newspaper, or talking to one of the kids about their homework. Frankie became quite self-sufficient, growing up quicker than kids whose parents were home more often.

Any day looked pretty much like another, as Frank walked through his front door, usually with his best friend, Eddie Schultz, in tow. Frank had become Eddie's friend more than a year before when the younger lad got cornered by a couple of bullies. Frank found out later the bullies were friends of 'Snake' Barron's. 'Snake'—the meanest kid around, would beat up anyone with little or no cause. Most kids backed away when he walked by.

The bullies, Ernst—another German, but the other kids disliked him so much they called him Hitler, and Eric—a Norwegian they called Red after Eric the Red, pushed Eddie into an alley as he walked home from school one day. By total accident, Frank witnessed their sudden departure from the sidewalk.

As the boys disappeared between two buildings, Frank wandered over to see what they were doing. When he realized they were going to beat the little guy, Frank stepped in the way and pushed the bigger two off.

"Go pick on someone your own size," Frank growled.

They grumbled the usual lines of bully-shit and took off.

"I could have handled them myself," Eddie said, offended.

"I'm sure you could have."

Chapter 3

Frank sometimes felt embarrassed by his family. A few years before he was born, his sister, Maddy, died. While he didn't understand everything that happened, he knew the Schultz home felt happier when he and Eddie entered. Something dark lived in the Mattich home, something Frank couldn't describe or understand.

"What's it all about, Frank?" Eddie asked, one grey, fall day.

"Well, no one likes to talk about it, but I know this much. One night Maddy complained about a bellyache and Mom said Dad ignored it. We don't go to the doctor's much. Anyway, it was her appendix. And it burst. She got real sick and had to stay at the hospital."

"Wow. I went there once 'cuz of a fever. I hated it."

"Yeah well, Dad spent every minute he could with her. You know, sitting by her bed. My Mom didn't sit with her as much because she had to be home for the other kids. But one time Dad went home because the nurse told him to get some rest and she would watch my sister closely. To hear Mom tell it, he shouldn't have left. Anyway, somehow her stitches tore out. She died before Mom and Dad got back to the hospital the next day," Frankie finished, weakly.

"But it wasn't your Dad's fault," Eddie offered with compassion.

"I know, but my Mom still won't talk to him about it."

"Wasn't that a long time ago?"

"Before I was born. I think Mom still blames him, though."

17

"Wow, that's tough."

"Don't tell anyone I told you, okay, Eddie?"

"I won't tell. Let's go eat."

"Okay."

A few minutes later they walked into Frank's home.

"Hello, Eddie. Would you like to eat with us?" Sarah Mattich's soft voice invited Frank's friend.

"Yes, Mrs. Mattich. Thank you."

"Frankie, tell your father dinner is ready," his mother said, giving him a hug.

"Don't coddle him so much, Sarah. He's gonna turn into a sissy."

"Look how tall he is, Joseph. How can anyone ever think he's a sissy?"

Frank's dad harrumphed and sat at the table.

With so little to do in the house except get volunteered for extra chores or homework, the boys spent all available time outside. Late summer drifted past and school started, but the warm weather lingered on.

"Want to go play some basketball?" Frank asked Eddie when the meal had finished.

"I gotta go home," he replied, forlornly.

"I'll catch you tomorrow."

Eddie left and Frank headed for the court which was really just an old parking area where someone planted a hoop. Three guys were there. Frank didn't know them—they were new in the neighborhood. But he'd come to play.

"Hey, guys," he called.

The shorter of the three looked over. "Hey, kid. What're you doing here?"

"I'm going to play some ball," came Frank's humble reply.

"You can't play. You're too short. Why don't you go home to mommy, kid?"

"I came to play some ball," Frank repeated, determined.

"Oh, you came to play some ball?" the boy taunted.

"Leave the kid alone, Dante," one of the taller boys called out. "You'll make him cry."

Frank wasn't going to cry. He stood his ground and even took a step forward. If he'd been facing 'Snake' Barron, he'd probably get his ass handed to him. But 'backing down' wasn't in Frank Mattich's vocabulary.

"Oh," the shorter one said. "A tough guy. So what do you think, tough guy. Want to play some two-on-two?"

"Sure," Frank answered without hesitation.

"My name is Dante DeMayo. These are my big brothers. That's Luciano, over there. People call him Lucky because of the gangster. And this one is Angelo, but we call him Skippy," Dante said softer. Then... "You got a name?"

"My name is Frank. People call me Frank."

"Well, Frank, or should I call you Frank, how about you and Skippy play me and Lucky?"

"I hate it when you call me 'Skippy', Dante. Quit it or I'll pound you," Angelo said.

Dante offered him a raspberry.

Frank looked at Angelo, who towered over him. *This is going to be a piece of cake.* "Okay. Two-on-two," he repeated.

Dante's ball looked to be in better shape so Frank tossed his aside. They didn't waste any time getting down to business. Dante threw the ball into play and Luciano caught it quickly. When he drove to the basket for his lay-up, Frank went to block his path. But Luciano plowed right over Frank, knocking him to the hard ground.

"Hey, kid," Luciano called. "Are you okay?"

"I'm fine." Frank gave no indication that he'd been winded by the fall. *So, that's the way they want to play.*

"Two points," Dante called out.

Frank threw the ball in to Skippy, who held it away from Dante's long reach, then began to dribble. Frank ran across the court and 'accidentally' bumped Luciano off the court just in time to catch the pass from Skippy. He jumped up and made the point.

"Tie score," Frank gloated. "You okay, Lucky?"

Luciano dusted himself off but looked otherwise unscathed. "Yeah, I'm okay." He smiled but his eyes looked crazed.

"Good," Frank said. *That Luciano guy is really enjoying this 'tackle basketball'.*

In a half hour the score was 40 – 38 with Luciano and Dante in the lead. Frank felt tired and pain spiked from a few bruises. Darkness began falling and he'd have to head home soon, but he couldn't walk away just like that.

The ball came into play again. Frank had control. Suddenly Luciano ran across and caught him in the arm, knocking him off balance.

"Foul!" Frank called.

"What do you think this is, the NBA?" Luciano chuckled.

"Hey," Frank reminded. "We still gotta have *some* rules."

"Well, we can have rules tomorrow. We gotta get home. It's late."

"Maybe I'll catch you guys again real soon," Frank uttered as he bent to pick up his own ball.

As Frank stood, Luciano was there. He glared down at Frank with a scowl, hands on his hips. Frank had to crane his neck to look him in the eye, but he didn't back away.

"You're okay, Frank." Luciano's face broke into an unexpected smile.

"Thanks, Lucky. So are you."

On his way home, Frank had one recurring thought. *Those guys are crazy.* After a while, Frank realized he liked *crazy*.

Chapter 4

"Don't ask my brother why we call him 'Skippy', okay?" Dante asked. His first day at school filled with class changing and new teachers, Frank showed him around. They sat together at lunch.

"Why not?" Frank asked around a mouthful of bologna sandwich.

"He'll get *really* pissed."

"He's a big guy. I don't want him pissed at me."

They ate for a moment in silence.

"Why *do* you call him 'Skippy'?" Frank dared. "He doesn't seem to like it very much."

"Skippy used to date a girl named Julie Watts. When they walked home from school together they'd hold hands. One time they were actually skipping."

Frank chuckled.

"It's funny, but he gets pretty ripped about it," Dante explained.

The boys laughed heartily. Frank and Dante became friends, hanging with Eddie as often as possible.

Later in the year, at some afterschool function, Eddie and Frank discovered a guy trying to do silly magic tricks with cards outside the auditorium. At first Eddie thought it was some school function and turned away. But when he saw Dante standing in the small crowd watching intently, he decided to join. Frank followed.

The guy sitting at the table shuffled the cards and moved them quickly. He seemed so determined, but he couldn't make the cards move quite right. Eddie watched and laughed.

"Hey, Dante," Frank called. "Who is this guy?"

"Some goon trying to be Harry Houdini."

"He needs a lot of practice," Eddie offered.

"What are you, their mascot?" the guy said to Eddie, who stood a foot shorter than Frank and Dante.

Eddie immediately felt threatened. He'd always had a pretty face for a boy. After fighting his way through most of middle school, Eddie toughened and most of the other guys didn't want to mess with him anymore—even the ones who had beat on him before.

But obviously this card playing idiot didn't know about Eddie's reputation. This *mascot* was going to wedge the guy's ass into the toilet seat and…

"Deal the cards, you little weasel." The growling sound spewed from the chubby mouth along with a few crumbs of a Twinkie. "It's my turn."

About a dozen kids, standing around watching and betting, suddenly had somewhere else to be. The card dealer didn't show any fear as he looked up at the school bully. Eddie recognized Barron right away. Aptly nicknamed 'Snake', Eddie couldn't remember if he ever heard the kid's *real* first name. Frank and Dante stood close by. Eddie moved off to the side, ready to jump in and get down to it.

"Okay," the dealer said passively.

Houdini moved the cards with a practiced hand. Eddie watched, amazed. The kid didn't look like he needed as much practice as Eddie first thought. Three cards lay on the table. He put them face up at first so everyone could see, then he turned them over. He looked Snake in the eye, obviously having mastered the art

23

of distraction. The trick in con games like these was to keep the other person's eye looking away from the cards on the table. It only took a moment.

He shuffled the cards around, mixing their positions to confuse, getting them into a spot that resembled the original appearance. Without knowing which card was which, they all looked alike, and it seemed wiser to guess.

"Find the queen."

Snake Barron studied the cards intently. His breathing sounded like bull snorts. There were no marks on the backs of the cards, no way to tell them apart. He seemed to be searching for some insight or divine intervention, something to give him a clue, maybe just an intelligent thought. With no outward signs to choose from, Snake picked randomly.

"This is easy," he said with mock confidence. "The one on the left."

"Your left or mine?" the kid in the chair asked, politely. His manners seemed only to aggravate Snake and make him snort even deeper and quicker.

Snake pointed.

The kid flipped the card over and they all viewed a king. The bully slammed his fist to the table, a vein in his temple throbbed in frustrated anger. He threw down another dollar and leaned close. Eddie could smell Barron's breath. The Twinkies did nothing to cover the stink of beer.

"Deal again."

This time, Snake watched the cards intently, despite efforts to draw his focus away. The dealer moved his hands side-to-side—side-to-side, overlapping and under-lapping with no regularity. Eddie didn't know where the queen hid, anymore than Snake. Snake leaned close to the cards.

24

Barron picked the card he believed to be the queen and lost, again. A couple more tries and he'd lost all his money. In true, simple-minded form, the fat troll moved forward. He reached out and grabbed the dealer's arms, pulling him up and closer.

Dante moved forward and wedged himself between Snake and his intended victim. Frank and Eddie moved up behind him. For a few moments, tension hovered around them, but together they stood against Snake, unwavering. Some of the other kids—still standing nearby but at a distance—held their breath.

Snake looked up into Dante's eyes. A moment of hesitation flashed across Snake's face. Despite knowing Dante to be many pounds lighter, Snake decided on prudence. Eddie remembered an old adage about discretion being the better part of fear—or something.

The bully walked away in a huff, striding toward the road to escape an embarrassing loss of face that only made him angrier. A few of the other kids dared to snicker at his back. Smiling and waving a hand full of dollar bills in the air, the card dealer had won a rather large victory over a power that claimed to have so much authority.

"Ice cream, anybody?"

"What's your name, Slick?" Frank asked.

"Victor Horvath."

"Slick Vic. I like that. I'm Frank and these are my best buds, Eddie and Dante."

"Pleasure," Vic said without enthusiasm.

Maybe he don't want any new friends, Eddie thought. *Or maybe he's just an asshole.*

"That was great, what you did to Snake!" Frank exclaimed. "How'd you do it?"

"A good magician never reveals the secrets of his trade."

"Yeah, well, when you're good, we'll forget you told us," Eddie said. "Now, come on. How'd you do it?"

"The trick is to keep the cards moving. When you move the right card to the left you set it down and pick up the one already sitting there."

"Of course," Frank said. "That makes sense. But I watched. The card wasn't where it should have been. You slipped it over somewhere."

"That's right. After the first couple moves, I didn't *always* switch cards when I moved to the other side. Sometimes I held onto the same card and brought it back instead of the other one."

"Well no one deserved it more than Snake," Eddie chanted.

"So maybe I don't need so much practice after all?"

"No, you *need* the practice. But Snake is stupid enough to lose, even to you."

"*Thanks*," Vic sneered.

"Hey," Frank added. "I don't care what Eddie says. I think you were great."

"*Merci, Monsieur,*" Vic said in a really crappy French accent.

Chapter 5

In the weeks and months that followed and the four became almost inseparable, Frank noticed that Vic had a sharp mind. The others joked about him becoming a brain surgeon. Vic told them he wanted to be a lawyer—they made lots of money. He said *slight-of-hand* was one of the skills necessary to be a lawyer. Vic claimed he practiced often, but you'd never know it watching his clumsy performances.

Frank never heard Dante mention what he wanted to be when he grew up. But he had no doubt Dante would marry and have lots of kids. Only twelve and he already went whichever way his dick pointed. Frank and the others knew a little about sex, mostly what they'd learned from other kids at school. The three didn't know if Dante ever *had* sex with a girl, but he sure *sounded* experienced.

He talked like he knew how it really felt. The other three sat and listened in awe when Dante rambled on about some conquest or other. And they learned more about sex from Dante than any other source. Without knowing if any of it was true, Dante really made it sound great.

Two streets over, a girl named Cathy Vincenti had eyed Dante on several occasions. She had, what Frank's mother would call—with distaste—a *reputation*. This, above all else, fascinated all the boys. They wanted to meet the girl with such a magical thing in her possession. They wanted to meet a girl who would show them her body parts. Cathy stood tall for a girl and her ass wiggled provocatively when she walked. As was common among Italian girls before they had kids, Cathy had a lithe, skinny figure.

This didn't deter Dante from sniffing around as soon as she gave him one of those girly looks from the corner of her eye. Frank thought most of the rumors about her were probably exaggerated. Then he saw the look she gave Dante and changed his mind. No *good* girl would look at a boy's crotch like someone staring at an ice cream cone.

No matter what anyone else thought, Frank had seen Dante disappear down Railroad Street toward Cathy's house on several occasions. He didn't follow and Dante could have been going almost anywhere. But somehow, Frank *knew* Dante might be experiencing something they all dreamed about—the magic and mystique of a girl's naked body.

Frank never considered what he wanted to be when he grew up. His ultimate goal—*the American dream*—just like his father. Nothing more. Although Frank saw a different path to the dream—through sports, perhaps—the end result needed to be the same.

Chapter 6

The crack of the bat sounded just like rifle fire and the ball bolted into play. The October sun sank with an orange glow, still on the warm side but weakening. The ratty, worn ball arched through the air with the grace of a ballerina, unaware of the impact awaiting it. Vic caught it effortlessly and Frank was out.

The boys switched sides. The inning was over. The alleyway behind their houses offered little room to play ball, yet the four managed easily. They walked past each other, smiling and exchanging hand slaps.

"Here comes Babe Ruth stepping up to the plate!" Schultzie announced as he always did before his turn at bat.

"Why you always gotta be the Babe?" Frankie asked.

Vic and Dante stopped to join in the good-natured argument before the game continued. "Yeah," Victor admonished, "why can't you be a Pirate? Like Ralph Kiner or Clemente?"

"Because the Babe is the best baseball player ever," Schultzie stated stubbornly.

"What's that got to do with you?" Vic asked, taunting him.

"Hey, come on, you guys. Let's play. He can call himself whatever he wants," Frank concluded, turning toward Victor. "He's still just Eddie Schultz. Nothing any of us can do about that."

Vic snickered.

"Hey!" Eddie objected. "What's wrong with being Eddie Schultz? You guys should be so lucky."

"Yeah," Dante chimed in. "I should cut my legs off at the knee and see about having half my brain removed so I can be just like you."

"And we could all call you Lucky, like your brother," Frank added.

The three boys laughed, but Eddie didn't join them.

"Very funny, guys. You just wait," he called out, indignantly, as the others made their way to the field. "One day I'll be as famous as the Babe. Just wait and see."

"Hey," Dante called from the field. "I've only got about a hundred or so years to live. You think we could play a little ball while we wait?"

I'm not going to let them get me with their talk. I want to play ball when I grow up. What do they know? Frank's two years older than me. He's too old to understand what I'm going to be. Vic thinks 'law' is the only profession on Earth. And Dante is only interested in getting laid. What do they know?

Eddie focused his eyes on Frank's swinging arm winding up for the pitch. Laying the bat out in front of him, Eddie tried to give Frank an idea where to put the ball. Determined to show them what he was really made of, Eddie swung hard when the ball came toward him. He pushed the heavy wood—with all his might—around toward the fence behind where they played.

The bat struck nothing but air. Eddie looked at the wood, searching for holes. When he found none, he returned to his stance, ready for the next pitch. He would get it this time. He'd hit that ball into the middle of next week.

The ball flew toward him again, slicing through the air like a jet plane. Straight and fast, the ball went right over the plate and Eddie twisted hard. The bat sang and Eddie could feel the vibrations into the handle. He dropped it and rubbed his hands together.

After hitting the ball past both Vic and Dante, Eddie ran the unmanned bases with one hand waving at the imaginary fans all cheering him in his mind. He rounded second but halted on third. No sense pushing the limit until someone offered him money.

Frank stood on the mound as Dante stepped up to the plate. Frank didn't look forward to Dante's 'at bat'. Neither did Vic and Eddie. Dante stood taller and had more muscle than the others. But it wasn't his homerun reputation that scared them—it was old man *Douche Bag*.

Frankie didn't think a meaner man existed anywhere in the world. Mr. Duchenbach lived alone. Being such a nasty man, Frank couldn't imagine anyone living *with* him for long. His back yard bordered the alley, too. Most of the alley was too narrow to be useful, but the one clearing large enough for a baseball game sat in back of Duchenbach's yard. His backyard caught more fly balls than Vic did. But Mr. Duchenbach, lovingly nick-named *Mr. Douche Bag*, collected their balls and wouldn't return them.

Dante hit the ball with his usual finesse. The ball splatted into the muddy back yard. *Douche Bag*—standing outside at the time—picked up the ball, examined it closely for a second, then went inside, taking the ball with him—as usual.

All four boys stood at the fence, pleading with their eyes. Though they'd called for him to throw back their ball, the slamming screen door signaled the end of all barter. Four solemn faces just watched in despair.

Frank spoke with sadness. "I had to collect soda pop bottles for three weeks and take them to the grocery store to get the deposits to scrape together the seventy-five cents to buy that ball."

With no more balls and no money, Frank sighed and sagged against the fence. Dante's face showed anger and his eyes grew

31

fierce. A little bit of that DeMayo crazy showed through. He stared as if he wanted to make fire come out.

"Someday, I'm gonna get that guy."

"Yeah, good luck," one of the others said, dejectedly.

Chapter 7

A few months later, as January ate away at any remaining semblance of warmth, Frankie got a brand new football for Christmas and the boys were tossing it around in the alley. This time Eddie fumbled, and the ball bounced into *Douche Bag's* yard. As the old man picked it up and headed inside, something very different happened—something that surprised the four boys.

Just before the door closed behind the old man, he turned and gave them a sinister smile. It was an almost imperceptible, evil thing that crawled across his face like spiders from a hole in the ground—just below black, empty eyes. His nostrils flared briefly, then the door shut, and he was gone.

At that moment, Frank *knew* the old man wasn't crazy or retarded. A deep seated meanness showed through his eyes when he smiled. Frank could tell the old man knew what he was doing and enjoyed that it hurt the boys.

"*Yebem Ti.*"

"What does that mean, Frank?" Dante asked.

"It's Croatian or Serbian. It means *fuck you.*"

The boys banged their fists on the fence, chanting a chorus of, "*Yebem Ti. Yebem Ti. Yebem Ti.*"

*   *   *

Two nights later, several hours after nightfall, the boys gathered around the front of *Douche Bag's* house. A layer of snow lay on the ground as they crouched against his front porch and discussed last-minute plans.

"Everybody got it?" Frank asked.

"Yeah," in chorus.

"Any questions?"

"Yeah," Vic said. "Why does Dante get to do the fun part?"

"Because I thought of it," Dante enforced. "Got a problem with that?"

"Uh—no," Vic answered, not sure if he should be afraid or burst out laughing.

"Okay, let's go," Frank ordered.

Vic took off running and crouched near *Douche Bag's* car. Frankie and Schultzie ran to the front porch and hid behind the glider. Dante stayed put. Once in place, they all nodded they were ready.

Vic opened *Douche Bag's* car door and took the pipe he carried from his back pocket. Once he got it jammed into the seat, he wedged it against the horn. Shattering the quiet of night, it sounded deafening. Vic shut the door and ran to hide behind a neighbor's car, next to Dante.

A couple lights came on down the street as the horn blared and Dante wondered if they might get caught by an ornery neighbor. Then old man *Douche Bag* jerked his front door open with fury. His eyes turned directly to his car.

"You little bastards," he called to the night. "I'll get you for this."

Wearing only slippers on his feet, the man ran through the snow to his car and disengaged the pipe. While the sound still rang in the air, Frank and Eddie slipped inside the house with a plan of their own.

Schultzie locked the door behind them and then went from window to window. Frankie collected their balls and anything else that looked like it didn't belong in an old man's house. *Douche Bag* headed back to his porch and tried to turn the knob. His face twisted with amazement. He pounded his fist against the door, looking more like a madman than ever.

"You little bastards! I know who you are!"

Inside, Frank saw through the window as Vic ran past Dante. The plan was for Vic to go around back to meet Frank and Eddie to help, leaving Dante alone to have his fun. Frank saw Dante stand. The lighter he'd *borrowed* from his father ignited quickly.

Inside, Frank and Eddie made their way out the back door and into the alley with arms full of their property and other various kid stuff. Dante pulled a bag from its hiding place and lit it, tossing it to the porch next to the old man. He ran away quickly without being seen. The old man heard the plop and turned. Seeing the fire, he reacted instinctively. He stomped it out. The bag, filled with dog shit Dante had collected, sprayed everywhere. Some even ran inside the old man's slipper.

"What the hell?" Duchenbach swore to no one.

Cold wind sent chills through the old man.

"See you later, *Douche Bag*," Dante called from down the street. "Don't forget to bundle up." A nasty laugh filtered through his voice.

"Shit!" the old man exclaimed as the odor drifted up to his nose. "Wait 'till I get you punks!"

After depositing their recovered treasure in Frank's back yard, the boys snuck back around to enjoy *Douche Bag's* dilemma. Wearing only a robe, slippers, a tank top, and his underwear, shivers wracked the old man's body. He stared into the night, his shoulders stooped in defeat.

Two months passed before the boys found themselves in that alley with another ball. Eddie fumbled again. He never did master the art of football. It fell into Duchenbach's yard. The old man stood outside sweeping snow from his steps. As soon as he saw the ball, he set down his broom and approached it. The boys held their collective breath.

He looked at the ball, then at the boys, and back at the ball. He bent and picked it up and stared at it for a minute. Then, with a shrug that seemed more for effect than anything else, he tossed it back to them. They cheered and slapped high fives. The man offered a grimaced smile, knowing they'd won. The conflict was over.

"We did it!" Dante exclaimed.

"Yeah," Eddie added, "we pulled off our first caper."

"Caper?" Vic asked.

"It's those little round, green things your mom puts on her ham," Frank said with a straight face.

"See what we can do when we work together?" Dante suggested.

"We can make a ham?" Eddie asked with sarcasm.

"No, stupid. We can get what we want."

"Don't call me stupid," Eddie shot back.

"Yeah, we can get what we want," Vic repeated. "We're like...*the Immigrant Gang*."

All the boys enjoyed a good laugh and returned to their game.

Then Frank remembered his manners and yelled back, "Thanks, Mr. Duchenbach!"

Chapter 8

After graduating high school, Frank went to work at Kennywood. That summer at the amusement park made his father so proud. It was just a job—minimum wage—but he felt more like a grown man for having it.

Working at a refreshment stand by the pool offered other rewards. Girls in the tiniest bikinis hung around that pool. Some people went to the amusement park for the rides, but the girls *loved* the pool. And Frank discovered he loved the girls.

At first he felt uncomfortable with his reactions. He certainly didn't want to become like Dante, chasing anything with a skirt. Hell, even the DeMayo's pet cat was female! And while Frank responded to the girls in a manner he thought might be wrong, it felt really good.

Frank had only been working there a couple weeks when Vic dropped by for a visit.

"How's it going, Frank?" Vic asked, eyeing a wiggling ass to his left.

"Going good now, Vic. Job doesn't pay much." Frank waved his hand. "The customers pay with refreshment tickets, so I don't handle any cash."

"How much is 'not much'?"

"Sixty bucks a week."

"That sucks."

"You know it."

"Well, knowing you, you'll think of some way to make some real money off this—," he rolled his eyes over the little refreshment shack, "—thing."

"Oh, I already have. And here comes opportunity's knock, right now."

Wendell Jones looked like a little kid, but he was actually only a year younger than Frank. He pushed a cart around—one of those silly vendor contraptions—selling ice cream sandwiches. He approached cautiously and slipped something into Frank's hand. Then he wandered off.

"What the hell was that?"

"What was what?" Frank replied, trying to sound innocent and failing.

"Come on, man. What have you got going on here?"

"Well, you see," Frank leaned in closer so he didn't have to speak so loud, "I give Wendell my ice cream sandwiches, which he sells for cash. No refreshment tickets with him. I keep two-thirds and he gets the rest."

"Wow, cool. How much do you make?"

"I can make as much as an extra three hundred on most weekends. All I have to do is wash out the soda pop cups and reuse them to keep my inventory accurate."

"Frank, you're still my hero, man." Vic smiled fully, enjoying the continued success of his friend.

The summer wore on. Frank knew the job wouldn't last much longer as the amusement park closed for the fall and winter season soon. He considered his options but always came back to the same conclusion. He wanted to go back to school.

"Hey, man. How you doing?"

Frank turned, surprised, recognizing the voice.

"Hey, Schultzie. What's up?" They slapped hands and smiled.

"Just trying to cool off. Hey, Frank, you remember my girl, Patty?"

Frank turned to the girl standing next to Schultzie—a pink ribbon tying her pony tail back. Frank thought she had a pretty-enough face. Kind of a 'girl-next-door' look, although no one living next to Frank looked even half as cute. Eddie had been completely taken with her for almost a year.

"Of course. Good to see you again, Patty." Frank offered a friendly smile.

"Likewise, Frank."

"And," Schultzie said, reaching behind him, "I'd like you to meet someone else."

Frank couldn't be sure how he managed to miss the other girl until then. She couldn't have hidden completely behind Schultzie and Patty, but there she stood—smiling. Frank felt like he was looking at the stars. His heart fluttered and an awkward smile came on his face.

"This," Schultzie continued, "is Connie. Connie, this is Frank."

"Hi," Connie said sweetly. Her smile grew like the sun rising in the morning. Frank stared at her beauty, speechless. His hand came up automatically, without any thought.

She took it to shake, but Frank didn't move his hand up and down, he just held it firmly, gently, and stared, mesmerized. Connie stared back into Frank's eyes and they both lost themselves in the moment. She giggled at his helpless clumsiness. His mouth floundered, making his lips quiver.

"Frank *usually* has more to say," Eddie quipped.

After that moment, Connie and Frank stayed together day and night. Every waking moment became part of the romance blossoming between them. Picnics were Frank's favorite. But they sometimes returned to the pool on his days off and even played ball together. Frank's friends rolled their eyes. He sure was hooked. He fawned over her every moment.

Chapter 9

Frank felt adored. Connie stayed with him all the time. But right now he sat on the couch in her parent's home, nervous. He'd become stagnant, almost to the point of not wanting to try. He hadn't meant to quit anything, but life got so complicated. He just needed a little time. But Connie would want answers. For a change, Frank had one to give.

"Frank, you know I love you. And you've been talking about doing so much more with your life. But it looks like you've given up, all of a sudden. What are you going to do?"

"You mean for a job?"

"That's one possibility, yeah," she said.

"You're not worried, are you?"

"Just curious," she cooed, but Frank suspected she wasn't sincere.

"Well, I thought about going to Florida and becoming a beach bum. I'd look pretty cool in one of those straw hats. And my legs aren't so bad, either."

"I'm being serious, Frank. Do you have a plan?" Connie pleaded.

"I've got a couple ideas."

"Mind sharing some?"

"Well, I was saving this as a surprise for you," Frank said, reaching into his back pocket. "I received an acceptance letter from California State College."

"California?"

"Yes. Right here in California, PA. I'll only be forty-five minutes away."

Connie's eyes opened wide. "That's wonderful." She reached her arms around his waist and pulled him close. "How, when, where? I'm so proud of you. What are you going to major in?"

Frank leaned his head back and smiled. "I counted at least four questions in there. How about the most important one first? My major. I really like kids so I thought I'd become a teacher. Then I can help shape young minds."

"I hear the dorms are very crowded."

"I heard that too. Too bad I won't get to find out."

She looked at him curiously.

"I'm going to commute."

"Really?" She didn't bother to hide the excitement she felt.

"So, I guess you're stuck with me."

Seats, mounted in declining rows, faced a stage proudly decorated with red and black—the school colors for California College. None were empty, except those occupied by the students now standing on that stage. They, too, were adorned as the stage— red and black.

A row of lesser dignitaries sat on stage facing the audience. One chair sat empty, its occupant stood behind the podium struggling with each new name—many he'd barely seen more than once on a file tab.

On the other hand, Frank knew the Dean all too well. Frank Mattich wasn't the kind to get into any trouble, but the man's face had been plastered on every news letter, every bulletin, every advertisement. His politician smile clung to his face like acne on a teen.

"Frank Mattich." The P.A. voice echoed around until it sounded mushy and unclear.

Frank stepped forward, remembering his earlier instructions. *'Shake with the right hand, take with the left.'* It seemed a bit silly at the time, but as he stood there, achingly aware of all the eyes on him, the limerick returned and he managed to keep from screwing it up.

He walked down the stairs, around the small U-turn, and stood in front of his seat. The line would not sit until they all returned. Then the next row would go, and the next, and so on. The entire process moved at an agonizingly slow pace, but it gave each student a chance to enjoy his moment of pride and accomplishment. Frank had done things in his past—like taking that money for ice cream and the *douche bag* caper. However, none thrilled him as much as feeling this rolled parchment thrust into his hand.

That felt better than sex, he thought. *Well,* he reconsidered, *maybe not quite.*

Frank stood waiting for the rest of his row to return so he could sit. Several minutes later they were all there and Frank rested once again on the chair assigned him. Three more rows still waited to go up there. Now, with his diploma in his hand and feeling Connie's eyes burning into the back of his head, he looked forward to going through with the plans he'd made with her.

The Dean called another name and Frank looked up. Two more people stood in line, waiting to collect their parchment from him. The last line, the last two people, the torture was almost over. Frank's legs tingled with anticipation—or had they simply fallen asleep?

The last name came and went, the closing speeches were made. Caps flew. Even the people Frank hadn't been friends with wanted to hug him. Some of the bigger guys picked him up, yelling loudly—something unintelligible.

Vic and Dante couldn't be there for the celebration.

A couple years before, when they were still in high school, Cathy Vincenti became pregnant. Frank's mother called it *disgraced*. Frank's father said she got herself pregnant, but Frank felt pretty sure it took two. Cathy's parents hardly ever showed themselves in public. No one knew who the father was and Cathy wouldn't say.

Dante didn't attend family functions, he stayed out of the homes of the other guys, he even missed baseball practice. Vic and Eddie just figured Dante was getting weirder as he grew up, but Frank had a feeling the two were connected. After all, he'd seen Dante head down Railroad Street toward Cathy's place too many times.

Frank tried to convince Dante that Cathy had a reputation. But Dante didn't waver. He *knew* he'd fathered a child. He rambled something about a connection and Frank soon gave up any idea of convincing his friend.

Cathy's young body couldn't bear the strain of giving birth and she died. Something had been wrong with the baby. The doctors didn't know what. It died only a few hours later. Frank remembered his mother blaming the girl for not taking better care of herself. Frank's father blamed the damned doctors. Cathy's parents blamed Dante. Dante agreed with them. Dante's parents just mourned.

Dante didn't fare very well with life in general after that. It seemed to spiral downward for him and every step forward came with at least two backward. Frank's studies kept him busy, but whenever he got the opportunity, he visited his old friends. It hurt him to see Dante so down. Two years before Frank graduated college, Dante enlisted. Shortly after, the Army shipped him to Nam.

Vic, on the other hand, had a stroke of good fortune. The magic set he got as a child really paid off. After school he put on a few small shows and developed quite a following. Frank never thought the 'Vic Show' was very impressive. Even though Frank had no first-hand experience, he often saw a number of mistakes in Vic's act. Perhaps he saw because he *knew* Vic too well and had seen all the tricks so many times.

But a Pittsburgh club owner either hadn't seen the errors or chose to ignore them, because he hired Vic and kept him on. What reason the man might have for hiring Vic, Frank couldn't fathom. But he managed to run over there one night to catch Vic's show and it looked like the same old Vic doing the same old tricks. In his favor, Frank noticed Vic smoothed out some of the wrinkles. Maybe it would really pay off for him this time.

One thing Frank knew for sure. If Vic ever hoped to make it in the *real* world, he'd have to come up with a better name for himself and his act. *The Illusory Reality of Victor Horvath* didn't exactly roll off the tongue. And as cool as *Victor Frankenstein* might sound, it had already been taken.

With Vic and Dante out of town, only Eddie made it to watch Frank in his cap and gown. He'd taken over managing his father's bar and it had begun to flourish. Despite all that, he came to watch Frank walk onto that stage. Frank's mother and father were there also and, of course, Connie. He could feel all of them staring at the back of his head.

Chapter 10

Frank got his first teaching job before that summer passed. And the next spring, he found the courage to approach the woman of his dreams. They sat in the park, watching kids play, a question pulling at his heart. The sun shone, although a chill—left over from winter—still hung in the air like the smell of a scented candle.

"Connie, I wanted to talk to you about something."

Connie stiffened.

"I've never really understood affection."

"I know, Frank," she replied with a wry grin. "We've been dating for a while."

"I'm not sure how to show it."

"You don't have to tell me," Connie said, with conviction.

"But I know when people feel about each other the way we do, they usually spend their lives together."

"Yeah, that's true. What are you getting at, Frank?"

"Well," Frank stammered. "Your mom and dad are married. My mom and dad are married."

"Frank, that's what people do," Connie explained.

"That's what I'm saying. Would you like to…"

Connie remained silent, though she leaned forward and listened closely.

"…you know."

"Know what, Frank?" she asked, her voice little more than a squeak.

"Would you like to…marry me?"

Tears welled in her eyes and Frank thought he might have said the wrong thing. He'd gotten so good at that. This time—he was mistaken.

All Frank's friends made it for the wedding. Slick Vic pushed to the front to make sure he got a handful of rice in Frank's face. His show in Pittsburgh finally flopped. Frank felt bad for him, but he'd expected it. Dante, fresh back from the war only two weeks prior, looked quite fit for having been a P.O.W. for a while. Both were now working in the steel mill. Eddie, of course, was best man, again taking time out from running the bar. He'd taken it over completely when his dad died in November.

Frank and Connie left the church and headed to their honeymoon. A short trip to the Poconos—to a secluded cabin Frank had arranged in advance—provided them time in romantic bliss. They'd been together for years. Of course they were intimate. And yet, somehow, the isolation, the intrigue, the romance, the mystique, the marriage certificate—there was something about a 'honeymoon' that brought them on a new and different journey of discovery and exploration. They learned about each other in a way they hadn't during their regular, daily lives. Frank and Connie were lost…in each other.

Once they were settled back in Duquesne, and back on track with normal life, Frank took on extra jobs as a recreation director and assistant basketball and baseball coach. Vic and Dante didn't come around for a while, but Frank didn't have any free time to give them while he worked three jobs. Eddie hardly ever came around at all. The bar kept him quite busy most days, but Patty kept him content most nights.

Not too many months later, Frank and Connie moved into a bigger, better house in West Mifflin. The purchase reminded Frank of his dream, and they'd stepped up to a better class neighborhood than Duquesne. Connie walked in, rubbing her belly, now big with child. Frank saw her struggling with the steps and moved to help.

He felt nervous about the birth. It hadn't gone so well for Dante and Cathy. Frank's own mother had lost two children. Two sisters Frank never met because they died before he was born. While he didn't sink into despair over them since he hadn't known them, he *did* mourn the loss. Frank wasn't sure how he would cope if Connie lost their child.

"Honey, I love the house," Connie said, snapping Frank back from his thoughts of fear. "It's all because of the money from those extra jobs you've been working. I know it's been tough, but it's really paid off."

"The jobs have kept me out of the house a lot."

"Apparently not enough," she laughed, looking down at her nine-month belly.

"Anything for you, Sweetheart, and our future family," he added, placing his own hand on her expanded midsection.

All Frank's fears dissipated when he and Connie carried home their beautiful baby girl. She brought a feeling of magic to the entire home. Over time the family grew again. Two beautiful girls ran about playfully without a care. Connie, being raised in a proper home, took great care of her house and her children. And when Frank came home from his jobs, she took good care of him as well.

Frank felt happy, content with his lot in life, until the night when the midnight phone calls began. Sarah Mattich died less than six months after Joseph. Both were taken by cancer. Frank and his family hardly had time to recover.

A third phone call came soon after. Frank answered without fear. He had no more parents to lose. Little did he know how bad it could still become. He remembered hearing someone say bad things came in threes.

48

Connie looked up at him as he came back into the room. She spoke tentatively. "Honey, what's wrong?"

Frank inhaled and sighed deeply. He went over and sat beside her on the sofa. His shoulders slumped, and he stared at the floor in despair. He didn't want to turn away from her but he didn't know how to tell her the truth. When he looked at Connie's face he knew he had little choice. He swallowed his emotions.

"The teacher's union is going on strike," he finally let out in one quick breath.

"Do they think it will last long?"

"Aw, they don't know a damned thing," Frank said, still aggravated.

"What are you going to do?" Connie sounded apprehensive.

Frank stiffened, as if he'd just then made a decision. He remembered back when the steel mill union went on strike. He'd overheard the conversation between his father and Karl Schultz about the picket lines and scabs and a bunch of things Frank didn't understand at that age. The next day, Frank and Eddie—at the ripe old ages of twelve and ten—snuck down to the plant and watched the drama unfold.

Hundreds of union workers had gathered, carrying signs of protest. Dozens of police, dressed in riot gear, guarded the gates. Walking down the street, Frank saw cops escorting scabs coming to break through the picket lines. Frank shuddered as a pang of fear shot through him.

His dad and the others stood in the path of the approaching police line. The two boys felt the anger in the air. Frank left his hiding place and ran to his father. Something told Frank this situation would turn bad.

"Dad! Dad!"

"Frankie? What are you doing here? You have to go home. Get out of here." He glanced warily at the approaching police line as he spoke.

Frank's instincts were proved correct. The two groups clashed violently. Frank saw billy clubs flying and strikers fighting back. Several people hit the ground, one of them covered in blood. He didn't look too good. The wild melee became too confusing for Frank. He and Eddie scrambled to safety and hurried home.

Two days later, as Joseph Mattich rested in his chair nursing a bandaged right eye and a sore wrist, Frank heard a knock at the door. They weren't expecting any company, and Frank's friends never bothered to knock. The knock grew persistent.

"Mr. Mattich?" the stern voice asked when Frank's dad opened the door.

Frankie, feeling the sudden rise in tension, ran over and sidled up next to his dad. The suits on the other side of the door stood straight and starched as Joseph Mattich looked at them. Both wore sunglasses and thin ties. Frank stood stiff with fright as his dad stared them down.

"Yes? What do you want?"

"We're with the F.B.I." They showed their I.D.'s.

"So?"

"Did you know Ken Baker died, today?"

"Ken Baker? Wasn't he the security guard supervisor?"

"He died from injuries incurred during the riot at the steel mill."

"I didn't know the man. Poor Ken."

"All we want, Mr. Mattich, is a name. Just give us a name."

"A name? How about my name?"

"Who hit Ken Baker?"

"How would I know?"

"Someone must have seen something, Mr. Mattich."

"I'm sorry, but I have nothing else to say to you."

"It'll go a lot easier on you if you cooperate with us, Mr. Mattich," the second agent insisted.

"You can't threaten me. I've done nothing."

"You were there," the agent stated, pointing at Joseph's bandaged eye.

"I told you," Joseph insisted, pushing the door toward the jam. "I have nothing to say. Would you please leave?"

"Mr. Mattich, please!"

"Good bye."

Joseph Mattich pushed the door into the jam. Frank heard the loud clack as the bolt sprang into its slot. He peeked past the curtain to watch the suits. One of them nodded to the other and they turned to leave. Frankie wasn't sure what just happened or what *would* happen in the future. They'd threatened it could get worse. Frankie didn't know what they meant by that.

"Yebem Ti."

"What?" Frank asked.

"All they want is a name." Joseph Mattich shook his head in disgust.

"You knew who it was? And you didn't tell them?"

"Listen to me, Frankie. You *never* rat on your friends. You got that?"

"But Dad, they said it would go easier. Does that mean they'll make it harder?"

"They're just trying to frighten me."

"But you could have just told them."

"There is no reason to rat on your friends, Frankie. *Ever.*"

"But they said that guy died."

"Yes. A sad day. A very sad day, indeed."

Frank now looked firmly into the eyes of his lovely wife, as the memory faded. "My father fought hard for his union. How could I do any less?"

Connie sighed in acceptance.

Frank had been a good teacher and never missed a day. But the superintendent of schools sat bleakly behind his desk and recited a story about cutbacks and necessities, all the while preparing to drop the bad news. The union and the school board agreed to end the strike with a substantial increase in wages across the board. However, that meant the school couldn't maintain as many teachers.

The all-American life was snatched from Frank's hand without so much as an apology. The money had bought a house and started a family, but hadn't brought them out of the working class. Frank didn't mind the union strike or the job loss nearly as much as he hated not having crossed that threshold to independence.

Although, with so little money left over at the end of every month, it would have taken many more years. Nevertheless, Frank could almost taste the success. He could almost grasp it. He reached for it, smelled it, he thought of little else. His heart sank.

Chapter 11

Frustrated, he couldn't just sit around the house, so he walked to Schultzie's bar and sought the strength of his friends. They, of course, all sat around a table, drinking and laughing loudly. They wore their softball uniforms.

"What's up, guys?"

They all looked up.

"Hey, we're supposed to play against Riley's bar today, remember?" Eddie asked.

"Not really," Frank said, dejectedly. "I guess I forgot."

Slick Vic had turned into a five-foot-nine bundle of muscle from playing basketball and baseball. He had a charming good look about him that attracted the ladies. His smile disappeared when he looked at Frank.

"They cut you, didn't they?" Vic asked.

"Yeah. From everything."

"Come on, Frank. It's going to be all right."

Everyone nodded in agreement. They were nothing if not enthusiastic.

"Life isn't fair," Frank bitched, sounding very sorry for himself. "A man tries to be a good, hard working citizen and as soon as times get tough, they toss him aside like yesterday's garbage. It just isn't right. I gave my all to be a good teacher and coach."

"All the kids love and respect you, Frank. And Principal Michaels speaks very highly of you," Casey interjected. He and

Solly, two cops that came by the joint regularly, had both become friends with Frank's crew, almost like an extension of the family.

"What good does it do me?"

"Frank, why don't you get suited up and come play with us? You're scheduled to play anyway."

"I'm not sure I feel up to it, guys."

"Come on, Frank. You know you'll feel better if you're playing."

"I don't know, guys. I don't want to ruin the game for everybody."

"It'll be fine. Come on. Your uniform is in the back. Get dressed and take out some of your aggression on the other team."

"Yeah. Maybe you're right."

"Hey, I don't mean to bring up bad memories," Dante said, "but you played after your dad died and you kicked ass."

Frank felt the beginning of a smile grow on his face. "Yeah, I remember. That was a great game."

"So, come on. What do you say?"

"I say…" he hesitated, looking around at his friends, "…let's play ball!"

They all cheered.

But the celebrating really cranked up when they returned. They beat the crap out of the team from Riley's Bar. Frank played like a pro, but the real MVP was Eddie Schultz. Every time he got up to bat he slammed it out of the park. In the field, nothing got past him. He seemed to be everywhere.

"Damn, Eddie," Frank said. "You always promised you'd become Babe Ruth. I guess you made it."

"You kicked some ass yourself, Frankie."

"Yeah, I guess I did," Frank admitted.

"I think the two of us could make an unstoppable team by ourselves," Eddie suggested.

"Frank," Vic said. He paused and looked around at the rest of the guys sitting at the table. "You know we're your friends and we're concerned about you. We came up with an idea. This town hasn't had a gambling joint since Mingo died. We all like to play cards and we think we could help you start your own place. Nothing fancy, just some cards and the like."

"Casey and I already asked the city fathers," Solly inserted. "They gave the OK. The only thing you have to do is give the 'numbers and sports bets' to their *man*. This is a no-lose situation. You get a percentage of all these bets without taking any of the chances."

"Wait a minute," Frank interrupted. "You already asked the city fathers?"

"Well, yeah. Wouldn't you want us to check it all out before we wasted your time?"

"Then you didn't *just* come up with the idea."

"Okay, Frank, you caught us," Casey admitted. "We've been thinking about it for a while, but we didn't know how to proceed. We don't want to run the place, just play some cards."

"Yeah," Solly added. "We didn't even know *who* we could get to run it. We just want a place where we can all hang out...and play cards," he added, waving his hand at Casey. "You'd be great."

"And the guy with the coffee shop at the lower end of our building is retiring," Schultzie added. "You could take his spot, rent free for the first two months. It has a nice back room where you can put in a couple tables for the games."

Vic and Dante stood near Frank. He towered over both of them now, but Dante grabbed his arm and pulled him aside, his grip unrelenting. He walked Frank to a corner for privacy. Solly and Casey might be part of the big circle, but they were still cops and Dante didn't fully trust them, even though Frank did.

55

"What the hell's the matter with you, Dante?" Frank asked, pulling his arm free and rubbing against the pain.

"What? Oh, did I hurt you?"

"Dante," Frank spoke with care. "We've been friends a long time. Ever since you've come back from that awful place, you're not the same guy. I know you don't like to talk about it, but what the hell happened to you over there?"

Dante looked away. To Frank it looked like Dante was struggling with an inner beast. When he looked back, it appeared he'd made up his mind. He leaned against the wall.

"When I first got there, I saw thick jungles and exotic plants. It was hard to breathe from the humidity. Dangers from the local wildlife were hazardous. The G.I.s never heard of some of the animals. That was one of the first things I learned when I arrived.

"But the ultimate danger came from the gooks. We were fighting people with no morals while trying to retain Marquis of Queensbury rules. Our hands were tied. You've heard the stories. Some of us didn't even have ammo."

"Yeah, Dante," Frank said, shortly. "I've heard the stories."

"Kids," Dante continued, "carried bombs in shoeboxes, sold us poison chocolate bars, or hid grenades in helmets or under dead bodies. There were so many other booby traps and sneaky tricks, I lost count. And the girls weren't any better. Cute smiles, petite bodies, and so willing to please, they could maneuver a G.I. into almost any dangerous situation. That's how I got screwed in the end.

"I'd heard the stories about girls with razor blades up their cunts. I even saw a guy with his dick shredded." Dante shivered. Frank felt a twinge of discomfort, just hearing about it.

"So I always checked a girl out before entering—so to speak. I'd look and carefully insert a finger, searching around for anything, you know?" Dante moved his finger around in the air as if demonstrating for Frank. "Of course, there were other stories about dangerous bugs or even poisonous liquids they'd been immunized against over months, with medical treatment. These things would be inside a girl, waiting for some unsuspecting soldier to stick his dick in. No amount of looking or inserting fingers would prevent some of those injuries.

"But I hadn't heard about them, so I figured I was safe. Fortunately, I remained that way. My screwing came about in a different way.

"There was this one girl in particular, Ting. I'd been with her on several occasions. Her tiny tits and perky nipples reacted quickly." Dante stood a bit taller, thrusting out his chest. "We'd lay together sometimes for hours, having sex and resting, then having sex again. Her moans were so arousing—so genuine—I kept going back. It's like she was really turned on by me, you know? And I pumped many days of tension into her willing body."

Dante nudged his elbow into Frank's arm as if he'd just shared some dark secret.

"So how'd you get into trouble, pal?" Frank asked.

"I didn't know it, but her family originally came from North Vietnam. I mean, how the hell was I supposed to know? They all look alike. Well, blood's thicker than water. She seemed so interested in me and enjoyed our time together.

"She'd invited me to her place on several occasions, so I thought nothing of it. But one time we were going at it and a couple North Vietnamese soldiers burst into the room. I guess she hadn't locked the door. I never noticed."

"Too busy thinking with your little head?" Frank asked.

"Hey, it was good sex—great sex! She opened her legs and invited me inside. She had her feet in the air and me pounding into her. Then these two guys—big by Vietnamese standards—quietly walked right in. At first I was far too lost in showing the girl what

American men were made of to notice much of anything else. She felt *that* good. I didn't even see them until they grabbed my arms.

"You know when they lifted me up, they were careful to get my dick out of the girl without hurting her. I guess there was no sense damaging the merchandise that could still be so useful.

"But do you want to hear the worst part? As they dragged me off her, I managed to look back. At first it was just protectiveness. I thought we were *both* being abducted. But then I saw. The girl still lay on the cot, her eyes rolled back and her tongue kept moving, her nipples still pointing at the ceiling, her finger rubbing quickly on her hard, little clit. I heard the moan. The girl was still having her fucking orgasm. Like I didn't even need to be there.

"Well that's when I knew she'd done it. I knew she made arrangements for another American soldier to bite the dust. Before we were out the door, she came, real hard. It seemed like she got off on me being taken away like that!"

Frank stood, shocked.

"They carried me, one under each arm, without clothing, through the building and out into the street. There, a car sat a few feet away. The two men tossed me inside the back seat. One guy got in the back with me and the other in the front with the driver. They didn't bother tying me up. I was naked, where could I run? They drove crazily and I tossed in the seat. I wanted to throw up.

"When the car turned onto the jungle road, I figured I was in deep shit. This wasn't gonna be no drive in the country with the in-laws. They took me right out of the warmth of her pussy and brought me to that P.O.W. camp."

That must be the worst, Frank thought. *Dante saw it coming.*

"The camp sat less than five miles outside of town. American soldiers partied in that town, so close, and yet they didn't even know. I tried to see everything, already planning my escape.

The car brought me to the middle of the compound and stopped. A big, wooden X stood solitarily, acting as sentinel or idol.

"Soon, I felt pretty sure, I would be shedding *my* blood at that altar, or some other one just like it. And then they pulled me out of the car and tied me to the X. I struggled, but they overpowered me. My arms spread out over my head, my legs wide, my dick just hanging loose in front of my balls, I stood completely helpless, and vulnerable. Naked.

"The two men walked away, smartly. For a long time I just hung there, food for the vultures. A loud bang to the left caught my attention—a spring-loaded door on one of the huts. A shorter man approached, a hand-made, wooden door bounced against its frame behind him. Though small in stature, the man commanded an air of superiority. Others saluted and cowered before him.

"He approached me and stood there, only a few inches away. I could smell the *kim-chi* on his breath."

"What's that?"

"It's a fermented cabbage dish with onion, garlic, and chili powder. It's a favorite of most oriental countries. I learned to like it…more or less.

"Anyway the man put his hand on my chest. No pressure, he just rested it there, all the while he stared into my eyes. He spoke in Vietnamese, the other soldiers laughed. Then he slid his hand down.

"It was *really* uncomfortable, you know?—him touching me down there. I wanted to vomit. But he wasn't being friendly. He pinched one of my balls between his two fingers and held it tight. Agony and nausea shot straight into my stomach. I tried not to scream—I didn't want to give them the satisfaction. I didn't want to show any weakness. But it hurt so bad, you know?

Somehow, in only the course of a few minutes, this had become a battle of strength between us and I had no chance of winning. I thought how much fairer the battle would be if they

59

would have untied my hands, just for a minute. Then the pain in my balls got too bad. I don't remember much after that."

"That's pretty intense, buddy," Frank said with compassion.

"Not as intense as the next thing I remember."

"Oh? Are you sure you want to talk about this?" Frank asked, wiping sweat from his brow.

"You asked."

"Yeah," his voice sank. "I guess I did."

"Besides," Dante continued. "I'd like to get this off my chest.

"For several months, I don't remember much. It's mostly a blur. One night I woke hearing strange noises. They carried out most of their tortures at night when the prisoners remained disoriented from what little sleep they were able to get. Also, most torturing took place in plain sight of the other prisoners as a means of motivation. A prisoner pulled from the cage for interrogation would be more likely to cooperate if he'd witnessed several of his fellow P.O.W.'s tortured before.

"I didn't really know the man they pulled out that night. It was difficult to get close to anyone in the camp. But, on some deeper level, everyone became close. All were fellow prisoners and all would escape or even kill the enemy if possible. From a common cause rose an unspoken camaraderie. So each time someone got pulled from the cages, we all watched. And we all shared the pain.

"The 'X' stood in the middle of the compound for torture in front of everyone. But if they wanted to torment someone closer to the cages, several individual poles were placed in the ground. The poles were made of small trees and had metal rings held on by long, heavy bolts through the diameter of the trunk. They stood firm and strong. Once you were tied to it, you couldn't free yourself, unless

60

one of the gooks tied a haphazard knot. But they all seemed quite expert at knot tying. Probably all fucking Eagle Scouts."

Frank chuckled uncomfortably.

"To the best of my knowledge, the man's name was Joe. But the gooks called every American, Joe. They tied him to the post. His resistance drew everyone's attention and we came to the front of the cages and watched—helpless against an enemy who would resort to such means.

"The man stood, breathing quickly, eyes wide, as he waited in terror for whatever was coming. The short leader—we'd all nick-named him 'General'—approached. Didn't any of those guys sleep? He carried a machete. Joe's breathing became faster, jerkier. He began hyperventilating. Saliva dripped from his mouth. The rest of us in the cages screamed our objections, but they didn't listen to us. We didn't lose respect for Joe, only grew more hatred for the Vietcong. That didn't make it any easier for the man tied to the post.

"The General sliced the knife across Joe's body, cutting the clothes off and leaving little trails of blood. Joe screamed more in fear than in actual pain. The cuts were minor. But we weren't all out there to have a party and Joe knew it. Something bad was coming. So he stood there screaming, his skin full of goose bumps, his dick shriveled, drooling in terror. He began to blither.

"The General stepped back and I saw Joe's eyes, wider than humanly possible and moving with twitchy, spasmodic motions. His hands, tied tightly to the mast, gripped and loosened repeatedly. Piss shot out of his dick, some falling on the General's shoe. The short man looked down at the mess, then back up at Joe. He seemed like he might erupt. Then he did. In laughter. I didn't understand, but I couldn't pull my eyes away.

"The General stood to the side, laughing. Joe's legs froze, his lips trembled slightly, he quivered all over in horrific anticipation. I didn't know what was going on. You see, they weren't asking him any questions. The General walked close to Joe.

"He started touching Joe in the groin, like he'd done to me. Laughter would have been inappropriate, but I tell you honestly, that's what I wanted to do. I wondered if the General might have more than a few homosexual tendencies. He stroked Joe until the man couldn't help but get a little hard. That's when the General swung the machete.

"Joe screamed in a way I'd never heard before. But I couldn't see anything. When I looked down, I saw lots of blood running down his legs. His screams had become some kind of unintelligible blubbering, as delirium overtook him. Considering how much blood flowed between his legs, I guessed he wouldn't last much longer. That was probably for the best.

"The rest of us in the cages stood horrified. Our cries for decent treatment suddenly abated. Some vomited, some turned away and cried. I just stood there, fighting off the laughter."

"Wow, that's tough," Frank offered.

"Don't you see? If I'd let it out, they might have noticed me. Then I would have been tied to the post. I choked it down with all my strength."

"I understand."

"No, you don't. *I was afraid!*"

Frank said nothing.

"I couldn't make myself look away from the horror in front of me. When I close my eyes at night, I can still see Joe just as clearly as I see you right now. I watched as the General then took both Joe's testicles. He tossed them away like they were ping pong balls.

"Then the General spoke to us. He managed to speak in pretty good English. *'You have no manhood.'* He walked near the cages, holding Joe's dismembered penis, waving it in front of us all. *'We will take it from each and every one of you. You do not deserve dignity. You do not deserve honor. If you live to return to your homes, you will be but half men. Then maybe your country will learn its lesson. If we take all your balls, you will not have enough of them left to dare ever attack us again.'*

"The General paced as he lectured. I began to count his steps. I don't know why. I heard a child's sing-song playing in my head, matching the beat of his footsteps. I felt giddy and needed to sit down. I found a spot and just fell over.

"I looked down at my bare feet. They had dirt all over them. I thought that was about the funniest thing I'd ever seen. I laughed until I was exhausted. They did *not* take me out and tie me to the post.

"Next thing I knew, the dawn's light struck my eyes. I don't know what really happened to Joe. But when I *did* look up, no one was tied to the pole. My cheeks hurt real bad. One of the other guys told me later that I'd laughed almost continuously—all night. He told me I laughed at the puddle of Joe's blood, too. But I don't remember any of it.

"I could see Joe's balls, lying on the ground, but no sign of his dick. I've often wondered if the General took it for a personal trophy." Dante laughed and Frank watched him with concern. "Maybe they could sell it at the market. Those Vietcong eat some unusual things, you know. Anyway, I laughed until I passed out from exhaustion."

Dante gave Frank an appraising stare. "So, sorry I hurt you but sometimes I just react.

"Well, I can see why you don't really trust anyone."

Dante wasn't the same man who'd left only a few short years before to go fight in that exotic land. Sometimes, like when he'd grabbed at Frank's arm, Frank wished for the old Dante to come back.

Dante motioned for Vic to join them. "Listen, Frank," Dante whispered, making sure no one else came close enough to hear. "All the guys at the mill love to gamble. We can bring them in, too."

"Yeah, Frank. I went to a joint over in McKeesport, a few weeks ago. The place was jumping. I wrote down some of the stuff they did." Vic stepped up next to them and pulled a piece of paper from his shirt pocket. "First, you must have good food. The guys will appreciate that."

"I think between all of us, we can cook up something," Dante joked.

"Dante," Frank said with conviction, "the only thing *you* can cook comes out of a box. And sometimes you cook the box!"

"Well, that's okay," Dante defended, "sometimes I like to eat the box."

"*Sometimes*?" Frank returned, his voice dripping with innuendo and sarcasm. "Are we still talking about food?"

64

"Anyway," Vic interrupted, "next, you should only have poker games. The other stuff gets a little rowdy and takes up more room. Besides, all the guys know how to play poker. And the last thing—take only five percent of the pots. Any more than that is greedy, and the guys will quit coming. Besides, that's five percent of every pot and you don't even have to play."

Frank felt a bit like he was on a roller coaster. First he'd gone way up, riding the teaching express, then the union went on strike and he plummeted down. But now, with renewed hope from his friends, Frank felt the beginning of optimism rising within. In a few years he might be able to get that down payment on something better for him and Connie.

"You guys have got this all figured out, haven't you?" Frank asked, rhetorically.

Always well focused, his mind played with what kind of business he wanted to be in. He enjoyed the night life and occasionally dreamed of owning a cabaret or a disco. He really liked the music. However, a nightclub would keep him out of the house almost every night. That meant, no time with Connie.

In the meantime, he saw nothing wrong in forging ahead with plans for a gambling joint. In fact, it sounded like fun.

Chapter 12

Every day saw a handful of steel workers trod into Frank's little gambling joint. Occasionally a new face joined them, but most were regulars. Of course, a few of the patrons came from other jobs in town, as well. Frank made note of some principle city officials, police officers, and one doctor, but denied none entrance. All were welcome and *all* spent the same color of money.

Dante and Vic held true to their promise. They helped set things up and got the word out and they covered for Frank when he couldn't be there to run the place. Frank made sure the food was good. People spent money, and the house profited.

Even though a significant amount of money had to be rolled back into the business, Frank managed to stash some away at every turn. His nest egg grew and he felt hope again that one day his dream might come true. Every day Frank went to the joint, looking forward to another exciting evening of gambling and camaraderie.

But Connie had reservations and she voiced them often. Frank didn't understand her attitude or her reluctance. He was doing it all for her—for his family—but she resented him taking so much time away from home and she didn't trust the legality of what he did. She spoke lovingly but harshly.

"God, it's nice to have an early night," Frank said resting his head against the sweet-smelling pillow. Connie always managed to get the sheets and pillow cases smelling so nice, like summer flowers floating on a gentle breeze.

She lay next to him, barely breathing, remaining motionless. Frank knew she was concerned again. No summer flowers swam through her head. He often wondered if something during the day didn't upset her and get her worrying about it all. Maybe someone she spoke to, told her about their *perfect* life and it ate at her that she couldn't brag about him. Or maybe she felt Frank's discontent. Perhaps she didn't even know what caused it, only that she often went to bed feeling irritated with him and his absence.

"Yeah," she finally responded.

"What's wrong?"

"It's nothing."

"Honey, it's obviously something." Although he didn't want to hear it all again, Frank knew it would be better if she brought it out in the open.

Silence.

"You know I can always tell," Frank said intimately, placing a hand lightly on her hip.

Connie twisted and looked into Frank's eyes as best she could in the dark.

"Can I ask you something?" she queried.

"Absolutely," Frank said with mock confidence. He considered making some comment like, *'You already did'*, but that kind of sarcasm usually didn't help with her.

"I just want to know how legal all this is."

"How legal all *what* is?"

"Come on, you know," she scoffed.

"There's nothing going on here," he tried to reassure.

"There's *something* going on here. I can see there's money coming in the house."

"I'm just working for it, hon. That's all. Now, come on. Tell me. What are you worried about? Really."

"Frank, I worry about you, all right? I'm worried that you're going to get caught."

"If I'm not doing anything wrong, how can I get caught?"

"I'm not stupid, Frank. I know that if you get caught, you could be in *real* trouble."

"Honey, it's fine. Nothing is going to happen." Frank looked deep into her eyes. "It'll be fine. If anything, I'd just get a slap on the wrist. Nothing major."

Connie remained silent.

"Besides, I'm making enough money so we can live a good life. Ten times what I made as a teacher. Even with all three jobs." He held out his hand to her.

"The school board called today."

"Oh," Frank said, hesitantly.

"They've offered you your old job back."

"Are they going to give me a raise?"

"No." Her voice sounded disappointed.

Frank said nothing.

"Is money all you think about anymore, Frank? The good life?"

"It's what we want, right?"

She shook her head in agreement, but the hesitation still lingered in her expression, which Frank managed to see—even in the dark.

"Okay, so there's nothing to worry about," Frank said, like a lawyer in a closing argument. "Right?"

He leaned in to kiss her forehead. When she didn't retreat, his confidence returned. He'd convinced her, he'd won. He almost believed it, himself. But it was a shallow victory. It would only last until the next day when she confronted him again. And the entire cycle would play over again. Frank just wanted to provide for his family. He couldn't be blamed for finding a way to make life better for them. Surely not.

Frank tried to shake it out of his head.

"I love you, Connie."

"I love you, Frank."

He slid his arms around her and pulled. She came willingly and they hugged in the night. He felt her relax a little. He moved his hand up her back to massage and play with her hair. Then he released her. They both rolled away from each other and Connie quickly went to sleep.

For the day, at least, he lived free from the persecution she bestowed upon him in her almost nightly ritual. It seemed more or less like taking medicine. As soon as she got her daily dose, she calmed down and became pliable.

The elusive dream, however, haunted Frank day and night. Caught up in the fever of making more and more money, Frank knew he wouldn't be so easily satisfied. A down payment wouldn't be good enough for his wonderful wife and his three beautiful girls. He wanted more.

Some people might say once you got started making money, you couldn't stop, and enough would never be enough. But the truth that haunted Frank's dreams was the belief he might only have one real shot at that success and he couldn't go half way. One slip up and he would get knocked back down. *The world loved to knock a man back down while he tried to get up.*

Connie worried, Frank consoled, and the girls grew. All the while, he looked ahead to a brighter future. But very little changed, until a few months later. Vic and Dante stayed late at the joint, playing poker with a couple guys.

"Frank," Vic stated after everyone left except their table, "you know we all love to gamble. But, we need to make some more money, you know?"

"What are you talking about? I'm making a great living. A hell of a lot better than teaching."

"Sure. You're making a great living. But what about us?"

"I don't know that I want to get involved with anything else, guys."

"Come on, man," Dante said. "This is small change. You could do so much better. And we could sure use a little something extra in our pockets, too."

"What are you talking about?" A respectable part of Frank wanted to say, *forget it*, right then and there. But another part of him, the part that wanted to have a secure life and run his own business—his American dream, the risk-taking, daredevil part perked up to listen further.

"Well," Vic got quiet even though only the five of them sat around the table. "Pete and Tommy here, have an idea about how to make some extra dough."

"Extra dough," Frank repeated, doubt evident in his tone.

"Hey, what'll it hurt to listen?" Vic challenged.

"I don't know. I have a strong feeling we're not talking about a legitimate venture and Connie doesn't even like *this*." Frank waved his hand to indicate the gambling joint.

"Listen up," Dante said forcefully. "You're the man of the family. You wear the pants. You have to make the decisions about what's best for them. Connie can't do it for you. What does she want you to do? Slave in the mill? Drive yourself into the ground? Die young like your dad? All the while getting older but you don't have a pot to piss in…ever. Is that what she wants?"

Frank hesitated for a moment. Then he looked at Vic. "I guess it won't hurt to listen. What have you guys got going on?"

"Pete? Why don't you explain your idea to Frank?" suggested Dante

Pete didn't seem like the type to be coming up with ideas. Frank half listened as Pete leaned closer and rested his elbow on the table. A shock of brown hair fell in Pete's face as he spoke. It annoyed Frank and he kept swishing his own hair out of the way as if that would somehow help.

"Tommy and I know the mill like the back of our hands. There's this stuff, cans of it. A chemical called Molybdenum. We all just call it 'Moly'. The stuff is used in making steel."

Frank looked a bit confused.

"The stuff is very valuable," Pete insisted.

Tommy jumped in with enthusiasm. He directed all his energy at Frank as if he thought he could do a better job of convincing than Pete had. He spoke with his finger extended, though it didn't point at anyone or anything in particular. He just waved it around like a music baton.

"We have access to them. Vic and Dante have a way to smuggle them out of the mill."

Frank looked first at Vic, then Dante. He couldn't believe those two were falling for such a stupid idea.

"We figure," Dante added, "we can bring out about twenty cans a week. If we don't get greedy, we can do it for a long time."

"Then what are we supposed to do?" Frank asked, exasperated. "Drink the stuff? Or do you propose to start your own steel mill?"

"We thought," Vic said softly, "with your connections, you might know someone who would buy them."

"Me? What the hell do I know about the steel mill?"

"Nothing," Dante answered. "But you know people. Maybe you know people who might want this stuff."

"What do you think, Frank?" Pete asked. "Are you interested?"

71

Frank's right index finger twitched—something that only happened when he felt money coming his way. The new deal *could* be sweet if no one fucked it up. He hated to admit it, but the guys were right. He *did* know people—maybe people who could sell the shit. Maybe people who would buy the shit. The money counter in his mind calculated all the additional cash he could put away. "Let me make a couple phone calls." He headed over to his desk.

"Hey, fellas," Frank said, coming back to the table quickly, making everybody jump. "I can get you two hundred dollars a can. Twenty cans will make four thousand dollars. How you split it up is your business."

"Holy shit!" Tommy said. "That's fantastic! That couldn't have been any smoother." He turned toward Frank and stood. "These guys said you were the man, but you really came through on this one." He extended his hand and Frank shook it.

"What do you guys think?" Tommy asked. "Let's get started right away, okay?"

"Okay."

"That okay with you, Frank? Any reason to delay?"

"None," Frank answered. "This will be a good deal if no one fucks it up."

"No one here is going to fuck it up, Frank," Pete said.

"I trust you mean that."

Tommy and Pete stood and left.

"Frank?" Vic inquired.

"What?"

"You haven't said much."

"What would you like me to say?"

"What do you think of the deal?"

"I gotta admit," Frank conceded, "at first I thought I'd just heard the stupidest idea ever."

72

"You really thought we would bring you something worthless?"

"What did you expect?" Frank asked. "I don't know anything about the mill."

"And still you went along with it."

"In the end, I trust you guys. I thought you knew."

Chapter 13

Frank had good reason to smile. Genuinely pleased with the new venture, they decided how to cut the profits. His contact had actually offered him three hundred a can. Frank would make an easy hundred for each one and the guys got the other two. That meant a hundred dollars a can profit for Frank and all he had to do was drive the stuff one mile to his connection. If he didn't need to keep his contact a secret, he could have done nothing and made money.

Frank knew Vic and Dante. They wouldn't steal an empty candy wrapper from a whole bowl full of them in Frank's home. But Pete and Tommy were opportunists. If they'd met Frank's connection, what would stop them from bypassing Frank and going direct? By cutting Frank, Vic, and Dante out, they could have sold it cheaper, and made more money. So Frank made the only smart business move. He drove the stuff for the last mile, every delivery. Thus, the *Steel Mill Mafia* was born.

They brought in one extra guy. Kemo kept inventory and did all the ordering for the mill. His American Indian blood showed through in his high cheek bones and dark, piercing eyes. They called him Kemo because of the Lone Ranger and his Indian friend, Tonto. Tonto used to call the Lone Ranger, Kemo Sabe, which meant White Friend.

Kemo kept the stuff coming through the mill, altering the ordering sheets to reflect the increased need without it looking suspicious. So Kemo kept the orders coming, Pete and Tommy moved the stuff to a safe location, Vic and Dante removed it from the mill, and Frank delivered it to his connection.

Frank didn't really want to drive the stuff at all, but it wasn't so bad. He remembered an old movie called *Sorcerer* where some guys had to carry old dynamite, leaking nitro. All they could use to move the stuff were a couple old trucks. They needed to close a burning oil rig. He quickly put it out of his mind. No one mentioned if this stuff would explode and Frank didn't really want to know. He drove carefully and kept his mind on the dollar signs— and his dream.

At twenty cans a week, Frank took home an extra two grand. As the weeks turned into months, the five men smoothed out their operation and it ran like clockwork. In six months, Frank pocketed an extra fifty 'G's.

The best part for Frank was that Connie didn't suspect most of it. Or she never let on if she did. Because they lived so well off the profits from his gambling operations, Frank managed to bring the extra money into his home without drawing much attention to it. But for a while, being a poor boy from Duquesne, he felt like a king. And yet he wanted more, always more.

The night Dick approached him, Frank had joined one of the card games at his joint. He did that from time to time when an empty seat needed filling. Frank enjoyed the thrill of betting.

The voice cut in, a whine that irritated to the core. "Hey, Frank. I need to talk to you." The man worked at the mill. Frank knew him. He'd come to the joint on many occasions, playing poker. He lost his fair share, and when he did, his temper flared out of control. To Frank, he seemed a little shifty, not able to hold his mettle if faced with a hard decision. He behaved like a guy with a drug problem. His real name was Richard. The guys all called him Dick. It wasn't just short for Richard.

"What the fuck, Dick. I'm in the middle of a game."

Dick floundered. "It'll only take a second. Come on, please! It's important."

Frank sighed with resignation. He'd have to leave the game and deal with the asshole or be bothered by him all night. "All right, God damn it. You're interfering with my game, so keep it short. I was winning."

"Like hell you were," Vic corrected.

Ignoring Vic, Frank looked around the table and said, "Would you guys excuse me for a moment? I'll be right back."

Frank got up and walked off to one side. Dick followed. "Now, what's so damned important, Dick?" Frank asked in a husky whisper.

"Look. I know what's going on at the mill."

Frank stood fast. This would be the end. This weenie would turn in their operation and the money train would stop. Frank decided not to jump to conclusions. *Just play it cool. I don't know 'nada'.*

"What the fuck are you talking about?" Frank spat.

"Don't play with me. I have proof."

Great. This asshole is going to fuck up our deal. I knew somebody would, sooner or later.

"You can't have proof of something that isn't happening."

"Frank, quit playing. I want in."

"In...to what?"

"I know you are getting cans of Molybdenum out of the mill. I want in," Dick insisted.

Frank glanced away

"Come on, Frank. I could really use the extra cash."

Frank remained silent for a moment and Dick stared him down. He wasn't going to give it up. Frank didn't feel right about it. This didn't concern his friends so he wasn't cheating them. But this guy, Dick, was nothing more than a jitterbug. One day he would twitch and get somebody hurt. Frank didn't want to be that somebody.

"If I was doing what you say, and I'm not saying I am, why would I bother to let anyone else in?"

"Because if you don't I'll blow the whistle."

Frank felt cornered. "Fine. You want in?"

"Yes, please!" Dick pleaded.

"All right. I'll give you a shot and see what you can do. I can get two hundred a can. I want half. And I don't want you taking too much. That sort of shit will get you noticed, real quick."

"Okay, Frank. Anything you say. Thanks for the shot."

"Yeah," Frank said without enthusiasm.

"You won't be disappointed," Dick tried to sell himself.

"You better pray I'm not. It won't go well if I am. Anyone who disappoints me regrets it."

"I know, Frank. You're a stand-up guy. Everybody knows that."

"You screw this up and I'm liable to stand up…on your testicles. You know what I'm talking about? We don't bust knee caps like they do in Little Italy. We aim a little higher." Frank added as an afterthought, "We're classy."

"You don't have anything to worry about, Frank," Dick replied, spittle coming out of his mouth. "I can do this. And I could *really* use the money, so I'm motivated to do it right."

"And by the way, Dick-*head*, don't ever threaten me again."

Frank went quietly back to his game. "Thanks for waiting, guys."

Chapter 14

For several days Dick brought out one or two cans at a time. Frank assumed he only intended on taking five to ten a week. That sounded reasonable. No need to draw attention. From Dick, Frank took two hundred so he could still net an extra thousand or two a week on top of everything else. No one cared if Dick made some extra money, too. After all, he was taking all the risks.

But by the fourth night, Dick put so many cans into the trunk of his car that it almost dragged on the ground from the weight. When he hit a bump, sparks flew and metal scraped against the concrete.

One of the guards, actually a good friend of Dante's, later told Frank he could look the other way for most things, but this was different. Another guard stood at the shack with him. They had to step in front of the approaching car. Of course Dante's friend suspected what was in it. But it was too obvious to hide from the other guard. So they stood together in the narrow part of the road, in the direct path of the oncoming car and waited. When Dick saw them, he panicked. He accelerated and rushed through them as the two guards jumped out of the way—barely avoiding serious injury.

When Dick came around to the joint later to bring Frank the new load, he swaggered like a peacock.

"Frank, I got some stuff for you!"

Frank turned. Dick swallowed hard and walked toward him.

"I got a great load. You should see. It was easy. I got—," he almost choked.

"What the fuck did you think you were doing?" Frank said, just above a whisper.

"Frank, what's wrong? I got a load for you."

"I'll take it, too. Because it'll be the last."

"What do you mean?" Dick tried to continue the innocent act. "I can do this every week. We could—,"

"Dick, I have friends in the mill."

"That's great. So do I. With a little help, w—!"

Frank grabbed him around the neck and slammed him against the wall. "I know what happened tonight, asshole."

Dick's mouth fell open. "Oh."

"You stupid son-of-a-bitch. You're lucky they didn't catch you! You put our whole operation right out of business."

"But Frank, I—,"

"None of us can bring anymore out. They'll be on to us, now. They'll fortify the guards. That place will be like Fort Knox. They got security up the ass, you know. All they gotta do is make a phone call." Frank paced. "Why did you have to get greedy? I told you to only take a few."

"But they won't miss even *that* many. There's only about a dozen."

"A dozen! With what they weigh? And your car has bad fucking shocks."

"I just thought—,"

"No! No, you fucking didn't. You don't. You can't. You're so fucking stupid." Frank threw up his hands and turned away in disgust.

"Frank, I'm sorry."

Frank turned quickly back to face him. He stepped up to the man and placed his nose less than an inch from Dick's. He'd just lost more than three-thousand dollars a week income because some blundering idiot couldn't maintain his self control.

"Oh, you're sorry? *You're sorry?* Thanks to you we can't take any more of that shit. But it's okay because *you're sorry*. In that case, instead of being mad at you, maybe I should be buying you a beer. I mean, after all, you are *SORRY*."

Fear distorted Dick's face into something almost comical. Frank didn't feel in a humorous mood. Not in the least. Dick stared at the floor, accepting the fate for his stupidity. Silence filled the room and Dick looked like he was about to piss his pants.

"You know what? Get the fuck out of here! You've pissed me off and I want you out. Just get the fuck out! And stay out!"

Dick looked from one side to the other as if he couldn't make sense of it. Wasn't Frank going to *hurt* him?

Frank reached out and grabbed Dick's shirt. Dick stiffened as Frank pushed him toward the door. Paralyzed with fear, Dick stumbled. He tried to step toward the door but never took his eyes off Frank. Finally, Frank's patience reached its end.

"Vic, Dante!"

They came from the other room. When they got next to Frank, they waited. Dick's eyes grew twice their original size, and he stumbled even more.

"You might like to know that Dick, here, just fucked up our Moly deal. Please *escort* his worthless ass out of here."

Vic and Dante turned and looked at Dick. Their eyes met and Dick just about melted where he stood.

"But, F-Frank, what about the cans I got?"

"Leave 'em here," Frank said. "I said I'd take 'em. But you ain't getting shit. I'll take them in payment for…" He couldn't form any more words. His temper had reached the top of his head and would explode at any minute, like in one of those old cartoons. He turned to Vic and Dante again. "Get 'im outta here!"

"Our pleasure," Dante said.

They each grabbed an arm and picked him up. He faced backwards as they carried him out the front door and into the parking lot.

Dante looked at the piece of shit he carried. "Where's your car, Fuckface?"

"There."

They slammed him into the car door and opened the trunk. Vic and Dante both let out a whistle, looking at all the cans inside. Dick rubbed his head and tried to stand.

"Some of these cars have excellent trunk space, don't you think, Mr. *Mayo*?" Vic sneered.

"Well I rather think they do, Mr. *Slick*," Dante replied. "I bet you could hide a human body in here."

Dick slid a few more inches away from the trunk as Dante and Vic stacked the cans there in the parking lot.

"I might have to get one of these for myself," Vic added, good natured. "I might have need to dispose of a body."

As they passed in front of Dick, Dante stopped and grabbed the man's balls. He gave a gentle squeeze.

"Don't ever think about stepping foot in here again or we'll cut these off and shove them down your fucking throat! Got it?"

Dick shook his head, excitedly.

"That'll be just about right, since his name is *Dick*," Vic added his measure of sarcasm.

"Look at the bright side. If you catch me in a good mood, I might sauté them in garlic butter first."

Vic chuckled. "Yeah, Dante's become quite a chef."

As they walked away, Dick turned to get into his car, to get away. He fumbled with the door as if it were locked. A voice stopped him.

"Oh, and Dick?" Vic called.

Dick turned to see what new horror faced him.

"Have a nice day."

"I'll get you back for this, Frank," Dick yelled toward the building, though Frank couldn't possibly have heard. "I needed the money, but don't worry about it. It's no concern of yours. *Stand up guy*, my ass!" he finished, more to himself but still out loud.

Dante wondered if the man might be losing control. "Who's he talking to, Vic?"

"Beats me."

Vic and Dante went back into the joint, talking and carrying one can each. The two made several trips back and forth. Frank's eyes widened when he saw just how greedy Dick had gotten. One thing for certain, he'd walked away from the *Steel Mill Mafia* with only a reprimand. Not many people would be able to make such a claim in the future. Later Vic heard Dick only received a reprimand at work, as well.

Chapter 15

Alexander Graham Bell once said 'when one door closes, another one opens'. Life has a way of supporting his philosophy. Frank didn't live his life by it—he couldn't—but it often happened that way. A couple days after Dick fucked up the Moly deal, a new arrangement fell in Frank's lap. A different kind of chemical.

The front room of his joint looked a lot like a drug store coffee shop. Seven small, round tables stood far enough apart for people to walk between. He never hired a waitress. Thin wire chairs offered patrons a place to park their asses. Frank kept it down to two chairs per table. This meant, when the seats were full, anyone else had to take their coffee to go. Frank didn't like crowds.

The group he hung out with on this particular night was his usual—Vic and Dante. They were holding a *meeting*. But the only business in progress at the time had to do with the poker tables…and drinking.

"Frank, our boys in the mill still need to make some extra money. This couldn't have happened at a worse time. But you know those guys, they've always got something cooking. Since they can't get the Moly anymore, they thought this might be a way to get some cash. I was wondering what you thought about it."

Dante threw a couple bags on the table. The plastic slid across the smooth surface a little and stopped near the opposite edge. The bags sat next to each other—one green, one white.

Frank stared at the table. He recognized the substances within the bags. One had been turned green by the marijuana inside. The other was filled with white powder. Frank sucked in a breath.

"Holy hell! Slick—go lock the door. Are you guys fucking crazy?"

Vic went over to the door of the coffee shop in front of the joint and locked it. Then he set the dead bolt for extra security. He quickly returned to the table so he wouldn't miss anything.

"Slick and I agree with the guys. The mill is our domain. We don't have to worry about the law. Strangers would stick out like a sore thumb." Dante stated the obvious, but he could be a bit naïve, and Frank often suspected he liked to hear the sound of his own voice.

"Yeah, but we need you, Frank," Vic added. "You have all the connections. We're going to need some good ones for a deal like this."

"Come on," Dante wheedled. "You know it won't work without you."

"Besides," Vic continued. "What kind of friends would we be if we neglected to include you in our newest endeavor?"

"Endeavor?" Frank repeated in disbelief.

"Adventure?" Vic asked. "Safari? Mission?"

"*Your mission, Mr. Mattich,*" Dante added, "*should you decide to accept it...*"

Frank couldn't suppress a laugh. "Only for you two dummies, I'll see what I can do."

Frank lay in his bed that night, tossing more than just an idea in his head. Tangled in the sheets and sweaty, he got up. The clock read 2:30. In the living room, he paced, talking to himself—not entirely silent.

"This is way bad, Frank. Once you go down this road there may be no turning back. And what about going back to teaching? No," he answered. "I want more. But how the hell am I supposed to—."

"Frank?" Connie's voice floated across to him.

He started.

"What's the matter, honey?"

"I'm just thinking about another job. I had some ideas."

She went to hug him and he withdrew.

"It's okay to show me affection, Frank."

"My father."

"What about him? Is he here?"

"No. He wouldn't hug me when I was young. He said it would make me homosexual."

Connie laughed and Frank felt hurt that his sincerity gave her such humor.

"I think it's safe to hug me, Frank. Even if you do, you won't be gay."

He hugged her. "I know, honey. It's just that…well, old habits die hard."

"Habits? Frank we've made three beautiful daughters together. I think it's safe to assume you can touch me."

Frank smiled wanly, staring out the window. A strong wind had picked up at some time in the night. He could see tree tops in the distance swaying from one side to another. He could hear his father's voice inside his head. He could hear Connie's too. But his own voice told him to move forward. Take the risk and see where it led. Go for the gusto. Ride the thrill wave just a little longer.

"Well, I'm going back to bed now, Frank," Connie's voice called as if from a great distance.

Frank simply nodded at her. He never saw her leave the room.

85

*   *   *

The next day, Frank met with a strange gentleman. His new contact kept to the shadows. Running the poker joint, Frank became acquainted with a number of people of lower moral standards. Frank only had to locate a connection he felt comfortable working with. He didn't want to deal drugs with a man who would rat him out to avoid arrest.

Frank arranged to get some coke and weed. That was the easy part. Moving it could be another problem. He felt a bit like the 'Godfather', with Slick and Dante as his trusted lieutenants and the men under them—underlings. After a while Frank managed to get things moving smoothly, despite the bumpy beginning. The business quickly became profitable.

Frank watched his dream come into focus again. All this stuff was just the means to that end. He knew it. He saw no harm in laying out more cash at the track. It just meant he could possibly win more. After he put it all together, his life with Connie would be so much better. He wanted nothing more than to be with her and work with her. One idiot may have ruined the Moly deal—but now money flowed his way once again.

Frank knew better money could be made with better connections. As with any business, more volume meant more profit. And, of course, higher quality product meant more buyers. All Frank had to do was oil the machinery a little and things would move along even quicker.

Frank's stomach churned with excitement.

Chapter 16

Sitting at the table enjoying the horse races at Waterford Park in West Virginia, with the sun reflecting off the drink sitting in front of him, Frank watched Dante leading a dapper, middle-aged man toward him. They approached without hesitation. Frank stood to hug his friend and greet the newcomer.

"Frank, this is Nick. We were in Nam together," then he added, as if Frank didn't know, "Vietnam. Nick lives in Cleveland."

Frank shook the man's firm hand and admired the sincerity in his eyes.

"Nick, this is my good friend, Frank."

"Hello, Frank."

"A pleasure, Nick. Have a seat."

"Dante and I went through hell together in that damn war." He pulled out a chair and sat down. "I know what a straight up guy he is. He speaks highly of you. I guess that means I can trust you."

"Any friend of Dante's..."

"This kind of trust doesn't come easy—not for me." Nick stared thoughtfully at Frank as if appraising his character.

"And I appreciate it, Nick," Frank said, adding a nod of thanks toward Dante.

"I'm not going to mince words with you," Nick said. "We have common business interests. I'm going to introduce you to a man from Florida. He brought a load of weed and coke to Cleveland. I had a group who normally moves it for me, but two of their leaders had some bad luck."

"Bad luck?" Frank asked.

"Yes. They ran head first into some bullets. Damned inconvenient."

"Not exactly a picnic for them, either, I imagine."

"I suppose you're right about that," Nick said, his lips twisting into a wry grin. "So are you interested?"

"In catching a bullet or having a picnic?"

"In making a deal." His grin faded a bit.

Frank sat back. He glanced at Dante, though he didn't want his opinion. Nor did he expect Dante to say anything. The Italian rarely did. Frank brought a finger to his lips as he thought about all the problems doing business like this might create. But doing the deal with a friend, or the friend of a friend, certainly took some of the worry out of it.

"Sure," Frank finally answered.

"Think you can handle it?"

"Is there any reason to think I can't?"

"It is a much larger quantity than you're used to handling."

"I know. But I think it's time to move out of the little leagues. We'll handle it."

"Good. If he likes you, he'll probably agree. Excuse me for a second, would you? I'll bring him over."

Frank nodded his acceptance. Dante still said nothing. Frank looked in the direction Nick had gone. He was already returning with another well-dressed man, a Latino.

"Frank, this is Jorge," Nick said as Frank stood to greet the newcomer, extending his hand in welcome.

"Jorge."

"Frank."

When the final negotiation was over, Jorge and Nick stood, made their goodbyes, and left without further words exchanged.

"Well, what do you think?" Dante inquired when they were completely out of sight.

"It went well. Jorge said he was going to bring some product over to my house Sunday."

"To your *house*?"

"Yes, around noon."

"On Sunday."

"That's what he said."

"What about Connie?"

"She's going to have kittens," Frank said lightly, "*if* she finds out."

"How's she going to miss that?"

"Well, she and the girls will be gone for the day, Sunday."

"Really? How convenient."

"Her mom is in the hospital, smartass. They're going to visit her. She doesn't know anything about drugs. I'd hate to think how she'd react."

"Yeah, I'll visit you."

"Visit me?"

"In whatever hospital she puts you in."

"Aw, you know Connie doesn't have an aggressive bone in her body."

"Except maybe when you put yours in her."

Frank offered an enigmatic glance and watched the next race, clutching his tickets as if his life depended on winning. Dante sat and enjoyed the rest of the day with him but placed only a few bets. Frank won a comfortable take for the day, as usual.

He went home with a good feeling about the deal, despite not knowing the guy personally. In this sort of business, not knowing a guy could be an asset—or it could bite you in the ass. But Frank's instinct told him this would be a good ride. As long as he managed to stay in control. And *if* he managed to keep it from Connie.

Chapter 17

When he heard the doorbell Sunday morning around eleven, he discovered that a bite in the ass could come in many different forms. He opened the door and came face to face with Jorge, dressed a little more casually. His bright colored polo shirt belonged in the tropics, and contradicted the incognito attitude Frank thought they should all have while doing such business.

"How are you, Frank?"

Frank looked over and saw a large box truck parked in his driveway. All the markings had been removed which Frank thought looked rather suspicious. Two muscular Latino men stood next to it. Frank felt a bit inadequate. If they were bringing that much stuff, he didn't know how well it would move. He worked a small town with only one major outlet, the mill. And it went without saying, not everyone there used the stuff.

"I don't know," Frank said doubtfully. "What's in the truck?"

"Just the product you wanted."

"I wanted? How fucking much is there?" Frank suddenly felt sure the conversation he'd had at the track did not cover *this*.

"Only a thousand pounds of marijuana and five kilos of coke."

"Only!!!"

"It's what you wanted."

"It's wha—."

"Hey, Frank. You'll love the prices."

"Huh?"

"I don't want to take them back to Florida," Jorge added.

"My wife, she doesn't know about any of this. I can't imagine how pissed she'll be if she finds all this shit in our house."

"So, what are you saying, Frank. Are you trying to back out of the deal?"

"No, I'm…I guess I expected a lot less."

"I understand. Look, I'll be deeply indebted if you can help me out, Frank."

"Deeply indebted?"

"There could be more deals in the future. Perhaps something smaller next time? Or we might be able to work around your schedule better on the next load."

Frank sighed. One way or the other, he'd been stuck with this load. If he wanted to retain his 'stand-up' reputation, he had little choice. He looked at the truck and tried to think of a good excuse to tell Connie. Nothing came to him. Surely he'd need to hurry and move the stuff out quickly.

"Okay, Jorge. Let me open the garage."

They backed the big truck near the house and Frank sucked in his breath as he saw the stacks of boxes inside. The two Latinos moved twenty boxes into Frank's garage and then grabbed the five one-kilo bricks of cocaine. Once inside, it looked so much larger to Frank.

No way Connie would be able to park in there when she returned.

"I'm going back to Cleveland for a few days. I've got business to clean up. I'll be back next week. I'll come by and see how you're doing, okay?"

"Yeah, just remember, my wife doesn't know. Keep it simple, okay?"

"I can be discrete."

91

Frank looked at the man's clothes with doubt. "Good. Have a nice trip, Jorge."

"Thanks, Frank. I'll talk to you soon."

Jorge and his men got into the truck and left. Struck with a sudden epiphany, Frank walked into the garage and stepped up on a bucket. He closed the garage door and then disconnected the automatic opener.

"Slick," Frank almost yelled into the phone as soon as he got back into the house. "Get Dante and bring him over here, pronto. No questions, just take my word, it's important."

As soon as the car arrived, a minute later, Frank went to the door. Only Vic got out.

"Where's Dante?"

"He couldn't make it. Something important came up."

"I'm almost afraid to ask."

"That's probably just as well, Frank. There's a new waitress over at Riley's bar and

Dante wanted to take her for a test drive."

"Figures. Anyway, take a look at this," Frank suggested.

He took Vic down to the basement and showed him all the stuff in the garage through the connecting door. Vic poked his head through and stared wide-eyed. Vic Horvath, lifelong friend and trusted companion, politely began to laugh—heartily.

"Hey, it's not going to be a laughing matter if Connie finds this stuff. You and Dante have to get your men together and start moving it."

"Right away?"

"Tomorrow, Vic."

"Frank, let me ask you something. Is it really worth having this stuff brought right to your own home like this?

"I told you I'll probably have to make other arrangements."

"But even this once, you're taking a mighty big risk."

92

"Short notice. I didn't have many options."

"I hope there's a good profit margin."

"Hey, you'll love the prices," Frank echoed Jorge's words.

"Huh?"

"It's a great deal for us, if we can move it. And it's really the only thing we have flying right now."

"If you say so, Frank. What are you going to do about Connie?"

"What do you mean, what am I going to do *about* Connie?"

"Well, I didn't mean it like *that*. I don't expect you to dump her body somewhere. I just meant you can't have stuff coming *here* all the time."

"You're right. We'll have to work out an alternate location to do business. For now I've disconnected the garage door opener."

"What good will *that* do?"

"I'll just tell her it's broken and I have to fix it."

The other man looked at him in disbelief.

"Hey, I had to think of something quick. You got a better idea?"

Vic shook his head. Soon after, he got in his car and managed to get far enough down the street for Connie to not notice when she pulled in. Frank sat at the table, enjoying a late snack. When Connie came in the door she looked upset.

"What's wrong with the garage door?"

The girls came in around their mother and headed for their own evening routines. Frank looked into the beautiful eyes he'd fallen in love with and knew he couldn't tell her the lie he'd been practicing. If she looked into the garage, she would see the packages and he'd be found out. The closer to the truth he remained, the better he'd feel and the more likely she might be to believe him.

"I disconnected it so no one could open it," Frank answered.

"Why?"

"Well, some of the guys dropped some packages off for a couple days. I said I would watch them until they came and got them out."

"Watch them?"

"You know, *store* them," Frank rationalized.

"What's in them, Frank? Drugs?" Her voice rose.

"I don't know," he lied. A lie he could live with. A lie that was necessary.

"Come on, Frank. You don't know?"

"Honest."

"How could you not know? Didn't you ask?"

"They'll be gone shortly."

"Shortly? What's shortly? Two days? Two months?"

"I said a couple days, and that's what I meant."

"A couple days."

"Honey, don't worry."

"Don't worry? Are you crazy? We have three, beautiful little girls here and we could lose everything over this. And you tell me not to worry! Do you even know what your youngest looks like?"

"I've been out of the house a lot," Frank replied, matter-of-factly.

"We hardly see you anymore."

"Connie, it'll be okay. I'll have the stuff out of here in a couple days. I've got connections."

"Connections?" Connie swung her head from side to side. "Connections, Frank?"

"Connections," Frank answered with pride.

"Do you even *hear* yourself?"

Frank looked away.

"So, what are you now?" she continued with ferocity. "A drug dealer, Frank? Nothing but a filthy gangster? Is that what you are?"

"Don't be ridiculous."

"Is that what you *want* to be?" She yelled as loud as she could while still retaining control over her volume. She didn't want the girls to overhear.

Frank slid his arms around her and pulled her close. "I'm no gangster."

"If you look like one and act like one, then you *are* one." She pushed against him, slightly. "What else can you be?"

"Don't judge a book by its cover."

"If you meow like a cat and purr like a cat, I'm not likely to mistake you for a duck."

"I'm no gangster. I'm the same guy you married."

"Are you? Are you, really?"

"Of course, I am. Look at me. Do I look so different to you?"

"Yes. Yes, you do."

"But I'm the same guy," Frank protested.

"No, you're not. You've changed. We've both been kidding ourselves. This isn't something temporary. It's who you are. The same guy who cheated with the ice cream sandwiches at Kennywood. But now you're in deeper than just ice cream, aren't you, Frank?" she said as her head lowered. "This is something much bigger."

"Much bigger, honey. And a lot more money."

"And a much bigger hole for you to be buried in." Her voice calmed a little.

Frank pulled Connie tighter and looked at her eyes.

"I still love you. Nothing can change that."

"I know, Frank. I know," she sighed.

Frank kissed her.

"I tried to do it the right way. You know I did. But the system took all that away from me. And I was so close to the dream. It just wasn't right, Connie. You know it's true. So, if I beat the system now, it's only fair, right?"

"Fair? Since when is life fair? And what is fair? *An eye for an eye*? They hurt you, Frank, and that's the truth. But that doesn't mean you can ignore whatever rule you choose, break whatever law you want to. We're supposed to be civilized. But you seem to be enjoying this life way too much."

"So I enjoy my work. What of it?"

"What good is having the American dream if we're no better than animals? What good will that dream be if you're in jail, Frank? Answer me that."

"I just want to catch a break, Honey," Frank pleaded. "This is for my family. I'll take that break however I can get it. For the girls. For you."

"What's in the garage isn't for us. We don't use it and we don't want it here."

"No, you don't. But I'm *doing* it for us."

"Is that what you tell yourself, Frank? When you kiss your girls goodnight? Is that why you're hardly ever here anymore? Are you afraid to face them? Afraid they'll see what you're turning into?"

"Honey, my father worked in the steel mill. He worked sixteen hours a day and was hardly ever home, either. Schultzie's dad did no better, running the bar and cleaning and keeping the books. Hell," Frank continued, trying to make light of the conversation, "one time Eddie told me he forgot what his dad looked like."

Frank offered up a little chuckle. Connie did not.

96

"Listen, Connie," Frank forged ahead. "Sometimes a man makes these sacrifices for the sake of his family. He leaves early and busts his ass all day, hardly seeing the ones he loves. And as far as getting arrested is concerned, there are always dangers—in any job. You remember what I told you happened at the mill that time? That steel beam fell right on my dad's head. Christ, Connie, he got a concussion and a neck injury. Not to mention most of his teeth were shattered. His dental work was never right after that."

Now Frank's breathing had increased, faster and deeper. *This is like exercise*!

He tried to force himself to relax. "Look, honey, I'm no better or worse than anyone else. I'm working a job, that's all. A dangerous job, maybe. But, in my opinion, the rewards are well worth the risks. It's like hazardous duty pay."

"Frank," she began. Her voice sounded so dejected, defeated. Its tone took the joviality right out of Frank. His smile fell away and his hands fell in his lap. He didn't know what would come next, but he felt obligated to concede to her.

Frank waited.

"Promise me, Frank. No more of that," she said, pointing toward the garage.

Frank sighed and looked down. He hesitated a bit, but if she grew concerned about his apparent lack of commitment, she never said. He sucked in a deep breath and looked up at her.

"I'll get rid of that stuff, and no more. I promise."

Connie kissed him, but couldn't manage a smile. He kept his promise to get the stuff out of the house.

Chapter 18

"I never imagined I'd see this much money," Vic said, touching it, running his hands through the bills with reverence.

Dante sat with Vic at one of the tables of the joint, playing in a pile of money. Smiles consumed their faces. Frank paced around, worried about how to keep Connie from finding out anything about his continued dealings. The irony almost made it humorous.

Criminals and drug dealers were easy to work with, but Connie—a man had to be like a master criminal to slip one by her. And when she caught you, she could be ruthless. In truth, Connie had never done anything to him, other than make him feel embarrassed about what he did for a living. Sometimes, for a man, that was far worse. He felt less of a man when she looked at him with disappointment. A simple look, and he felt like a worm. But wormy or not, this life called to him, smothered him in honey and warmth. Frank wanted more.

"Can we keep doing this?" Dante asked. "This is my kind of fun."

"You can have fun without a woman sitting in your lap?" Vic asked.

"With fun like this," Dante replied, holding up a wad of bills, "I could have a whole harem, and not just on my lap."

"I saw you at the club the other night," Vic continued.

"We went together, dummy," Dante retorted.

"I saw you when you went over to that girl."

"What girl?"

"The one with the red sweater." Then he leaned over to Frank and whispered behind his hand. "Like it makes any difference."

"Oh, her," Dante answered. "So?"

"You didn't show her money to get into her pants."

"No, I showed her a baggie with some coke in it. That stuff works better than olive oil to get a girl's pants off."

Frank and Vic both let out a sigh of resignation. Dante would always be Dante.

"So, Frank," Vic said, returning to the previous conversation. "What about doing more?"

"I got a call from Jorge. He was real impressed with our work. We took a large load and made it move."

"Yeah, we're like…professionals," Dante swooned in jest.

"So, we can expect more?" Vic asked, remaining serious.

"He says he has another load waiting for us. All I have to do is give the word."

"The gospel according to Frank," Dante continued to quip.

"Waiting? Where?" Vic asked, ignoring Dante altogether.

"West Palm Beach."

"West Palm Beach? Florida?"

"The only one I know of," Frank replied with sarcasm. "Is there another?"

"How the hell are we supposed to get it?" Vic asked in disbelief.

"We go there and bring it back."

"Aw, we gotta be our own delivery boys now, too?" Dante asked.

"Hey," Frank insisted. "You want the deal or not? Remember—."

"You'll like the prices," they all said in unison.

Vic and Dante looked at each other and shrugged. The choices were limited and the money spoke to them, *called* to them. They didn't want to give up what was laid on the table. Money like that would make life grand—perhaps even a couple *hundred* grand. And soon enough a wise man could retire.

"Sounds cool, Frank," Dante conceded. "We go down there, have some fun in the sun, and get out of this dreary Pittsburgh weather for a short time."

"And we don't have to pay for shipping and handling," Vic added, "like when you order out of the Sears and Roebuck catalog."

"Hey," Dante asserted. "I like the Sears and Roebuck catalog."

"Of course," Vic taunted. "There are pictures of women in their underwear."

"Well," Dante hedged, "yeah."

Vic focused. "We'll just take a few days off work, like a short vacation."

"That brings up something else," Frank added, ominously.

Vic and Dante looked inquisitively at each other, then turned back to face Frank. Neither one dropped their smile.

"It looks like this could become a regular thing."

Their smiles broadened.

"It might interfere with your jobs at the mill," Frank added with compassion.

"If it's regular enough," Vic began, "we'll just quit our jobs."

"Yeah," Dante added with enthusiasm. "The money's better, that's for sure."

"How's Connie going to take you being gone so much?" Vic asked.

Frank smiled. "She seems to have calmed down since I bought her a new car and have given her piles of money to spend on herself and the girls. I've also made arrangements to take them all to Harrah's Marina in Atlantic City to see Bill Cosby. That should keep her a little preoccupied."

"Yeah," Dante added. "Funny how the women like the green. Money or coke usually gets you over with them. Either one can get you all the pussy you could want."

"Hey, Frank," Vic added. "This is all fine and dandy, but what about the joint? Who's going to keep an eye on it while you're gone all the time? It can't be Dante or me. We have *some* life outside this place and it sounds like we might be traveling with you some of the time."

Frank averted his eyes.

"Frank?" Dante asked, feeling a bit empathic.

"I don't know how to tell you guys." Frank felt like an idiot. He should have discussed this with them sooner, but it seemed like such a let-down. He didn't want to disappoint anybody, but life beckoned. His index finger twitched.

"What is it, Frank?"

"I've been thinking about closing the place. I mean *really* thinking about it."

"What? Why?" Vic asked.

"You have a good thing going here, don't you?"

"Yeah," Dante said with hesitation. "You make enough money, right?"

"So why close it?" Vic asked again.

"You know about the people who have been protecting this place. Politicians and policemen, they help keep me safe from prosecution."

"Yeah, we know. Some of them come in here to play, that's why they protect it. What about them?"

"Well, they got voted out of office."

"Oh, shit. Can we get to the new group?"

"I got word the new group is going to have me raided."

"What? Why the hell would they do that?"

"Probably so they look good to the voting crowd. And they probably want to get their own man in here to control their own joint. It's the American way."

"Bastards."

"Anyway," Frank continued, "we're making so much money with the drugs, I didn't think I needed to be aggravated by more crooked politicians."

"Or straight ones," Vic inserted, not entirely joking.

"You guys know how I feel about *them*," Frank said, already knowing they knew the answer.

"One step above cockroaches?"

"One step *below*," Frank corrected.

"Hey," Dante spoke up enthusiastically. "I hear they got a lot of cockroaches in Florida. We can go down and crush some."

Frank looked at him, confused. Sometimes Dante's mind didn't reside on the same planet as mere Earthlings.

"It might make you feel better," Dante finished.

"I'd like to crush some of the two-legged kind that took over."

"Yeah," Vic added. "We heard a rumor the other day. They want to close the mills in the area."

"Really?" Frank asked in disbelief. "That's honest, working-man profit there. How many do they want to close?"

"ALL of them. Duquesne, Homestead, McKeesport, every single one. That'll probably kill your gambling business anyway. Dante and I will be out of work. This place will go to hell real quick. Everybody will want to do drugs to escape the crap of daily life."

Frank smiled. Maybe this would work out, after all. Certainly no harm in making a profit, especially when everyone else would be in the unemployment line. Maybe Connie would appreciate his *work* a little more then, but not likely.

"The corporation got their man, Reagan, as president," Dante filled in. "He doesn't care about the steel workers."

"These small mill towns will turn into ghost towns," Vic whispered.

The other two nodded.

"Poor Schultzie," Vic continued. "His business will suffer."

"We'll have to help him out, somehow," Frank said, firmly.

"Yeah," Vic and Dante chorused.

"The question is, will he accept our help?"

"Why wouldn't he?" Dante asked.

"His life is different now. He's become...respectable."

"Eww! Why'd he want to go and do a dumb fucking thing like *that*?"

"It comes with the business. He's even hired an extra bartender."

"What's next, is he gonna sell stock in the place?" Dante sounded disgusted.

"A kid by the name of Zack," Frank continued.

Vic and Dante rolled their eyes.

Chapter 19

Stuck in Florida, Frank spent as much free time as he could muster golfing. Bars were nice enough and, as it happened, a necessary evil, but Frank never felt like he wanted to be a bar hopper. High rolling at a casino more appealed to him. Golf was considered the rich man's leisure.

The Florida courses offered beautiful grass and warm sunshine. Fresh air, that's what Frank wanted when he relaxed. And a little exercise never hurt. Dante often spent his time at the local beaches, usually trying to watch the beach babes through hungover eyes, but occasionally he joined Vic and Frank on the green.

One day, Frank and Dante sat in the clubhouse at the bar. After a frustrating game of swatting the ball half way around the world, sometimes a little drink took the edge off the bad score. Frank and Dante waited for Vic to return as he finished off his eighteen with another group. Big windows lined the wall facing the course and they saw Vic approach while he was still many yards away. Fortunately for the players, and their drinks, the glass windows were unbreakable. The last hole brought the players back, full circle, to the clubhouse.

Vic took his turn, focused his club, swung almost perfectly, and knocked the ball into the medium sized lake. Some of the small crowd in the clubhouse noticed, but none commented. Most of the players had sliced into that drink at one time or another. Dante, on the other hand, laughed out loud.

"Uh-oh," he said to Frank. "Slick just hit his ball into the water. I don't think he saw where it went."

"Yeah, nobody rides with him because he gets so uptight when he plays."

"I don't think he likes the game."

"Really? I wonder why he continues to play."

"It's probably just for status," Dante said. "Jack Nicklaus is one of Vic's heroes."

Just then, Vic's cart pulled up to the lake. He looked a little red in his face as he eyed the lake. He turned and stormed back to the cart. All eyes watched the drama unfolding outside the window.

Vic grabbed his bag of clubs and carried them to the water's edge. With a massive effort, he lifted it over his head and threw the entire thing in the water after the ball. A soft laughter spread over the crowd in the bar as they watched Vic get into his cart and drive off. The laughs lingered after the cart went out of sight.

"The sad part is," Frank said to Dante, "that was a fairly new set of Calloway's. They cost a pretty penny. I guess easy money isn't worth as much as the hard earned kind."

"I don't think Vic cares how hard he had to work for it. When he gets pissed about something like that, there's no talking any sense to him. He has to have his little temper tantrum. Just stay out of his way until it's over."

A couple men standing near the bar where Frank and Dante sat, watched the whole thing, a little less interested than the rest of the club.

"He won't leave them in there," one man said to the other.

"I wouldn't bet on that," Frank answered.

"I'll bet on that," the second man said.

"Me too," said the first.

"How much do you have to lose?" Dante asked.

Frank glanced at Dante and then back to the two men. "Five? Ten? Are you brave enough?"

"I'll bet a hundred bucks," the first man answered with confidence.

His friend nodded. "I'll take a hundred."

"Put your money on the bar, gentlemen," Frank said.

Frank and Dante anted up, as did the strangers. Moments later, Vic came back into view, still driving his cart as if he wanted to roll over some pedestrians. He stopped at the lakeside and got out. After rolling up his pant legs and removing his socks and shoes, he waded into the mucky water.

"I told you he'd be back."

"Yeah, hand over your money." The two men gloated.

"Now, just wait a second," Frank said. "Let's just wait and see what he does."

Vic walked into the water, almost to the depth where his rolled up pants would get wet. He reached his arm down and searched for the bag he'd discarded. As soon as he found it, he lifted the weight up and cradled it close to his body.

The sound of a pin dropping would have shattered the silence that had fallen over the place. Everyone heard the bet. Everyone watched Vic with earnest. Not one eye strayed away from the scene outside. Even the waitress stood still and watched.

Vic searched through the pockets on the side of the bag. He came out with his Rolex and car keys. He put them both in his pants pocket and threw the bag out into deeper water. The entire place collapsed into hysterical laughter. Even the two smug strangers chuckled.

Dante looked at them and smirked. "A pleasure doing business with you gentleman," he said as he picked up the money from the bar. The two men stared at their money as it disappeared into Dante's pocket.

"That was almost as good a scam as that time you got that girl to have sex with you and you only gave her a baggie of crushed aspirin," Frank whispered to Dante.

"Yeah. That was the best blow job I ever had."

"I think the best part was what she gave you afterward," Frank scoffed.

"She was just trying to tell me she appreciated how good I tasted."

"Are you sure it wasn't her IQ?" Frank laughed.

Chapter 20

The Tropical Twilight Club in West Palm shone with neon and colored flood lights. The all-too-familiar palm trees framed the entrance. The throb of the bass hit them at the door. The three men walked in expecting another evening of great entertainment. Of course the most interesting drama generally entailed watching the Dante production, to see which lucky lady would win the leading role for the night. His success rate beat the odds by far. And this time he had some *real* coke. Frank and Vic sometimes felt a little envious.

They sat at a table, and listened to music played far too loud. The dance floor held several couples in varying degrees of intercourse. Lights swirled overhead but left the corners shadowed for intimate liaisons. Frank and Vic watched as Dante hit on a very pretty blonde with incredibly long legs. From the look, he scored once again. He walked toward them.

"Hey guys, I think I'm getting lucky tonight. She is really fine."

"I don't know," Vic said. "I'm getting bad vibes."

"Vibes, *schmibes*. You're just jealous."

"I don't think so, Dante," Frank said after studying Vic's expression. "He doesn't look jealous to me. And it's not like Vic to get involved with your…affairs."

"Yeah," Vic agreed.

"I requested a slow song. You just watch us grind." Dante turned to leave.

"Don't do it, Dante," Vic called after him.

"Eat your hearts out," he answered back over his shoulder.

Frank and Vic sat watching, unwilling to get further involved. Vic's expression showed a sense of discomfort.

"Something isn't right, Frank. I can feel it."

"You think she's trouble? Maybe a narc?"

"N-n-no, not really. Just something…something wrong."

"It's not like you to be timid. Getting superstitious in your old age?"

"Maybe, but the feeling's tugging at me. I can't put my finger on it."

"Let's hope when you do, it's not *too* late," Frank suggested.

Dante and the blonde were kissing passionately, still tamer than what some of the other patrons were doing on the dance floor. Dante's hand slid down to her ass. She leaned into him with enthusiasm. The music seemed to pulsate just for them. Dante thrust his hips against her and began working one hand into the crack of her ass, through her dress.

Suddenly he stood back with a stunned look on his face. He pulled his arm full back and punched her in the mouth, knocking her to the floor. Frank and Vic stood up, ready to get into the action if Dante needed any help.

Dante returned to the table so fast he almost ran. Frank and Vic questioned with their eyes, but no answer came. When Dante spoke, his voice sounded as immediate as his steps had been. Apparently he didn't want to waste any time explaining.

"Let's get out of here!"

"What the fuck happened?" Frank asked.

"Hurry up!" Dante insisted, as he turned and marched toward the door.

They ran outside, not looking back. There could've been a hundred guys following, all ready to defend the beautiful lady's

109

honor. Of course, most men didn't give two shits about her honor—
they were only interested in her pants.

As it happened, no one followed them. The trio reached the
car and Frank cornered Dante, grabbing the door handle before he
could open it.

"Okay, enough. I asked you what the fuck happened. Now
tell me."

"I gotta get…get outta here. You can't leave me here."

"Leave you?"

"Can we just go? Please?"

"What are you talking about? Leave you?"

"I just want to get the fuck out of here. Is that too fucking
much to ask?"

"Talk to me, Dante," Vic asked, "why the fuck would you hit
a beautiful woman? Is that the secret to your success with them?"

"Fuck you."

"*Fuck me?* After the way you treated her, I'm going to have
to decline. I like the kind of guy who touches me gently—"

"Look," he interrupted, lowering his head. He took a deep
breath to steady himself and began to speak just above a whisper.
His sheepish tone was barely audible. "I don't know how to say
this."

"Just spit it out, Big Guy."

"Well, we were dancing, you know? And, after a while I
began to feel something hard come up between us."

"So?"

"It wasn't me!"

Frank stared at him while Vic, who put it all together a
second faster, began to laugh uncontrollably. A few moments later,
Frank's smile washed over his face and he couldn't get it to go away
long enough to act compassionate to his friend.

"Now I know what was bothering me," Vic shouted.

"Can you be a little fucking louder?" Dante hissed.

"Oh, sorry. But I thought I saw an Adam's Apple."

"And you couldn't fucking tell me?"

"Hey, shit-for-brains, I tried to warn you. But you were thinking with your little head again," Vic said, pointing down at Dante's crotch. "Don't blame me. Besides, you always say you're looking for new sexual adventures. She, I mean *he*, might have been the best fuck you ever had."

"How would you like to feel my foot up your—," Dante began, angrily.

"Hey, Dante, chill. You know he's right. You get your dick hard and you don't always think straight. We always knew, one day, it would get you into trouble. I guess I never thought it would be like this," Frank finished with a chuckle. "But if you *really* want to stick something up someone's ass, why don't you go back in there and get with that blonde. At least she looked hot. Unless you'd rather be with someone who looks like Vic."

"You guys can go fuck yourselves," Dante yelled. He grabbed the handle again, flopped himself down on the back seat, and slammed the door hard—rocking the car. He crossed his arms over his chest, which rose high with heavy breathing. He looked like a sulking child. Frank couldn't keep the smile from his face. He looked at Vic.

"Want to get out of here?"

"Did you want me to go back in and ask if the blonde needs a ride home?"

Frank chuckled. "Just drive, will you?"

"Yeah, I think the excitement is over. This place won't have anything else going on tonight."

"Unless…," Frank began.

"Unless?" Vic asked.

"Well, you know, if other guys hit on her, I mean *him*, we might see a lot more shit. There might even be an old fashioned bar brawl."

"Or some guy might be stupid enough to go with her/him," Vic added. "That would be a laugh."

They both looked at Dante to see if he might be game. He sat in the seat and stared at the floor, determined not to be drawn in.

"Maybe not," Frank suggested.

They got into the car, Vic at the wheel.

"You guys want to stop somewhere so I can buy some antiseptic mouthwash or chewing gum or something?"

"Maybe you'd like some kerosene?"

"You guys are a riot. Just find a fucking store, will you?"

"Well, we *do* need gas," Vic said as he started the engine.

"Just think," Frank joked, turning toward the back seat. "You might never have been troubled with constipation again."

Vic crumbled into hysteria. He managed to regain control before putting the car into drive.

"Asshole."

"Yeah, that's what he/she wanted. Your asshole."

Dante made a noise of disgust and spoke no more. Just a few minutes down the road, Vic sat upright.

"Hey, there's a gas station. Let's pull into that one."

"Why that one, Vic?"

"I think I saw a sexy blonde with a red dress."

Dante snorted air out through his nose.

112

Chapter 21

Frank and his 'gang' met many people in their travels, even the occasional celebrity. Lots of people enjoyed what they called 'recreational' drugs.

One, an ex All-Conference linebacker, Ted, believed he could take advantage. Frank knew some people thought he might be stupid and easy to outwit because he was well mannered. Obviously Ted thought that because he tried such a stupid stunt.

He managed to swindle fifteen thousand dollars from Frank and the boys. They handed him some money to make a buy and he returned with some lame-assed story. They trusted him a bit too much. Then he just left. He probably thought he'd pulled a fast one.

So, late one night, Frank and Dante showed up at Ted's house. His driveway was poorly lit—dirt with patches of grass growing in uneven spots—giving the appearance of being an unused road. Frank pulled the car up to the front yard and honked the horn.

"Now, you know the plan. Be careful. He's a real bad ass. He didn't make All-Conference because of his tremendous singing voice."

"Got it," Dante said from the passenger seat.

"This guy claimed his people stiffed him out of *our* fifteen grand. I told him we were coming by to help look for them."

"How do you know they didn't stiff him like he said?" Dante asked.

"Something about this guy isn't right. I'm not even sure there were any *people*."

"Right," Dante agreed.

The guy's rugged build looked bigger than Dante. He came down the steps from the raised house, looking very confused, wondering who the hell was disturbing him at this hour. After he passed the blindness of the headlights he saw Frank. He approached the driver's window with a friendly attitude.

"Hey Frank. What's up?"

"Hey, Ted. Shake hands with my main man, Dante."

Ted reached through the window to shake the hand offered in front of Frank's chest. Dante, well muscled himself, gripped the hand and held tightly. Frank rolled up the window, trapping Ted's arm. The window pinned him past the elbow so he was unable to free himself.

"Hey, what are you doing? Let go of me."

"Did you hear something?" Frank asked.

"'fraid not."

The two men in the car said nothing else. Frank put the car in drive and released the brake. The car began to roll forward. At first, Ted easily kept up with it, all the while calling to them to release him.

"Who the fuck do you think you're fooling with, you big dumb motherfucker?"

Dante looked at Frank. "Did he just call you a motherfucker?"

"I think he was talking to you," Frank returned.

"Hey, you're the one driving."

"It couldn't be me, could it?"

"And really, fucking your own mother? That's such a disgusting concept."

"Well, Dante, the only person around here who even *looks* like they might be stupid enough to fuck their mother is him," Frank said, pointing his finger toward the window and the guy outside it.

"Well, one thing I know for sure about motherfuckers," Dante said, knowing Frank would ask.

"What's that?"

"They drive a hell of a lot faster than this."

"Good to know," Frank acknowledged.

"You're welcome."

"No!" Ted shouted. "Don't!"

Frank accelerated. Ted still managed to keep up, although it became more difficult. Several minutes later, Ted slumped, exhausted, stumbling to regain his footing. He finally failed. They dragged him a little further to ensure his compliance. Frank pulled the car to the side and came to a stop. Frank released Ted's arm from his window and both he and Dante got out.

Looking down at Ted, lying in the dirt, he no longer looked so tough. Dante kicked him on his back. Ted groaned. Frank swung his own foot up and connected with Ted's ribs. Dante struck again, kicking the man's thigh muscle.

"What the hell are you doing? Do you know who I am?" Ted groaned.

"Yeah, you're a piece of shit."

"What the fuck do you want me to do?"

Frank squatted down and looked directly into Ted's eyes.

"Well, you could...die."

Just then Dante struck out with his foot again. Frank, still face to face, struck a right cross that twisted Ted's face hard to his right. Brass knuckles protected Frank's fingers from being broken. Blood trickled from the center of Ted's lower lip. Dante kicked again, this time at Ted's kidney. The man groaned in pain as he struggled to breathe.

115

Ted faded into semi unconsciousness, no longer reacting to each strike. Frank held up his hand and Dante stopped. The lump of flesh at their feet offered no more struggle. Dante leaned down and pulled out a pair of pliers. He reached over with them and grabbed Ted's nose. Frank could see the pliers squeeze and Dante gave them a gentle twist while he turned Ted to face him.

"Do you want to lie and say you don't have our money?"

Ted's dazed eyes rolled over toward Dante. He could barely keep his heavy eyelids up. He seemed unable to focus, and Frank thought maybe Ted hadn't heard. Before Dante could repeat his question, Frank leaned in closer. He looked directly into Ted's eyes. Frank showed no mercy and Ted recognized the truth as fear crept onto his face. He managed to keep his eyes open just a little better. He stared directly at Frank, not even glancing at Dante.

"Yes," Frank almost whispered. "You want to tell us, don't you, fuck-nuts? You don't want to lie again."

Ted shook his head as best he could, minding the pliers still holding his nose firmly.

"What does a guy like you need to rip off a measly fifteen G's for, anyway? Didn't you make enough being All Conference? Or is your little coke problem becoming too much of a burden?

Again he tried to shake his head.

"Maybe you should sell some of the shit you've got inside your fancy house. It'll fetch a better price and you won't get your ass kicked. Unless you *like* getting your ass kicked."

This time, when Ted tried to shake 'no', Frank could see the movement, a little. Frank focused harder, trying to see inside the man's mind. After some time, satisfied that Ted was no longer able to fight back, he glanced at Dante. Dante, catching Frank's signal, released the pliers and stood back.

"You wanted to say something to me?"

"No more, please."

116

"Oh, are you hurt? Maybe we can get you a doctor," Frank said, looking up to Dante. Then he dropped his head sharply to look back at Ted. "Would you like us to call one for you?"

"No, please. Please. I've got your money."

"I know you do. Where is it?"

"At the house. I can go get it for you."

"You're in no condition to make it alone. We'll go with you, won't we Dante?"

Dante just shook his head but Frank wasn't looking. Neither was Ted.

"We want to take care of you, *buddy*."

"Can you take me to my home?" the guy blubbered.

"Sure. It's the least we can do for a good guy like you, Ted."

They picked him off the ground, cuffed his hands behind his back, and dropped him without finesse into the big back seat. The guy sat there, leaning dangerously to one side, his eyes barely open even a slit, alone and bleeding. Frank stood outside the car, facing Dante with a smile. The Italian stood there smiling, holding up the pliers.

"You know," Dante said, breaking the night silence with his sharp voice, "I'll be damned if that Bob Vila guy wasn't right."

"What the hell are you talking about?"

Dante wiggled the pliers back and forth. "You just need the right tool for the job."

Frank laughed.

Chapter 22

Jorge's head bounced off the car fender. The dull thud echoed around them. For a moment it became difficult to tell which one was made of the harder substance. In the end, the car won out and Jorge's bloody face sank to the ground. His eyes rolled up and he collapsed into a semi-conscious stupor. He rolled to one side with a weak groan.

His dazed vision refused to allow him to focus on any one thing in particular. There were trees and a dirt road. He could see his own two feet and, of course, the car. He'd been introduced to the car. They were now intimate friends.

He gurgled something but blood kept him from forming words properly. It passed his lips and rolled down the side of his cheek and dripped off his earlobe. Whatever pleas came from his mouth intelligibly—fell on deaf ears. No one wanted to hear the babbles of an idiot.

Sometimes, a head-on wreck just could not be avoided, even by Superman.

Frank smiled.

"Frank, I thought he was giving us what we needed," Vic said, glancing out at the waters of West Palm. The hotel room stood bleak and utilitarian, but the Florida colors offered a friendly atmosphere. A potted Areca Palm in the corner added a touch of life. Back in his hotel, after pummeling Jorge, Frank paced in the good-sized room, curling past the two beds, searching for answers.

Apparently, Vic and Dante wanted some, as well. Frank explained the necessity of searching for new connections.

"Jorge *appeared* to be on the up-and-up," Frank explained. "But he's been stiffing us, you know. Haven't you noticed our shipments have been a little lighter lately?"

"I noticed, honest. I thought that's why we were watering them up."

"True, but he's been shorting a little more on each shipment. I got fed up with it."

"But Frank, you beat the crap out of him. I don't think he'll want to supply us anymore."

"I don't want anything else from that piece of shit, Vic. If I want to get fucked, I'll…"

"But, Frank."

"Just because we're nice guys, he thinks we're weak. It seems everybody thinks we're weak. Are you weak, Vic?"

"As a girl," Vic joked.

"Come over here and kiss me," Dante added in.

"Want to dance, Sailor?"

"Sure. But if you get hard I'll pull a '*Dante*' on you."

Both men laughed. Frank sighed and remained serious. He didn't think Jorge could be trusted and even after the beating he'd received, he might remain dangerous. The man knew too much and could talk, if given the proper motivation. Say, for example, he was arrested. Frank realized Jorge had changed—he'd probably started using the shit—and now he couldn't be trusted. Users were the type who would turn evidence to get a lesser sentence. It would be best to get as far away from him as possible. No more dealings, not even little ones to help him out of a jam. Cut the cord and be done with it.

"You guys shut up. I've got to look for some other sources. I'm not ready to retire and I won't deal with that fucker anymore. I want my dream, I want my own business. So unless either of you know someone else we can deal with, go play your games somewhere else."

"Sorry, Frank. What can we do to help?" Dante asked, sincerely.

"Yeah, Frank. Come on. Together we can do anything. It's always been that way."

"There's nothing you can do right now. A couple friends told me about this guy. His name is Ronnie. They said he's a good guy. That's the other reason we're here."

"Then why are you so glum?" Vic asked. "Sounds like you've already got the problem solved."

"It just sucks, that's all. I don't want to meet new people right now. Jorge had to fuck up a sweet deal. Reminds me of that fucking 'Dick' guy at the mill filling his trunk with all those cans of Moly and crashing *that* deal."

"Okay, things come and go. Out with the old and in with—," Vic began.

"Don't give me any fucking clichés, Vic. When one door closes on your fingers, another opens into your toes!"

"Uh, something like that," Vic said, tentatively.

"I'm not in the mood to be meeting new people. It brings an unstable element into our well-oiled machine. Anyone could be a snitch."

"Want us to meet him for you?"

"No, I gotta do this. Besides, you can't tell a snitch from a human anymore than I can. They look just like us. The cops train them that way. Otherwise they don't get their pretty diploma."

"Yeah, not to mention a cap and gown."

"Anyway, I'm meeting this guy tonight. You guys wait for me. When I'm done with him, I'll come around and fill you in."

"Okay, Frank. Whatever you say."

Despite Frank's apprehension, he felt a certain amount of confidence, as well. He'd made friends in the Sunshine State. More than he had in Duquesne, in fact. People who knew people, would introduce him to a friend, and pretty soon, Frank met possible connections.

This meeting went smooth and Frank returned with the good news. Slick Vic and Dante waited as he'd instructed them to do. They jumped at the door.

"Frank, how'd it go?"

"It went well. Absolute top quality coke, and he's willing to deal. If nothing goes wrong, we should continue to make a lot of money."

Frank dropped a package on the table. He pulled back some of the metallic tape and showed them the smooth, white block inside. Light shone off in tiny gold sparkles. Vic and Dante looked at each other and then back at Frank. They expected a deal, not a *deal*. Frank was still the man.

Frank suspected a dealer who used drugs usually caused the biggest problems in the business. Jorge licked his lips a little too often. But Ronnie looked clean, like Vic and Dante. Frank didn't think Dante actually used the stuff. But he liked to flash some to get girls. So, while he'd use up some of the product, it didn't interfere with his brain and he could still be trusted. And Vic—Christ, Vic squeaked when he fucking walked.

"How you gonna get it back to PA?" Vic asked Frank, looking at the bag on the table.

Frank didn't say a word, he just began unbuckling his belt and opening his pants.

"Hey, I know what you heard before, but I'm really not into that," Dante said, holding his hands up in front of him.

"Fuck you."

121

"That's what I'm worried about. I just had some."

Frank stopped and looked at Vic—no one else in the room.

Vic's eyes grew wide as he realized what Frank thought and he began to shake his head, fervently. "Hey, don't look at me. I'm still a virgin."

"Yeah, right!"

When Frank's pants were around his knees and his shirt was pulled up, the two men looked at him. There, hiding under the shirt and unseen while his pants were up, was a kind of girdle. Both men stared.

"What the hell is that?"

"Salvation."

"You named yours?" Dante asked, apprehensively. Frank scoffed at him.

A gallon freezer bag encased the kilo. Frank removed the rest of the grey metallic tape and shoved the kilo into a second bag. Then he slid it down into the girdle on his lower abdomen. He made several adjustments, like a man 'fluffing' his pillow, before he dropped his shirt back down. Then he pulled up his pants and buckled them. Lastly, he put on a sports coat to help conceal any odd shape that might be noticed.

"Are you actually going to try that at an airport?"

"Of course. Got a better idea?"

"We could drive?"

"Fuck that. Every time we do that it takes too long because Dante will have us stop at every strip club, you will need to stop at every gas station and rest stop, and I'll hit every restaurant."

"It'll take more time for you to get out of jail if you get caught at the airport with that shit."

"That's how we're doing it. You guys just walk ahead of me. Keep your distance."

"Okay, Frank."

"You know, Frank. I was just thinking," Dante offered. "If it slips any lower some people might think you're trying to brag about something else."

Frank laughed. "Let's get out of here. We've got a flight to catch."

The three men walked into the terminal and Frank strolled right through security as if it were a sunny day. The two overweight rent-a-cops barely glanced twice at him. No metal, no security risk. Frank shook his head and went into the men's room.

Once inside a stall, he transferred the dope to his carryon and walked out as straight as any businessman. He swapped it for an identical bag that Vic carried, just in case someone had been watching. Once on the plane, they put their bags in the overhead bins like everyone else, which usually remained closed the entire trip.

"That took a real pair of big ones, Frank," Vic said later.

"You know me. I got more balls than brains."

"Really? But you're the brains of the outfit."

"Makes you really stop to think, doesn't it?" Frank suggested.

"Oh, I don't know. I'd rather follow someone with balls any day," Dante offered.

"So you can punch them in the mouth?"

"Would you shut the fuck up about that? It didn't make me gay."

"Well," Vic persisted, "that much is true. He was leaning that way before he met her...I, er...mean, him," he said to Frank.

"Fuck you. One of these days, Vic, your childish sense of humor is going to get you into some real trouble."

123

"My childish sense of humor is only going to let me enjoy life. Hanging out with *you* is what's going to get me into real trouble, Dante. You're a crazy son of a bitch."

"That's me."

Chapter 23

The drugs kept coming and the quality remained top notch. The boys made lots of money. More than they had before. Frank could feel his dream sitting in his lap like one of Dante's women.

But the day finally came, in Duquesne, when Frank noticed a car following him. Somehow he thought it would never happen. And yet the car stalked him, not letting go an inch but keeping its distance.

He didn't know the two men inside the car, but the whole thing smelled and Frank didn't like it. After some wacky driving he managed to ditch them, but his nerves were electrified. Forcing his hands to remain steady, he turned and headed for Schultzie's bar.

He parked his car near the back of the lot and walked in, trying to act casual. He probably looked more like he'd been drinking, unable to keep his wobbly legs firmly beneath himself. He held his hand against the wall to steady his gait. He blinked rapidly as he stepped inside the bar.

"What's wrong, Frank?" Schultzie asked.

"Put the jukebox up real loud. Then you guys gather around."

Frank had a habit of having the music up loud when he wanted to talk business. If anyone tried to listen in or record them, Frank and his buddies wouldn't have to worry about anything being heard clearly. Vic, Dante, and then Schultzie came close and formed a circle around Frank. The music rocked the walls and even the furniture bounced a little.

"What is it, Frank?" Vic insisted.

"I'm being followed."

"How can you tell?"

"How the fuck do you think?"

The three looked at Frank with wide eyes.

"Look, I'm sorry, okay? I'm a little uptight. I didn't mean to take it out on you."

"It's okay, Frank," Vic said, softly. "I'm not sure how well I'd take it if I was the one being followed."

"What can we do?" Dante asked. "I mean, do you know who it is?"

"They're no friends of mine."

"Feds?" Dante asked.

"Could be. But to me, they all look alike."

"So, what do we do?" Schultzie asked, fear sneaking into his voice.

"Solly and Casey are due in shortly, aren't they?"

Eddie looked at his watch. "Any minute now."

"Let's see if they know anything."

Sure enough, several minutes later, Solly and Casey came in and Schultzie pulled them to the side. They still wore their uniforms. It made Frank a bit more uncomfortable. After watching a few minutes of intense conversation, Frank stepped toward them. Just as he took the first step, Schultzie waved him over. Casey motioned Frank into the kitchen. The cook hadn't arrived and they had a bit of privacy.

"Listen, Frank. This is a very delicate situation. I could lose my job if anyone found out I'm even telling you what I know."

"I appreciate that, Casey."

"Appreciation is nice, but I need your word. I know your word is good, Frank, so swear nobody will know what I tell you."

"I swear on my kid's lives."

Casey sighed deeply. "Wow, Frank. That's a hell of a vow. It's difficult not to believe a promise like that."

"You can trust me, Casey. What's going on?"

"The Feds are after you. They're going to bust you sometime this week. Something to do with West Palm Beach. It sounds big, Frank."

"What can I do, Casey?"

"Have a good attorney ready."

"Any recommendations?"

"Vince Murovich, he's in the book."

"Thanks, Casey. I won't forget this."

"Go see this guy. Don't wait. Do it tomorrow, Frank. See him right away, for the sake of Connie and the girls."

"I will, I promise."

Chapter 24

The inside of the office smelled like cinnamon potpourri. The old, majestic building had been remodeled inside to the finest standards, gold fittings, genuine leather seating, and designer lighting. But Frank's mind was overwhelmed with other priorities. He couldn't be bothered with the nuances of decorating.

The man behind the desk stood slender but not skinny. He looked like he worked out. He wore an expensive suit, cut well over his broad shoulders. He still had all his hair. To Frank, the dignified man strongly resembled John Wayne.

"Do I know you, Mr. Mattich?" Vince said as he shook Frank's hand over the desk.

"No, Sir. You don't."

"Why did you come to see me?" He sat back down, motioning for Frank to take one of the seats facing him.

"I think I've got a little problem." Frank's index finger twitched and forced his hand into his lap. He didn't want to appear nervous. In fact, Frank felt oddly confident.

"Of course. No one ever comes to see a lawyer if they don't have a problem they want to make go away. So why me, in particular?"

"I have friends."

"Commendable."

Frank furrowed his brow. "Some are clients of yours. They speak highly of you."

"If you give me their names, I'll see they get a discount."

Since Murovich was bent on cracking jokes, Frank decided on a more direct approach. "Can you take my case?"

"Well, why don't you start by telling me about it."

"I don't know very much, I haven't been arrested yet."

"Then how do you know you need a lawyer?"

"Can I just say a little birdie told me and let it go at that?"

"I'll accept that for now, but like I said, I'm not exactly trolling for new clients. So why did you choose me?"

"Well, a few associates were arrested recently. The case is in Florida and I don't know any good lawyers there. I hear you're a straight up guy and I can trust you."

Attorney Murovich leaned back in his high-dollar, leather chair and brought his hands together in front of his mouth. He didn't close his eyes, but he lowered them to the desktop blotter. He seemed to come to a decision very quickly.

"If I take this case—and I haven't said I would—it's going to be pricey. You understand that? I'll have to fly back and forth and I'll need somewhere to stay while I'm there. You're fortunate I'm licensed to practice in Florida, but I'll still have to enlist the services of an attorney that's based there. Not the most practical method of retaining a lawyer. I suggest you reconsider using a Florida attorney."

"Mr. Murovich, I've made the decision. I want *you* to represent me."

"What part of Florida are you going to be tried in?"

"West Palm Beach."

"What are the charges going to be?"

"Well I don't know specifics, but it will have something to do with drug trafficking."

The big man sighed, resigned. Frank remained determined—unmovable. "I will represent you, Mr. Mattich," Murovich finally conceded.

"That's great, Mr. Murovich. What do we do first?"

"Have your wife ready with the bail money. After the arraignment, she can get you released immediately."

"Released?"

"From jail."

Frank shivered. "Jail?"

"They won't send you to a resort. Did you think you'd get to bring your clubs and catch the front nine?"

"No, but I thought...well, I've never been arrested before."

"Or perhaps you thought I could simply snap my fingers and make it all go away."

"I like that idea." Frank chuckled.

"Sorry, it doesn't work that way."

"Can't fault a guy for hoping."

"Mr. Mattich, the first step in any case is to make an arrest—even though they're all innocent," Murovich insisted. "Then they're processed through the system and go before the judge. If the judge allows bail, he'll set a figure. You arrange to pay it and you get out. If you don't, you don't. It's relatively simple, you see."

"Any idea how much she'll need?" Frank asked, ignoring the sarcasm.

"It won't be cheap. Just give her access to the checkbook."

"But..."

"Look, Mr. Mattich. You don't have to do anything, just spend the time in jail waiting for your trial date. Or, you give her the money and you'll only be in there overnight. Maybe less." Attorney Murovich went silent for a moment. "It won't make any difference to me either way, Mr. Mattich. I'll be able to go home to my family no matter what you choose."

The lawyer didn't pull any punches and his statement jarred Frank more than any other. He paid Murovich a hefty retainer knowing more would soon follow. Plus he'd have to give Connie access to money for his bail. The dream had come so close only to be snatched away yet again. Deep in his heart Frank wanted to cry.

He agreed and left, shaking the other man's hand. Things moved very quickly in his mind. Each minute passed at light speed. Soon he sat on the couch in his own home, facing Connie's red eyes, watching tears flow down her cheeks. His heart hurt. He stared at Connie and bucked up his fortitude to speak without any shaking in his voice.

"The attorney said you should be ready with the money to bail me out."

"Bail?"

"Yeah, to get me out of jail."

"Jail." She shook her head in despair. "Maybe I should just leave you there, Frank," she answered in frustration. "I warned you about the results of this lifestyle. You brought this into our home. This is what happens to gangsters, Frank. You told me before that you weren't a gangster. But if you're not, why is this happening to us?

"Aw, come on, Baby. Don't be so upset. Everything will work out."

"You've said that before," she replied in a huff. "How am I supposed to keep from getting upset? And how long will you be going away? How long do I have to wait? And what about the girls?"

"And look at the life we live," Frank reassured. "Look at the places we've gone and shows we've seen. Things are great. I love you. Just do your part and this will all go away. I promise."

"Yes, let's look at the way we live. There's a constant fear that you'll go to jail for many years. I hardly sleep at night. The girls can't have a life with their father, because he doesn't live here anymore. And when he is here, he's bought them tickets to see another headliner they've never heard of. Or he has another expensive toy for them."

"If I hardly live here anymore, you'll barely notice if I go away for a few years, right?"

"Sarcasm, Frank?" she sneered and shook her head.

"No, I just thought that would make it easier on you, if you were used to me being gone."

"Believe me, Frank, things are NOT great. You haven't got a clue what would make this easier on me."

Frank took her hand in his. "I'll fix this. It'll be okay," he insisted.

"I hope so." She didn't sound convinced.

Chapter 25

"Frank, there are men in suits at the door. They're looking for you." Her quivering voice drifted upstairs to Frank who'd just stepped out of the shower.

He pulled the curtain in the upstairs bedroom window to one side and looked out at the scene on the street below. Several officers and men in suits stood in the street. He counted four pistols and two shotguns.

"I'll be right down." His voice didn't waver in the least.

He put everything of value in the top dresser drawer. No need to bring them, they'd be taken anyway. He took a couple deep breaths and headed down the stairs, feeling a little like a death row inmate walking that last, long mile to the gas chamber.

As soon as his feet landed on the first floor he was greeted with a scene from deep in his memory. His father stood there and two men in suits insisted on a name, someone who killed Ken Baker. His father, so strong and bold, told them nothing. Frank drew strength from the memory and stood a bit taller as he approached the two suits in his doorway, smiling.

"Hello?"

"Frank Mattich?"

"I'm Frank Mattich."

"Good morning, Sir. We have a warrant for your arrest."

"A warrant? For what?"

"From Palm Beach County, Florida, sir. For drug trafficking. Would you come with us, please?"

"Aren't you guys even going to read me my rights?"

"We'll get to that, Sir."

They walked him to the car as if he were a visiting dignitary. They cuffed his hands behind him and held his head as he ducked into the back seat. He looked through the window and saw Connie looking out the door back at him. Through the living room windows, Frank saw the three small faces of his beautiful daughters watching with tears in their eyes.

Frank could see his dream in his mind like a piece of paper with writing on it. The words spelled out a magic code that unlocked a safe with tons of money. The piece of paper had been caught by the wind, ripped out of his hands, and was being whisked in loops and swirls, finally flitting away out of sight. His hope sank. Frank felt as though his whole life was like Charlie Chaplin chasing his hat.

Long before they read Frank his rights, he'd already made up his mind to exercise the one to remain silent. Placed in a small holding cell, he felt like a misunderstood victim from all the horrible prisoner movies he'd ever seen.

Frank crouched on the cot looking at the room. Austere concrete block with green/grey paint made the walls seem endless and without corner. He saw no window with bars, nor skylight through which sunlight could enter. *So, I've already been thrown into solitary confinement and I just got here.*

As silence crowded in on him, Frank studied the walls inside himself even more. Clearly he wanted more than just a marginal living and had no intention of settling for less, but at what cost? Would the end justify the means? Would his family stay his. Truck drivers could maintain a lifestyle away from home, why couldn't he?

And the need crawled through his veins. The excitement of the lifestyle, the ups and downs of betting, the noise of a few hundred fellow human beings calling for their horse to win, these things tingled every spot of his body like electric shock. Could he ignore that?

Turmoil rolling through his body and mind, he tried resting his head down on the pillow-less cot. He found no rest. If he wanted to take care of his family at the level he wanted, he would have to continue to do what he'd been doing. He'd have to work even harder now that his money would be going to the lawyer. If they didn't send him to jail.

It felt like forever before the two guards arrived and brought him up to the courtroom. The arraignment went smoothly and soon Connie walked him out of the building. Only a few hours in jail and his eyes hurt from the harsh sun. It hung high in the sky, beating down on them furiously, reflecting sharply off the pure, crystalline snow.

"What time is it?" Frank asked, holding a hand in front of his squinted eyes.

"Almost two," Connie answered, looking at her watch.

"What took you so long?" he asked with a touch of sarcasm.

"Traffic was bad," came her short answer.

Chapter 26

After sleeping hard through the night, Frank got up early and headed straight for Murovich's office, taking only enough time to shower. He expected to spend the entire day there, but breakfast never entered his mind...or his stomach. Even the word *jail* sent cold chills deep into his soul. If the lawyer could keep him out of that dreary hellhole, Frank would happily put a large sum of money in his hands. Frank sat in the heavy, leather chair. The empty pit in his stomach decided at that moment to remind Frank about the missed morning meal.

"Frank, you are being charged according to the RICO act," the attorney said, shuffling a couple papers, stacking them neatly.

"RICO? Isn't he the guy who starred in the movie, *The Mobster*, with James Cagney?"

"Have your fun, Mr. Mattich. It's not *my* ass on the line."

"Okay, sorry. It's a defense mechanism."

The lawyer just sat quietly.

"What's RICO?" Frank resigned.

"Racketeer-Influenced and Corrupt Organizations Act. It's the law the F.B.I. put into service so they could come down hard on organized crime families for murder and kidnapping."

"But we haven't done anything even remotely like that."

"Doesn't matter, Mr. Mattich. The truth is, your organization is engaging in illegal activities for profit. Under such a broad heading, the Bureau can indict anyone they choose. The law's very purpose is to allow law enforcement agencies to arrest friends and family whom they suspect may have some involvement in the operation."

"That doesn't sound very constitutional."

"It's not. But the fact is, they have the authority. Like it or not, you are in serious trouble."

"Great. What are my chances?"

"As it looks right now, I don't think they have a very strong case against you. But you never know how a jury will rule."

"Okay. That sounds good."

"Not really, Mr. Mattich. Need I remind you that between eighty and ninety percent of defendants in federal trials are found guilty."

"What about the ones who aren't guilty?"

The lawyer seemed flustered. "*Eighty* to *Ninety* percent of defendants in federal trials *are* found *guilty*!" he reiterated.

Frank sighed. "Then what?"

"If you're found guilty, you could be facing fifteen years in a federal prison," the attorney said, matter-of-factly.

Frank's heart sank. He swallowed hard.

"I talked to the Feds," Vince Murovich continued. "They said they want to make you a deal."

"What kind of deal?" Frank leaned forward, resting his elbows on his knees.

"They offered to give you three years in a minimum security facility plus five years probation for the names of the others."

"The others. The other *whats*?"

"Don't play with me, Frank," Murovich spoke sharply as he sat forward. "I'm the guy you need on your side. I'm the guy looking for a way to get you the best deal."

Frank withdrew. This was the first time Murovich called him by his first name.

"I hate to coin a phrase," Murovich spoke sharply, "but, *be afraid. Be* very *afraid.* You are in a very bad position. The odds are against you."

"I see. What do you recommend?"

"I would seriously think about taking their offer. Give them the names they want."

"You mean *rat* on my friends?" Frank thought of his father, once again.

Attorney Murovich gently shrugged his shoulders.

"I can't do that," Frank insisted.

"Then you'd best hope I'm as good a lawyer as your friends told you." Murovich said without humor. He stood and offered his hand.

Frank made the appropriate gesture of politeness and got out of there as quickly as he could. Even though the lawyer was only telling him the truth, claustrophobia set in, fear of the consequences facing him. No wonder lawyers had such a bad rap. They could be scary even when they were on *your* side. He needed to see Connie.

"What did Vince have to say, Frank?"

"He said I'm facing fifteen years."

Connie lowered her head and sobbed.

"He doesn't think their case is very strong," Frank continued.

"Is that it?"

Frank held his breath. He knew Connie would get even more upset. *How did women figure these things out so easily?*

"What is it, Frank? What aren't you telling me?"

"They said if I give them names, they'll let me off with three years."

"Frank," her voice pleaded, "I know you don't like to rat on your friends, but you can't leave us for fifteen years."

"I don't *like* to rat on my friends? Honey, it's more than just what I like or don't like. This is a matter of honor, and I do *not* take it lightly. Not to mention my dad would come back and haunt me if I took the deal."

"But Frank, the girls will be adults by the time you get out! In case you haven't noticed, even the *baby* is no longer a baby. What will we do without you?"

"There's enough money for you to live on for a number of years. If you're frugal, it could last for five, maybe."

"You think money is all we need? You think that's what we care about?"

"I don't know. What *do* you care about?"

"Frank, I've been trying to tell you for years. What about being a father to the girls? They need that more than your money, Frank. The money is nice, don't get me wrong. But we never see you. You've missed every school play, field trip, and teacher's meeting. And I won't even mention the things that *didn't* happen that you missed, like when Tina didn't make it into cheerleading."

"They don't need money..." Frank repeated, matter-of-factly, "...until one of them needs braces or college tuition. Working hard is a man's way of showing love for his family."

"Being here with them is how to show love, Frank."

"Even if I had a 'nine-to-five' I'd have to be gone some of the time."

"Well, what do *you* think the girls would appreciate more?"

Frank hugged her and rubbed his hands over her back.

"Honey, I thought of this the whole ride home. It's tearing me apart. But I *have* to fight them. My father's words keep ringing in my ears. I can't ignore my upbringing. *You NEVER rat on your friends.* Did I misunderstand his words? Do you think he meant something different?"

"I don't think your father meant for you to abandon your family."

"It's difficult to make money sitting around the house."

"Let me put it to you this way, Frank. Your father instilled all these morals into you, standards you live by. He told you or you learned by his example. Right?"

Frank could feel the trap spring shut around him. "Right."

"But what are *our* girls learning from *their* father? When they grow up, what lessons will they pass on to *their* children? What legacy will you leave?"

"Connie, we have to weather this through. They don't have the case they think they do and Murovich is going to get me off. Just watch, I have a feeling."

"A feeling?"

"Please have faith in my decision, Connie. Stand behind me on this."

He hugged her again, feeling her body soften in his grasp.

"Okay, Frank. I love you so much. I just don't want to lose you. Understand?"

"I know, Honey. I love you, too."

"My Aunt Susan called from Florida."

"Susan, Susan. Is she the one that likes to hug a lot?"

"Is that all you can remember about her?"

"No. I remember she seemed to like your cooking. In fact I think it was starting to show on her."

"That's not very nice, Frank."

"Sorry."

"Anyway, her and my Uncle Paul made an offer I thought would be good for us."

"Oh? What offer?"

"She suggested the girls and I go stay with them in Jupiter, Florida."

"Stay *with* them?"

"They have that small motel. They're getting older, and they could use the help. Besides, they never had children of their own and I think they would enjoy having the girls around."

"I see."

"I think it would be a good idea, Frank."

"Is that the *real* reason?"

"What do you mean?"

"Come on, Connie. When Susan and Paul came up that summer, you had a miserable time. I can't imagine old age has made them less irritating. So, what's the truth?"

Connie sighed. "Well, the girls came home from school telling me the other kids have been saying some mean things. They're getting teased and I don't want to wait until someone gets beat up."

Frank's face stretched out long and sad. He stared at the floor but no crack appeared big enough for him to crawl into. He took a couple deep breaths and looked back up at his wife.

"I understand. When do you want to leave?"

"As soon as possible."

"I see," Frank mumbled. "Not wasting much time."

"Oh, Frank. No, you don't see. It'll be fine. You can stay with us during the trial instead of renting a place. Won't that be nice?"

"You mean...?"

"Yes, Frank. I'm not leaving you."

He smiled and went to her. Their embrace was warm and comforting.

Chapter 27

The move proceeded in an orderly fashion. The girls sang happily about the sunshine they would enjoy every single day, although there were a few '*miss my friends'* comments. And Connie had a new bounce to her step. Even Frank had a good feeling. All was well in the Mattich house, except for the upcoming trial. It felt a lot like having sunshine and rain at the same time. But Frank knew that meant the possibility of a rainbow afterward.

They stayed with Connie's aunt and uncle while Frank went to the courthouse every day. There was little difference from working a nine-to-five job. He dressed the part and sat in that courtroom, trying to look innocent to the jury—a fine, upstanding citizen. Sometimes it was hard to tell him from one of the attorneys. The trial dragged on for two months.

Connie ate poorly and lost quite a few pounds, although it wasn't a diet she would recommend. She sat in the courtroom every day, faithfully. Frank looked for her. He thought she looked lovely, but dark circles had begun to show under her eyes. He worried about her even though he needed to worry about himself at the time.

The fourteen other defendants sat in that courtroom, each with their own attorneys. There were originally thirty-nine indicted, twenty-four of which bargained their way out of court—accepting deals offered by the Feds. Frank didn't even know most of the guys. But they were all part of a bigger picture. Frank only wanted to look like part of the furniture.

Murovich assured Frank the case looked good for him and he wouldn't have to take the stand. This, according to Murovich, worked in their favor. Once on the stand, Frank's words could be twisted by the prosecutor to make him look bad to the jury. Avoiding it would be the best solution.

The only person who could identify Frank was Jorge. The prosecution still hadn't called him to the stand. Frank's attorney described it as a ploy, like holding back a trump card. They went through a number of testimonies that made Frank look bad, but Murovich disputed each of them brilliantly.

Frank began to see the light at the end of a long trial. No witness made a significant enough impact on the case to even slap Frank's wrist. Murovich had been right. The prosecution didn't have a very good case. It seemed they went on the premise that if you throw enough shit against the wall something is bound to stick. In the end, all they had was Jorge. But if Murovich couldn't discredit him, he could close the door on Frank's dreams forever. Frank knew the asshole couldn't be trusted.

Near the end of the trial, Vince Murovich entered the courtroom and sat down next to Frank without saying a word. That was unusual. Murovich lived up to his reputation for being an excellent trial lawyer. He was aggressive and manipulative. Basically, lawyers are like salesmen. They sell perception—a belief in the innocence of the person on trial. And the men and women of the jury are the potential buyers.

Murovich always instructed Frank at the beginning of each trial day. Although this usually constituted a simple rhetoric of manners, on occasion the lawyer would have useful advice about certain things that were going to be made public that day so Frank could be prepared. There was always *something*. Except this day. Frank wondered if the trial had taken a sudden turn for the worse and no one else noticed.

"What's wrong?" Frank asked.

"Nothing."

"Something has changed."

Murovich let out a long breath.

"Am I in trouble? Did something go wrong?"

"No. Be quiet."

Frank watched the morning court unfold. The prosecution stood and called for a private session. The courtroom cleared and Frank sat in the hall. In a very few short moments, they were recalled. Murovich spoke to Frank in a whisper.

"Jorge is dead."

"What?" Frank was shocked. "How?"

"He's been shot to death, crossing the street."

"An execution? Who would want…?"

"You mean besides you?" Murovich shrugged.

The judge, a middle-aged man with steel eyes, looked around the room intently. The crowd that had gathered in the courtroom from the beginning grew smaller as the months wore on. Murovich only cared that the reporters were still there, listening.

"The court has just been presented new evidence," the judge said in a firm baritone. "The witness, Jorge Dominguez, has been shot and killed."

A flurry went through the courtroom. The judge banged his gavel.

"Several defendants' cases will be reconsidered since Mr. Dominguez's testimony would have been crucial to these proceedings. We'll begin with the case of Frank Mattich."

Murovich stood. Frank copied.

"How does the prosecution wish to proceed?" the judge asked, formally.

144

Standing, "Your Honor, the prosecution requests a continuance while we search for further evidence against Mr. Mattich."

"Mr. Murovich?" the judge queried.

"Your Honor, searching for evidence suggests they do not have enough to proceed. It is a waste of the court's time dragging this out any further."

"A continuance is denied. Would the prosecution like to make any further requests?"

"Yes, Your Honor. The prosecution suggests the case be dismissed without prejudice."

Murovich jumped up. "I object, Your Honor. My client has no prior record. He is a family man. The case presented thus far has not warranted even a hint of doubt. The burden of proof has not been met and holding this over my client's head would be inhumane and unnecessary. It is a ploy by the prosecution to continue the case. I petition the court to grant *full* dismissal."

The prosecution desk buzzed with nervous tension. They talked among themselves. Being ignored wasn't the kind of thing many judges appreciated. He banged his gavel harder and called for their attention.

"Does the prosecution wish to proceed?" he asked again.

"Your Honor," the man finally said with a quiver in his voice. "The prosecution will accept dismissal *with* prejudice in the case against Frank Mattich."

"Mr. Murovich, the case against your client has been dismissed with prejudice. You are excused from the courtroom."

Frank turned a concerned face to his lawyer. "What does it mean, *with* prejudice?"

"It means they can't call you to trial for the same issue, even if they find further witnesses or evidence.

"Oh."

"That's a good thing, Frank. Be happy."

When Murovich had gathered all his folders and packed his briefcase, he and Frank rose to leave. Frank noticed the prosecution looking very dejected. Murovich wrapped an arm around Frank's shoulder and offered him a genuine smile.

"Ignore them," Murovich uttered, pointing to the other table.

"You were right, Vince," Frank said. "I didn't have to take the stand."

"There was a moment, Frank, when you were on the stand, whether you knew it or not."

"What do you mean?"

"I know what you do. And I got you off because you paid me to do so. I can usually read people very well."

"Look, Vince. Me and my boys aren't thugs, we're businessmen. We might kick some ass but we don't murder anybody."

"I know. And when I told you about Jorge, I watched. You reacted with complete surprise. If you had shown no emotion, or reacted in some other way, I would have known I was wrong."

"Wrong about what?"

"How I read you, Frank. You see, I never really thought of you as a thug."

Frank smiled. "Well, you've got a loyal client. I'll send my guys to you, if they get into trouble."

"And it will be a pleasure to meet each one, I'm sure."

With the trial over, and money paid to Vince Murovich, Frank's dream drained from him, once again. And once again he felt himself kick the hat just as he bent to pick it up. He watched it scurry away. But he remained a free man. Something had to be said for that.

Chapter 28

When the phone rang, Dante simply said, "You gotta come up to the Burgh, Frank. The guys want to throw you a party."

Over the phone, Frank could hear lots of noise in the background. "It sounds like the party already started."

"We're just getting warmed up. The *real* partying begins when the guest of honor arrives. When can I tell them you'll be here, Frank?"

Frank looked at Connie who seemed to understand completely. She waved her hand with a smile and said, "Go—play with the boys."

To the phone, Frank said, "I'll be on the next flight."

*　　　*　　　*

Schultzie's Bar vibrated from the jukebox set on maximum. About fifteen guys from the *Steel Mill Mafia*, and other guys Frank knew from the gambling joint, sat around tables—some even danced. They all sang loud and mostly off key. The song, *I Fought the Law*, blasted out of the jukebox, hurdling the guys into Earth-shattering brevity. They felt invincible.

Struggling to be louder than all the rest, Eddie Schultz led everyone to alter the words, singing; *"Frank fought the law, and Frank won."* Their jubilant voices rang out through the walls and faded into the night air outside. Frank could hardly breathe. Vic, Eddie, and Dante all gathered around him.

"Everyone's happy for you, Frank," Eddie said. "And, believe me, these guys don't have much to be happy about since the mills closed."

"What about you, Schultzie," Frank asked, concerned. "How will you survive?"

"I'll try to hang on." Eddie smiled. "Maybe I'll have to move to another spot in the future. This business is all I know."

Frank looked around. There were a lot of faces that made Frank feel good—friends who had been with him through some nasty shit and some pretty good times, too. But something bothered Frank. Something looked wrong and he couldn't put his finger on it. He hated that feeling.

"Besides being happy for Frank, these guys are thankful to him," Vic said. "He has not only helped them make a lot of money, but his refusal to talk kept them all out of prison. Bad enough losing their jobs, but it could've been worse. Much worse."

"Yeah," Schultzie agreed. "That's the truth."

The crowd continued to grow ever louder. Everyone wanted to hug Frank, or shake his hand. Some appeared so plastered they hadn't noticed Frank's arrival. As long as no one wanted to kiss him. That made him think of Dante's blonde. Frank smiled. Life could certainly be worse.

That's when it hit Frank. Dick. Dick Stinner, the asshole that ruined the Moly deal at the plant, stood among the group, laughing and singing. Frank felt a kind of hurt that any of his friends would think he had an interest in seeing Dick Stinner again for any reason—except maybe to smash his head into a car fender.

"What's *he* doing here?" Frank asked, coldly.

"Who?" Eddie said, swinging his head around. "Oh, Dick? Just a minute.

Eddie walked over and grabbed the man by the arm and led him back to where he'd been standing with the other guys. Frank began to fidget. He wanted a piece of this guy and he could almost smell it. The closer he got, the more intense the smell became.

"Frank," Dick said, offering his hand.

Frank didn't take it. "Dick."

"Look, Frank," he began, pulling his hand back. "I know there are some hard feelings between us, but I just wanted to congratulate you. This is a hell of a victory."

Eddie wrapped an arm around Dick's shoulder and patted him. He smiled at Frank. "Dick's all right, Frank. He's helped me out with some of my problems."

"He's helped you?"

"Yeah. He's managed to get me some side jobs and a few good catering gigs. Not to mention some of the...*other* kinds of financial assistance."

Frank realized what Eddie was talking about. He turned a glaring eye on Dick. "Eddie's our friend. We'll take it very badly if he gets into any trouble."

"No, Frank," Dick stammered. "We're good. It's mostly legit, anyway. Hey, look. I've got to get going. I just wanted to stop by to wish you the best, really." Again he stuck out his hand and Frank ignored it.

Dick turned and Eddie took the offered hand and shook it fervently. "We'll talk later, okay Eddie?"

"That'll be good, Dick. Take it easy."

"You too." Then he was gone.

"Be careful of that guy, Eddie," Frank warned. "He's not the most stable sort."

"I don't know the whole story of what went down with you two, but Dick's a good guy, Frank. He helps me out a lot."

"You said that before."

"Because it's the truth."

"Yeah, well, he can be trouble. So just watch it."

"He hasn't caused me any. Besides, like he said, most of the stuff he gets me is legit. I've gotten pretty good at the catering business," he finished with a broad smile.

"Well, why don't you cater us? I'm starved," Frank said.

"Yeah, Eddie," Dante joined in. "How about serving up something special—like a nineteen year old with big tits?"

"I'm fresh out," Eddie answered, matter-of-factly. "But I already made up some special platters in your honor, Frank. I got 'Pardon Chicken', free-range roast beef, and even a hard salami for Dante's enjoyment."

"I got my own hard salami, dumb ass."

"I'm afraid I couldn't keep the other guys from getting into them before you got here," Eddie admitted, ignoring Dante's comment. "But there's plenty left. Help yourself."

"Thanks, Eddie." Frank scanned the area again, this time looking for the food.

A number of people had wandered over to the bar for a break from the noise some dared call singing. Frank looked to the end of the bar and saw a man waving at him to come over. Frank didn't think it was meant for him, at first.

He knew most of the people in town by sight. Donnie Riley—who's brother headed the toughest Irish gang in Pittsburgh—wanted to talk to him. Frank walked toward that end of the bar, a smile firmly planted on his face.

"Donnie Riley. As I live and breathe. What brings you to the competition?"

"I heard the commotion. Thought it might be a riot or something."

Frank shook the man's outstretched hand. "How are you?"

"I'm doing well, Frank. You?"

150

"I feel like I just got a clean bill of health after having a terrible disease," he said, waving his hand around the room. "So, what brings you to this neck of the woods?"

"Hey, word of your stand against the Feds has been heard far and wide. I bumped into Eddie and he told me they were throwing this little shindig and I thought I'd crash. No one told me I should bring along some aspirin for the headache I'm going to have." He glanced around the room with a crooked eye. "Anyway, it gives me the chance to congratulate you, myself."

"That's mighty white of you, Donnie. Thanks. The kind words are always appreciated. Next week they're electing me King," Frank finished with a glance around the loud room. "Will you vote for me?"

"I'm not sure it'd be wise to vote *against* you, right now, considering how much popularity you've gained. I'd say, whatever election they want to hold, you're a shoe-in. But I think I'll vote from across town. The noise is annoying."

Frank scrutinized Donnie's expression for signs of sarcasm. He saw none.

"So," Donnie continued. "Why don't you do it?"

"Do what?"

"Run for office."

"No...thank...you. It may only be trading one kind of crime for another, but at least I can hold my head up."

"Yeah, you don't seem like the baby-kissing type."

Frank still searched for signs of insincerity, and still couldn't see any. But he saw something else. "Now tell me, why are you *really* here?"

Donnie laughed.

"Can't I just mean what I said? Do I have to have an ulterior motive?"

151

"You don't *have* to, and I'm sure you're sincere about the congrats."

"I'm sincere."

"Thanks, again. Now, why are you *really* here?" Frank repeated.

"Damn. I never could fool you, not for a minute."

"You're avoiding."

"Okay, you're right. I have another purpose."

"And what's that?"

"My brother, Mike, is getting out of Federal Prison in a few months."

"Yeah, I heard that."

"Well, he's impressed with the way you stood up to those Feds."

"He did the same thing when he went up."

"Yes, that's why he's impressed. He's in a Texas prison, did you know?"

"I think I heard that, too."

"You hear a lot."

"I got an ear."

"Looks like you've got two," Donnie said, looking at both sides of Frank's head.

"Yeah, at least I can't fly with 'em like some of these guys."

Donnie laughed. "Anyway, Mike has made some great Mexican connections."

"Good food."

"Yeah. Good, primo, green, Mexican weed."

Frank perked up a little, as the dream knocked on his door once again.

"Listen, Frank. This stuff is a hundred times better than that cheap Columbian shit. You sell less and make more. Interested?"

"I haven't walked away."

152

"Frank, there's a lot of money to be made with this shit. And you'd only have to deal with Mike, so that screws the RICO laws. How's that sound?"

"Sounds like I want to talk to Mike when he gets out."

"It's already being arranged, Frank. He wants to deal with a stand-up guy like you. In fact, he's kind of insistent."

"I'm honored. Mike's got a hell of a rep."

"I'll pass the word along to him."

The two men shook hands.

"I've got to mingle. After all, I *am* the guest of honor."

"Yeah, well, *Your Honor*, maybe you could get them to tone it down a bit."

"Somehow, I doubt that," Frank laughed. "Enjoy the party, Donnie."

"Thanks, Frank."

Frank approached a table where Vic, Dante, and Schultzie rested their singing voices. Next to them sat a table laden with food. Frank grabbed a sandwich and turned to his friends. They were laughing and sounded like they had a buzz going on. But they looked tired.

"Boys," he said, "I need a vacation."

"I can imagine," Vic mumbled.

"I gotta relax my nerves. I saw an ad that interested me."

"Hey," Dante insisted. "I know just the girl for you, Frank."

"Thanks, Dante. But not *that*. That's exercise. I need rest. There's this deal on a trip to Cancun next week. Anyone game?"

"Count me in," Dante answered almost before Frank could finish his question.

"Me too," Vic put in, sounding suddenly more sober.

"How about you, Buddy?" Frank added, turning to Schultzie. "My treat."

"Frank, I'd love to. But you *know* I can't. I got way too much to do around here."

"Yeah," Dante spoke up. "There's money to be lost."

"Hey, come on, Dante," Frank admonished. "If he's got a lot to do, he can't make it. It's cool. We'll miss you, Eddie."

"Thanks, Frank."

The party rang loud through the night and didn't break up until grey sunlight poked in through the windows. As they began to leave, they were forced to cover their eyes in pain, even thought the sun had barely risen above the horizon and the day remained hazy and dim. They looked like a group of vampires—cowering from the light and racing for the cover of their cars.

Chapter 29

The trio had no reason to get nervous going through customs this trip. They stood in the line like regular tourists. They carried no contraband, nothing illegal. Frank noticed the officers at the gate were leaner and more formidable than before. Nothing like those overweight ham steaks he'd seen in the past.

After a few minutes of waiting in line, a guard walked by with a dog that sniffed at everyone and their luggage. Frank eyed the beast with trepidation. But his feelings changed. He elbowed Vic, who just happened to be the closest.

"Look at that."

"Ow! Look at what, the new bruise on my ribs?" Vic howled.

"No, stupid. The dog."

"Aw. Would widdew Fwankie-Wankie like his Uncle Vic to buy him a new puppy faw Chwistmas?"

Frank looked at him with a condescending eye and a sneer on his lip. Vic backed down and smiled sheepishly.

Just then, the dog began to bark at one of the people standing in line about three people in front of Frank. Two uniformed men came over and escorted that passenger to a room behind the X-ray machine. Everyone looked out of curiosity, but they continued to move through the machine at a slow pace.

"You know what I'm thinking?" Frank asked.

"Sure, you're thinking…" Vic tapped his temple with two fingers and let his eyes drift closed. "…you're having a Big Mac attack."

"Come on, Slick. Get serious."

"I'm no fucking Kreskin, Frank. And you know they confiscated my crystal ball. They thought it was a crack rock."

A moment of silence fell between them. Frank took several deep breaths and just looked out the window. Finally, overwhelmed with frustration and curiosity, Vic broke the quiet.

"Why don't you just *tell* me what you're thinking? Wouldn't that be simpler?"

"We could get a dog that sniffs money and drugs."

"And hire ourselves out as airport security for less than minimum wage. What a great idea, Frank. We could get *jobs*. Good thinking, buddy. Why didn't I think of that?"

Frank stared. "You done?"

"No, but I thought I'd save the rest for the next dumb idea you suggest."

"Smart ass. We're not going to get *jobs*. But I was thinking we could rob drug dealer's cars. They can't report the crime to the cops and it's all profit—no investment. Except, of course, the dog," Frank added.

Vic looked at Frank like insanity had taken over his friend's mind. After a few minutes, though, Vic began to *see* the plan in action and a smile lit his face. It just might work. And there was more.

"I was just up visiting my sister," Vic said. "You know, the one in Penn Hills? Anyway, her husband's best friend, Tony, lives next door. Care to guess what *he* does for a living?"

"He's a fucking astronaut," Frank said with sarcasm. "You know they took *all* our crystal balls, Dummy."

"Okay, Frank. Don't pucker your butt, you'll get constipated."

"Look who's talking. You were pretty constipated a few minutes ago."

"But I'm funny."

"And what am I?"

"You never could get the hang of it."

"Whatever. What does your husband's friend's sister do for a living?" Frank asked, twisting the words purposely.

"My *husband*?"

Frank raised an eyebrow at him.

"He trains this kind of dog, Frank," Vic finally answered.

"And? Would he sell us one?"

"I think someone keeps close tabs on the trained ones."

"I'm sorry. I lost track. How does this help us, exactly?"

"Tony has this one mixed up shepherd. He's had all the police training and drug and money sniffing school, but the stupid mutt kept attacking people after his original trainer had to go on extended leave—heart attack. The force had to retire the dog real quick before he bit a kid or something."

"Yeah, they might get sued," Frank sobbed with a smile.

"They'd lose their shiny badges," Dante added in, "and have to wear old, rusty ones."

"You think this dog could work for us?"

"I think Tony wants to get rid of him, right quick. And no one cares what happens to this particular animal."

"Was the dog good at sniffing out drugs and all that?"

"As far as I remember Tony telling the story, the dog was a wizard. But the force won't touch him because of the liability."

"So we'd be allowed to buy it?"

"Only one way to find out for sure."

"Oh?"

157

"When we go back home, I'll talk to Tony about it."
Frank smiled.

Chapter 30

Eddie Schultz grew up with a face that got him into trouble, *lots* of trouble. But not in a way you might think. On Halloween, if he'd dared, Schultzie could have dressed as a girl and really looked the part. His mother often tried to get him to do it. Eddie emphatically refused, insisting he would not dress that way and he was *not* a sissy. They couldn't make him and he wouldn't do it.

This seemed to please his father no end. While Eddie's mother thought beauty an acceptable trait in a boy, his father often suggested busting Eddie's nose just to take away some of the beauty and give him a more rugged look. His mother profusely disagreed and would hide the boy behind her apron whenever his father made even the slightest move in that direction.

Frank laughed when he thought how Dante might react if he saw *'Sexy Schultzie'*, dressed as a girl. Even in men's clothes, suit and tie, Schultzie had a feminine appeal. His sweet face often shone through as meek and mild. However, Eddie Schultz was anything but. He'd grown up with that pretty face and he'd been toughened by it. And if you ruffled his feathers, he might be likely to kick your ass six ways from Sunday rather than look at you twice.

Eddie only went to the Holiday House in Monroeville to have a good time and mind his own business. He'd read Neil Diamond would be singing there. Eddie thought it might turn out to be a misprint or some similar excuse, but Neil was one of his favorite singers and Eddie would have driven ten times as far to see him. And if a girl just happened to fall into his lap while he watched the show, well so be it.

Eddie fared quite well with the girls, despite being prettier than most of them. But women appreciated a more sensitive side to a man. Eddie knew a lot of women didn't mind his less-than-rugged good looks.

"Hey, pretty boy."

The man was known simply as 'The Blade', supposedly a member of the Pittsburgh Connection—a real no-nonsense outfit. Schultzie didn't know the man from Adam. But he'd heard stories and people had described him, though none admitted knowing his real name.

For the most part, Eddie had been teased about his good looks for as long as he could remember and managed to brush off most comments. He ignored the well-dressed man at the table near the door and walked past. He'd come to see about picking up a woman. Maybe even getting lucky. And listen to Neil, of course.

"Hey, I'm talking to you, pretty boy. You doing a little cruising tonight, honey?"

Again, Eddie Schultz did his best to bury the urge to rip the guy's throat out. The man was beneath him and wouldn't be worth the aggravation that followed if he reacted rashly. So, he ignored the moron who heckled him. He looked like a gentleman. Eddie couldn't imagine what would cause a man of culture to call such things out loud in public.

"I might be just the guy to fuck you up that tight ass, pretty boy. I've got a big dick. Wanna see it?"

Schultzie looked back, watching, as the man grabbed his crotch and gave it a couple yanks. Reaching his limit of patience, Eddie stepped closer to the rude man. He looked down into the man's lap and smiled. Without warning, he doubled his fist and sent it crashing into the top of the chair seat, compressing the man's balls between his knuckles and the wooden seat. The creep howled. Eddie walked away, further into the club, as though nothing had happened.

Minutes passed as he looked around at the prospects before him. A warm-up band jumped around on the stage. To Eddie, their music sucked and he couldn't imagine a guy like Neil Diamond choosing such a band to tour with. *Maybe headliners don't get to choose.* But he listened intently, bouncing sprightly on the balls of his feet.

All but forgotten, the man came up behind Schultzie, hobbling a bit. He tapped Eddie on the shoulder. Eddie turned. A pile driver fist caught Eddie square on the nose. A bouncer approached them, outweighing each of them by fifty pounds, Eddie guessed.

"Take it outside!" he demanded, simply.

Eddie saw flashes of light in front of his eyes. But not being one to back down from a challenge, he walked out behind the other man, ready to take him on. The man, whom Eddie still didn't know, finally managed to stand straight, just as they arrived in the parking lot. He turned.

Face to face, they moved, carefully sizing the other up, searching for weakness. Finally a punch flew. Eddie's fist missed, he'd been anticipated. The guy returned with a blow to Eddie's gut. With the lights still dancing in his head, Eddie could only *act* tough. He continued to dance, playing for time.

When Eddie lunged the next time, the guy side-stepped and pulled Eddie's arm. This swung him around and his arms flew open for a moment. That's all his opponent needed. He thrust his fist into Eddie's chest several times. Eddie never felt anything like it. The pain shot through his body, all the way to his back—like bullets going through.

He couldn't catch his breath and his knees quivered. All this he could deal with, but when his eyes became blurry, Eddie started to worry. This fight wasn't going so well. He'd been beaten before, but not for a long time. He'd fought so much in his youth, making him tough—all because he had that girly face. Eddie Schultz wasn't the kind of guy to take shit from anyone. He learned to take a lot of punishment and he learned to give it back, too.

But this guy was just too fast. And too strong. His punches felt like an elephant stomping on him. Finally Eddie fell down and looked up at his attacker. He saw the man's fist open and he took something out of it.

Nothing made sense until Eddie looked down at his shirt and jacket. Some black substance stained them. The guy hit him with some kind of dirt? Eddie weakly raised one hand up and ran his fingers through the black liquid. Still confused, he brought the fingers to his face for a closer look.

He smelled it and looked again. As realization dawned, confusion sank even deeper. The substance was blood. But all the guy did was punch him. Could someone draw blood from a simple punch? Eddie never heard of such a thing.

The night had been cloudy and dark, but the parking lot lights usually kept things lit well enough for people to find their cars. Now the light began to fade. His eyelids grew heavier with each breath he took. People gathered around, but he couldn't focus on any of them. They spoke, so many voices, all talking gibberish—like different languages, all speaking at once, until Eddie couldn't distinguish any one sound from another. The sound washed over him like a blanket of noise resembling a steady buzz. Then he heard…

"Longfellow serenade…"

Eddie struggled, trying to focus, but everything blurred as if he viewed the world through a dust storm. Questions of sickness ran through his head. He wondered, perhaps, if he wasn't possibly dying. He could see a waterfall in the distance, and worried what would become of his bar.

"Such were the plans I made."

A sound, a wondrous noise filtered through and into Eddie's ears. He lay dazed, trying to identify it. Then he remembered why he'd come. The opening music, the crowd cheering, he'd missed it all. But that singular voice rose above it all, pouring out through the open door. Neil had begun to sing.

"For she was a lady and I was a dreamer..."

Eddie lay there, struggling to hear over the babble. A new sound drowned out the others. He tried to ignore it, to hear past it. He wanted to remember Neil's voice. But this noise overwhelmed everything. A loud, annoying sound—the last sound he remembered hearing before he went to sleep. He could no longer hold on. Even the deafening din couldn't keep him awake. He just wanted to sleep. Darkness swallowed him.

The sirens came up next to him and stopped.

Chapter 31

Frank knew the travel brochures boasted pristine beaches. They drew thousands of vacationers every year. But Cancun has very small beaches—and beautiful waters. A light ocean breeze kept most people from running for relief from the intolerable heat. Dante behaved as though he'd died and gone to the most perfect afterlife.

Near the pool, tables offered comfort at a discrete distance from the 'splash zone'. A few people sat, sipping drinks with colored umbrellas sticking up from them. A few girls sunbathed. Frank loved these tropical paradises for other reasons. The three men had the most delightful afternoon. Playing cards in the sun while mists of chlorinated water from the pool sprayed over them when anyone dove or cannonballed in created a perfect day.

"I really needed this, guys," Frank said out of the blue, winning another hand.

"After what you went through," Dante answered, "I'm surprised you don't need to get laid."

"Not everybody is Dante," Vic retorted.

"You should be so lucky," Dante replied.

"What I needed," Frank insisted, "was wide open spaces to remind me of the value of freedom."

Dante's focus remained elsewhere, despite gravity's effort to taint some of the beauty.

"Hey, Dante. How about paying attention to the game."

"Come on, Frank. I'm looking at all the hooters."

"Christ, Dante, those are sagging," Vic offered, pointing.

"I don't care if they're lower than they once were."

"I know, but those are poking out by her knees."

"Look, Vic. Let me educate you in the ways of female anatomy. Breasts are like coins to be used in a vending machine. A vending machine of taboo treats, get it? Even the saggy ones have value."

Frank glanced at the woman again and shrugged. He couldn't deny they were fun to look at. When she walked her breasts swayed with mesmerizing rhythm. Frank shook the image out of his head.

"Look at this," Dante said, temporarily focusing on his friends at the table. "I got this silver dollar when I was in Vegas."

"What about it?"

"Now look at this," Dante demanded, holding up a different coin. "This is a Mexican peso. I got it from my friend, Amigo."

"Again, what about it?"

"Look at them both. Feel this silver dollar and then compare it to this peso." Dante handed Frank the money.

Frank and Vic felt the two coins while Dante took another inspection tour with his eyes. All seemed well in *Breastville* and he turned back to the table. His casual gesture didn't go unnoticed by Vic.

"Is that drool I see coming out of your mouth, Dante?"

Frank turned from the coins and looked up.

"That's what it looks like, Vic."

Both men looked at Dante's empty glass.

"We'd better order him another drink," Vic said.

"Yeah, at this rate, he'll be dehydrated by dinner."

"You guys," Dante answered. "You're always so full of shit."

"Hey, my eyes are blue," Vic insisted.

"That just means you only fill up as far as your mouth. Then it all runs out."

"At least I'll never be all the way full."

"Did you feel the coins like I asked?"

"Asked, it seemed more like an order to me," Vic teased. "But I'm sorry, Dante. I felt them both several times and I have to tell you. Neither one feels like a woman's breast."

Dante offered him an evil glance. He turned to Frank.

"Honestly, Dante. I can't feel much difference," Frank offered, staying on topic.

Dante ignored Vic's taunting. "Precisely," he said shortly.

Vic sat forward, now more interested. "What are you getting at, Dante?"

"What I'm getting at is this. If they look the same, and feel the same, how would a machine know the difference?"

"You want to buy a lot of bubble gum?" Vic asked.

"No, asshole. What if these pesos work in the dollar slots in Vegas? It takes fifty pesos to equal one silver dollar."

"That's quite an exchange rate."

"Yeah. We could pull that handle fifty times for only the one dollar. I know the odds are against winning at the slots, but they're better than fifty to one. We could make a killing," Dante finished.

Vic and Frank sat up straight. Dante finally caught their attention. Frank thought his way through it, trying to make something workable they could use.

"Okay guys, how's this for a plan? Dante, you said you're going to Vegas with your Mexican buddy, right?"

Dante chuckled. "Yeah, we've been planning it for a while. But hey, Frank, I can postpone it if you need something."

"Not at all. In fact, it's right on time. Why don't we get a hundred dollars in pesos and you can try them in the slot machines

166

while you're there. That way, you can see if they really work. Vic and I will go home and check out this dog idea of his."

"Sounds like a plan, Frank," Vic said.

"A hundred dollars' worth," Dante said, distractedly, "that would be about five thousand of them, wouldn't it, Frank?"

"Sounds about right. Not enough?"

"No, that's good to start. We gotta be sure they'll work before we invest too much. I don't think they'll be worthwhile for anything else if this doesn't work," Dante said. Then he added, "Unless you're planning on moving to Mexico!"

Frank ignored the insinuation. "So, we all agree that sounds like a good plan?"

The men nodded in agreement. The card game—all but forgotten—Frank and Vic stood and headed back to their hotel room for an early supper. Dante, lingering behind, stared at the image of beauty lounging around the pool. Once he felt sure it had been burned into his brain, he turned and joined his friends.

"Don't be an ignoramus, Dante. Those girls don't want nothing to do with you."

"You're kidding," Dante chuckled.

"Don't get him going, Vic," Frank added. "We'll never get any dinner."

"How much you wanna bet, little man?" Dante challenged.

"Got change for a nickel?"

"You guys, knock it off," Frank insisted. "I want to get out of here *without* getting thrown out."

Both men looked at Frank and settled back down.

Chapter 32

Austere hospital walls—neither green nor blue but something in between—offered little comfort to Frank. He felt anxious and gentle colors did nothing to alleviate it. The desk nurse wore lavender scrubs with a light blue hem and didn't look very happy about being interrupted. She gave clear directions to the room he sought and still Frank felt more than a little lost. Every hallway looked the same, each room—like the last. Even the machinery littering the passageways didn't change. Sometimes, nerves could make you blind, stupid, and clumsy. Frank felt all three.

Finally—two-twelve. He gently pushed the door open and carefully looked inside. Room colors blended well with the corridor. The visible foot of the bed extended past the corner of the bathroom. All Frank could see were two feet buried under the blanket. The usual machine noises floated in the air, lending power to Frank's anxiety.

He never liked hospitals, even as a boy. A feeling no doubt carried over from his father's attitude about them. Perhaps, Frank thought, he'd see his friend die. Or maybe they'd put Frank in a bed and strap him down against his will. Nightmare images swept through his imagination as he stepped forward to see the face above the feet.

Drooping eyes with dark circles moved statically around the room. They finally settled toward the door and met Frank's. Frank tried to smile at the horror staring back at him, but found no happy thought, no optimism, not even an old joke he could cling to that would bend his mouth upward at the corners. Emptiness ate at his gut as he just stared at the wreck of a man lying in the bed, tubes running into his arms and wires taped to his chest.

Eddie Schultz was connected to more machines than the *Six Million Dollar Man*. With a valiant struggle, Frank shook the image of a stupid, old television show out of his mind and focused on his friend, lying helplessly on the bed before him.

"You should see the other guy." Eddie tried to laugh as he observed the look on Frank's face. He winced in pain and dismissed the idea of laughing again…ever. "No jokes, it hurts to laugh."

"Hi, Buddy."

"How you doing, Frank?"

"You know me, fit-as-a-fiddle." Frank splayed his arms out to show off his health, but only succeeded in reminding both of them that he could still stand and Eddie could not.

"You look like a big dick."

"How observant. I just happen to have one," Frank shot back.

Eddie broke his promise and laughed again, struggling through the obvious pain. Frank fought back a pang of regret for making a joke. He'd have to try and be careful not to do that again. Finally, Eddie regained control of his funny bone and began to breathe normally. His face relaxed back to the grimace of pain it had been when Frank first walked in the room.

"Hey, Eddie," Vic called, good-naturedly from the door.

Staring at the daunting task of finding their way around the maze of hospital gurneys, doctors and nurses, patients moving slowly, machinery on wheels, and other obstacles, Frank and Vic had gone in different directions in search of Eddie's room. The room happened to be in the hall Frank had chosen. He knew Vic would catch up soon enough.

169

"How's it going?" Vic continued his jovial attitude.

"Great. Want to organize a ball game?"

"Only if you'll pitch."

"I can be ready in an hour."

"Very good."

Eddie looked around. "Dante didn't come?"

"He's out in Vegas, doing an experiment."

"Dante? Doing scientific research? Hard to imag—wait. Does it have something to do with female body parts?"

"No. He's checking on some money ideas he had."

"Just as well he didn't come here, though. I've got this one nurse—," Eddie began.

Just then the trio was interrupted by the hottest little nurse imaginable, somehow made even hotter by the uniform. It's been said that women love a man in uniform. Well damned if the reverse isn't true as well. Frank and Vic stared. Eddie did his best to follow too, despite the pain.

The woman, possibly in her late twenties, stood just over five feet. Round in all the right places and filling out her nursing uniform like a pro, the room went silent as she came in and checked the machinery next to Schultzie. He held his breath. When she finished, she leaned over and made sure everything still had good contact on Schultzie's body. As she did so, Vic and Frank couldn't help but notice her short skirt riding up invitingly.

It was a tease beyond compare. She couldn't have managed any better if she worked in a strip club. She walked out of the room and all six eyes were glued to her ass. Like a cat watching a bug flittering around, each move she made was echoed by three heads. When she had gone and the door closed, all three released a breath they didn't realize they'd been holding.

"Dante would have never survived," Frank finally said with a sigh.

"You mean the *nurse* would have never survived," Eddie offered.

"Did you see her smile at me?" Vic asked as the other two looked at him in disbelief.

"I think she smiled at me," Frank taunted.

"Oh," Eddie sneered. "And how's that lovely wife of yours, Frank?"

"Yeah," Vic said, elbowing Frank in the ribs. "You're off the market."

"Doesn't mean I can't look."

"Besides, we would have known if she was looking at you, Frank," Vic returned. "She'd have had to break her neck looking up so high. Obviously, she was interested in the better looking of us. And that's me."

"You guys are screwed in the head. She smiled at me," Eddie confirmed. "And I can prove it."

"How the hell can you prove that?" Frank asked, genuinely curious.

"Simple. She smiles at me like that every day."

"I gotta say, Eddie, you're one lucky son-of-a-bitch," Vic conceded.

"Yeah," Eddie groaned. "I *feel* lucky. Don't I *look* lucky?"

"So, what happened, anyway?" Frank finally asked.

"I gots a boo-boo."

"No shit, Sherlock. Care to elaborate?" Vic snapped at him.

"Celebrate?"

"*Explain*, asshole."

"Oh. I got stabbed."

"Why'd you go and do a damn fool thing like that?"

"Nothing better to do. And it seemed like such a great plan at the time."

171

"Hey, Vic," Frank called. "Is *boredom* the mother of invention?"

"I don't know, but I wonder if that nurse will be the mother of my children," he replied, looking toward the door as if he could *will* her to return.

"Shut up, Vic. You're starting to sound like Dante."

"Damn, that sucks," Vic answered. Then he turned toward Eddie. "Well, Frank, Eddie *does* look a lot better. Maybe it's just some of that plastic surgery stuff all the Hollywood girls are getting."

"Fuck you."

"I might," Vic answered. "Did you get your boobs done, too?"

"I hope they're not too big," Frank chuckled. "Dante will never be able to keep his hands off them."

"You guys are so funny. Did you forget that laughing hurts me? Is that why you came here, to give me more pain?"

"Well I've always wanted to be a pain in someone's ass," Frank offered.

"You giving Connie a break, big guy?" Vic asked.

"Yeah, you know. For the holidays."

"What holidays? It's March, dipshit."

Eddie furrowed his brow—deep in thought. "Hey, how'd you guys know I was in here, anyway?" he asked.

"I went by your place. Zack was there, milling about, cleaning tables, that sort of shit."

"He told you I was here?"

"Yeah."

"And you came running right over to see me?"

"Well, we played a game of cards first."

"Comedian."

"Hey," Frank countered. "You asked for that one."

"Yeah, I guess I did."

"So, come on, Eddie. Tell us what happened."

"It's not as bad as it seems. I got injured, that's all."

"If it was minor, that fucking quack doctor in Duquesne could have patched you up. They brought you to the hospital in Monroeville for something more serious than a...*boo-boo*."

Eddie looked embarrassed. It's difficult for a man to be fully a man while wearing a paper dress that doesn't completely close in the back. He took in a deep breath, which hurt like hell, and spat out the story.

"I went to Monroeville. Can you believe, the fucking Holiday House finally got a headliner that I would want to see?"

"Who was there?"

"Neil Diamond."

"Wow, Eddie," Vic said, sincerely. "That's pretty cool."

"Not very cool, Vic. I never got to see the show. I got stabbed by this guy."

"Any idea who it was?"

"I'm pretty sure it was the guy they call 'the Blade'."

"Hey," Frank said. "If it's the same guy, I think I heard a rumor that he's part of the *Pittsburgh Connection*."

"Didn't Hollywood make a movie about them?" Vic asked.

"Yeah. It was called...wait a minute. I remember. It was called...*Goodfellas*, wasn't it?"

"That's right. I saw that. Ray Liotta played Henry Hill," Eddie managed to say.

"I've heard of that *blade* guy," Vic said. "He's a real bad ass, a tough son of a bitch. No matter what group he belongs to."

"Anyway," Eddie continued. "There was a fight. I didn't know, but he had one of those ball knives you hold in your palm. You guys know the kind? The blade sticks through between two

173

fingers when you make a fist. We were just fighting and I thought he had a hard punch."

Frank shifted uncomfortably.

"It was dark," Eddie continued. "I couldn't see the blade. But I saw blood. And everything started to look out of focus. Pretty soon, I woke up here with that pretty nurse bending over me and I thought I'd gone to Heaven. They told me I was out for a couple days from the blood loss."

"Yeah, you're lucky that knife didn't pierce your heart or puncture one of your lungs," Vic inserted. "You might have made it to Heaven. Then all the nurses would have looked like her. Hey, wait a minute! Maybe that's not such a bad thing."

Frank chuckled.

"It's not like you to get involved in a fight," Frank observed. "What was it about?"

"You know, I really can't remember. I don't know if it's just that I was unconsciousness for those couple days or something else, like maybe he damaged something, but the whole thing is mostly a blur. I heard too much blood loss can cause brain damage."

"You think you lost that much blood?" Vic asked.

"Yeah, I hear it takes quite a lot to cause any real damage," Frank added. "And in Eddie's case, we wouldn't know the difference."

"Thanks." He groaned again. "All I know is what the doctors tell me, and they say I lost a hell of a lot. And I'll tell you this for nothing, it hurts like hell when I even try to think about what happened that night," Eddie confirmed.

"Hey, Buddy. It's no big deal. The damage is done," Frank consoled. "Now it's time to just get well and back on your feet again."

"Are you going to press charges?" Vic asked.

Schultzie looked toward the wall. That 'embarrassed' look swept over his face again. Frank frowned. It seemed like a simple enough question. Frank unfurrowed his brow. Something was wrong, he could feel it. He decided to push.

"What is it, Eddie? You either are or you aren't."

"They made me an offer."

"An offer?" Vic began to sound irritated. "What do you mean an offer? What *kind* of offer?"

"Yesterday, these two guys showed up."

"Cops?"

"No. I think I recognized them."

"Who?"

"They're mafia lieutenants."

"From the *Connection*?"

"Yeah, I'm pretty sure. Maybe."

"So," Vic pushed. "What kind of offer did they give you?"

"They'll give me ten thousand dollars to *not* press charges."

"Ten thousand? That's not very much money."

"It's a lot to me. And they said they couldn't guarantee my safety if I didn't accept."

"Typical brute mentality."

"Are you going to do it?"

"The mills are closed," Eddie answered, matter-of-factly. "The money will help me keep my bar open. What else can I do?"

"When do you have to tell them?"

"They're coming back later today."

"Don't waste much time, do they?" Frank asked Vic.

"Life's too short to waste time on any one pair of knee caps."

"Well, I'm allergic to those guys," Frank said. "So why don't we get out of here and let Eddie conduct his business without shame."

175

"Yeah," Vic agreed. "We'll come by tomorrow and visit longer, Eddie."

"You take it easy, Buddy. And give that nurse a glance at those ten G's. Maybe she'll jump right in that bed with you."

"I'm not sure that's such a good idea, Frank. It'll hurt."

"Oh, don't worry about that, Eddie," Frank replied. "She's young and strong. She'll heal."

Outside the room, Vic suggested they pay for Eddie's hospital stay. Frank agreed.

Chapter 33

"Hey, Dante. How was the trip?" Frank asked, rubbing his eyes as he walked into Vic's kitchen. He tried to suppress a yawn.

"We keeping you up, big guy?" Vic asked.

"Fuck you." He smelled the wonderful aroma of fresh coffee. "Vic, you got a cup for me?"

"One cup of *Slick Vic's Lava Java* coming right up."

"You sure you want to drink that shit, Frank?" Dante asked.

"From you I want to hear about Vegas."

"Vegas was great," Dante said. "Vegas is always great."

"Did your idea work?"

"Come on, Frank. You know what they say."

Yawning again, "Uh…no. What do they say?"

"What happens in Vegas, stays in Vegas." Dante smiled.

"Well, whatever happened in Vegas had better start spilling out of your big mouth," Frank insisted, taking a sip of the bitter, hot liquid Vic handed him.

Vic looked a bit nervous. He didn't want his house messed up when Frank beat the crap out of Dante for being a jerk.

"Jeez, can't a guy have a little fun?"

"Sounds like you had enough fun," Vic inserted, hoping to quell the hostilities. "You went to Vegas, while we spent time in the hospital, and with a dog."

"Hospital?" Dante turned serious.

"Big building," Vic insisted. "Lots of guys in white lab coats."

"Did the dog get hurt?"

"No, but Eddie did," Frank explained.

"Eddie? Is he gonna be okay?"

"Yeah. There's no danger now, but he had a rough time of it."

"What happened?"

"Bar fight. We'll talk about it later, okay? For now, let's discuss new business. Did the peso idea work?"

"Shit, Frank, I'm sorry. You know I was just trying to have a little fun."

"I know, Dante. But do you suppose we can get serious now?"

"Yeah, sure."

"Hey, dummy," Vic interrupted. "You want to tell us about Vegas or not?"

"It worked great, Frank, Vic." Dante nodded his head fervently. "I made twenty-five hundred bucks."

"With only a hundred worth of pesos? That's fantastic."

"Yeah, then I lost it all playing Blackjack."

"Dumbass," Vic said, just above a whisper. "That's not so fantastic."

"Hey," Frank offered, standing to stretch and heading toward the coffee pot for a refill. "Let's look at the positive side of this. Dante had fun, right? That's all that matters."

"Yeah, right," Vic said, sadly

Dante looked sheepish.

"Okay, it *did* work," Frank said after a couple sips of java. "We gotta give him that. He lost a hundred bucks. Big shit. And it proves we can do it again. Anytime we need a little extra cash, we hop over to Vegas and bring back a couple grand."

"That's true," Vic said.

"And if we need a bigger score, we stay for a couple weeks."

"Yeah, we hit different casinos so they don't catch on," Vic added, enthusiastically.

"I think we got us a nice little deal there. Real sweet, don't you agree, Dante?"

Dante sat, slumped, still a little distracted. But he immediately lifted his head. "It's true, Frank. It was easy picking. How'd it go with the dog?"

"Not bad, actually. Come on, I'll introduce you."

They walked out to the kennel Dante had never seen. The Shepherd inside looked docile enough but able to change at a moment's notice or at the sound of the right command.

"Now, don't make any sudden moves. He doesn't know you yet."

"Got it. Should I cover my testicles or something?"

"If he wants them, he'll chew your hand off to get them. It's your choice. If you want to lose both, go for it." Frank smiled.

"I managed to keep them all through Nam."

Frank just nodded.

"This is Blitz," Vic said cordially, opening the kennel door. "And this is Dante."

The dog sniffed Dante's relaxed hand. All the while, Dante forced himself to *not* hold his breath, though he did keep a cornered eye on his testicles.

"You see, Dante," Frank instructed, "the problem we have with old Blitz is that he was trained using commands only in Hungarian."

"Hungarian, huh?" Dante repeated in disbelief.

"Yeah. That way, the suspects couldn't give the dog any commands of their own and get away from the cops. You know, some of those crooks are getting pret-ty smart. Unlike our men in uniform. I didn't have the heart to ask those idiots what they would do if they tried to apprehend a Hungarian suspect. There are a *few* Hungarians in Duquesne. I'm sure there are more elsewhere."

Dante dared a small laugh. Vic already had Blitz going back into his kennel.

"Vic has a paper with Hungarian commands. You should learn the basics. Vic can help you with the pronunciation. Some of the words are tricky."

"You speak Hungarian?" Dante asked Vic.

"Just a few words."

"Vic, that's amazing. I'm impressed."

"Well, not so amazing, I think."

"What do you mean?"

"I guess I don't do the dialog very well." Vic looked a bit dejected as he spoke. Then he looked up sharply and spoke louder. "I don't pronounce everything just the way the damn dog likes— fucking prima donna."

Dante laughed. "That's *dialect*, dumbass."

"Yeah, that," Vic answered.

"Hey," Frank interjected. "At least he's not saying 'bite' when he means 'sit'. That could be disastrous."

"True," Vic insisted, "but sometimes he looks at me like I'm crazy. It's the same look mom used to have when grandpa would say something stupid. He went senile early and stayed with us until he died. Remember, Frank?"

"I sure do. It wasn't all that long ago."

"Anyway, I'm not happy being looked at in that tone of voice."

This time both Frank and Dante chuckled. From inside the kennel, Blitz looked up at Vic and tilted his head, quizzically. Vic stood with his back to the cage while Frank and Dante faced it. They burst into full laughter.

"Sure, go ahead. Laugh it up, you assholes."

180

After catching his breath, Dante asked, "Have you tested him on drugs?"

"Sure, we let him smoke a joint with us. He turned into an asshole," Vic sneered. "Just like you."

"Come on, don't keep me in suspense. Can he sniff out drugs or not?"

"Yeah," Vic said. "We tried him with coke *and* weed. We even tested him with only money in the car. He was right on almost every time."

"Wow!" Dante blurted. "That's cool."

"We got some tools for breaking into vehicles," Frank said. "Vic's gotten real good at it, haven't you?"

"You know it."

"You're just all kinds of fucking smart, aren't you?" Dante asked, sarcastically.

"You'll have to practice that too," Frank told Dante.

"Being smart?"

"Breaking into cars, Dante."

"Sounds good to me, Frank."

"Yeah, Dante," Vic chuckled. "We wouldn't want you to strain yourself trying to be smart."

"But we didn't stop there," Frank said, smiling, ignoring Vic. "Dante, you should have seen Vic the other night. Friday, wasn't it, Vic?"

"You mean the night at the Marriott?"

"That's the night."

"Yeah, that was Friday."

"We were at the Marriott," Frank chuckled toward Dante. "Anyway, he put on dark glasses and carried a cane. Can you believe it?"

"So," Dante said to Vic, "you pretended old Blitz, here, was a seeing-eye dog?"

"You bet."

"Did that really work?"

"Oh man, did it ever. We got a hit on a couple cars," Vic told Dante. "And we learned the value of carrying walkie-talkies. Frank followed as lookout to tell me if security was headed my way. They came by once." Vic held out his hands like he was riding a surfboard. "I just acted blind and said I was getting some exercise." Vic put on his best 'cool dude' attitude like he could just sail through life.

"What happened then?" Dante could hardly contain his curiosity.

"This one guard tried to give me a hard time. Just another rent-a-cop who thinks he's Magnum or Dirty Harry, you know? So he looks at me and says, 'At night?' So I said, 'I'm blind. It don't matter to me.' They just laughed at me and took off."

Dante looked a little distant. Vic's funny story should have warranted a better reaction. Frank was just about to ask Dante if he felt okay when a light came on behind Dante's eyes.

"Hey guys, this gives me an idea!"

"Sorry, Dante. The dog can't sniff out pussy," Vic shot back, obviously irritated.

"No—shit—guys. Is that what you believe I'm always thinking about?"

They both looked at him scrutinously.

"Okay, it's probably true," Dante conceded. "But the best way to get pussy is with money or coke. So I think about those, as well." He smiled before speaking again. "Look guys, my Mexican friend lives in El Paso. His cousin is in charge of night security at a hotel there. For a little kick back, we can run this scam and security won't be a problem."

"And being just this side of the border, there's probably tons of shit there on any given night," Frank added, excitement beginning to pump through him.

"You got that right. And while we're there, we can have my friend run over the border to Juarez and get us pesos. If we throw in a grand each it'll give us a hundred and fifty thousand pesos."

"Christ, Frank," Vic exclaimed, doing a little calculation in his head, "that could be seventy-five thousand or more from the slots. From a three thousand dollar investment, over a couple weeks."

Frank shook his head. "If we win at the same pace Dante did."

"It'll be tough not to win back our three grand, Frank."

Frank thought for a moment. "Sounds like a fine plan."

The three smiled.

"This friend of yours, Dante, he got a name?"

"Yeah, Rudy. But we all just call him Amigo."

Frank and Vic looked at each other. "Amigo, huh? How original."

"It's Spanish for friend."

"I know what it fucking means," Frank scoffed. "It just seems a bit...generic."

"Hey, if you want to make a friend, *be* a friend. I'm going to go give him a call."

After he walked away, Frank looked at Vic.

"Amigo," he stated as if Vic hadn't heard.

"Yeah, friend," Vic translated.

"If you want one, be one."

They both smiled and shook their heads in disbelief. Just as Dante came back out, Vic's phone rang. After a short moment, Vic poked his head out and called to Frank.

"It's for you."

Frank took the phone from Vic, baffled since no one knew he was here. "Hello?"

"Frank," he heard Connie's voice, frantic on the other end. She sounded close enough to be in Pittsburgh with them.

"What's wrong, honey?"

"It's Janice." Frank saw his middle daughter's smile in his mind.

"What? Is she all right?"

"She's in the hospital. Frank, they think it's her appendix. They're operating."

Frank's heart sank. Images of a sister he'd never met, dying of a burst appendix before he was born, floated around his head like birdies in a cartoon. An irrational feeling overcame him—only he could save her. Tears blurred his vision.

"Where are Sara and Tina?"

"Uncle Paul has them. Aunt Susan is at bingo. There's no phone there. Frank, I'm scared."

"I'll be there as fast as I can, honey. Just hang on. And don't leave her alone with them."

He hung up the phone, not waiting for a reply. He practically ran outside.

"Guys, I've gotta go."

"Where?"

"Florida. There's an emergency."

"What about El Paso?"

"I'll meet you there." Then he was gone. Six hours later he hit the tarmac in West Palm Beach and rented a car.

Chapter 34

Two weeks later, with the crisis passed, and his daughter safely back home, Frank joined his friends in El Paso. The sliding door of the white van had been intentionally left open. The warm air felt different than Florida's—dryer—hotter. A couple palm trees looked out of place, perhaps transplanted from a more tropical location. Like Florida. Everything reminded him of Florida. That's how Frank felt—transplanted, out of place. Unwelcome.

El Paso felt arid, the air barren of life. The land—desert, yet full of a life of its own, though different than any other. Frank was distracted by the abundance of differences he could spot just sitting there in the van. This uniqueness reminded him he was far from home. Loneliness sank in, the kind you could still feel even in a room full of people.

By the time he'd arrived in Florida, Janice laid in ICU, recovering. The operation had gone through without a hitch. She would be okay, completely normal—minus one appendix. A voice deep inside Frank tossed around the opposite ideas of relief and regret for not being there.

But when the first score came, his mood lightened and he began to feel a little more positive. Life always offered options and after a week in El Paso, the trio accumulated more than thirty-five thousand in drugs and money. It would never be reported—not to the police or the internal revenue service.

They polished their routine. Frank stayed in the van as a lookout with the base walkie-talkie. Vic perfected his blind man routine with Blitz. He managed to stumble over a few obstacles that could be easily seen by a person with sight, which added to the realism. Dante acted as a friend of Vic's, out for an evening stroll— an escort. Dante held the other two-way.

As with traffic cops, they never knew what treasures, or dangers, lay inside any vehicle they approached. And sometimes the danger came from outside, as was the case with the custom black van. Adorned with gold-plated trim and high-dollar wheels, the vehicle screamed money.

Even before they got near, Blitz began to fidget, his keen nose sensing something in the air. Still ten feet away he went completely crazy. Dante keyed his radio and yelled excitedly to Frank who could have heard him without the walkie-talkie.

"Man, we found something. Something *big*, by the way Blitz is acting."

Frank started the engine and waited. He heard the mic keyed again and Dante's voice sounded quieter but more excited, almost reverent.

"Oh, my, God! There's coke, weed, and a suitcase full of money. Get over here quick, Frank. This is the kind of shot we came for. Looks like a million or two!"

Frank started driving in the direction he'd last seen Dante. But, to his right, he saw four Latino men running out of the motel. Although in control, his voice came out as a desperate yell. He almost forgot to key the mic.

"Wide awake! You got company!"

Dante turned and saw what Frank warned about. The Latino man in the lead held a gun, pointed in the air. That would change. Two more weren't far behind and stood close to him as bodyguards. The fourth lagged behind, struggling against the extra weight he carried around his mid section. He breathed heavily.

"Hey, you don't want to shoot," Dante called.

"Why not, gringo? You are trying to steal our dope," the man replied through his strong Spanish accent.

"Who's there?" Vic asked from beneath his 'blind' eyes.

"You've got a lot of dope here," Dante said. "There's enough to put you in jail for a *very* long time. I don't think you want all that noise from a gunshot. It might attract the wrong kind of attention."

The man with the gun hesitated for only a moment. Then, in a flash, he produced a cylindrical object from his pocket and began screwing it to the barrel of the gun.

"Now we won't have to worry about making any noise. How 'bout I take out your damned dog, first? Then maybe I shoot you in the balls, just for fun, eh?"

Vic, suddenly sighted, threw huge handfuls of money into the breezy, evening air. Money went flying like dead leaves in a fall wind. The Latinos were momentarily distracted. At the same time, Dante released Blitz, who seemed to know just what to do. He ran, growling, toward the Latino in front.

While the dog they had cursed occupied the man with the gun, Dante, as quick as lightning, ran to the man on his right and slugged him. The man crumpled to the ground in a heap. Dante offered the man one last kick and moved to the other one who grappled with Vic.

"Get the money. Get the fucking money!" the man yelled as he fought with Blitz.

Frank sped up with the van, bearing down on the men trying to grab their money out of the air. They were forced to dive out of the way and it left Vic and Dante temporarily free to retreat.

"Get in. Get in!"

Vic and Dante ran and jumped into the van, pulling on Blitz's leash, struggling to pull him in with them. The dog seemed more intent on resuming his attack. Maybe he liked Mexican. But they wrestled him in as Frank stepped on the accelerator. Bullets hit the metal skin of the van. Vic and Dante ducked.

Frank tried frantically to maneuver the van through the other parked cars and dodge the bullets at the same time. A few quick turns and he managed to escape the parking lot altogether. He swung his head around to catch a glimpse of his friends. Seeing them assured him they were okay.

"Is everyone all right?"

"No," Vic said flatly.

"Is Dante hit?"

"No."

"Then what the hell is it? What's wrong?"

Frank twisted his head again, taking his eyes off the road that was briefly devoid of cars. He knew he only had a few seconds to look away without the risk of hitting something. Frank became irritated at Vic for not simply answering his question, forcing him to chance having an accident. This was no time to be coy.

As soon as Frank saw Vic, he understood. Vic sat on the floor of the van, his long face drooping almost to his knees, holding the dismembered tail of the dog, cradling it in his palm. The dog offered a meek glance in Frank's direction—only moving his big, brown eyes. Dante struggled to stop the bleeding from the dog's tail stub. Just squeezing it didn't seem to be helping.

"Frank, can we find a vet? Can we find the dog a fucking vet?"

"I can't stop the bleeding," Dante added.

Chapter 35

Poor Blitz, there was no hiding his injuries. Wounded in battle, the dog faired up pretty well. With Vic stunned into silence, Dante bonded with Blitz. Perhaps his time in Vietnam gave him a unique ability to empathize with a captured animal. After they managed to find a vet willing to get out of bed and tend the dog, they went back to the hotel in El Paso.

The next day, the three men went back to see Juan, the security head, one last time. They sat in a parking lot, right under a large, yellow structure shaped like the eyebrows of a cartoon character. Dante ate a burger, but Frank had passed in lieu of *real* food. Vic thought the fries were probably safe, but eating them so quickly, one right after another, his stomach still suffered.

"You guys are lucky," Juan said with compassion.

With a super-sized order of fries churning in his stomach, Vic didn't feel so lucky.

"You ran into one of the nastiest Mexican gangs around."

"You know them? Friends of yours?" Dante asked.

"Not friends, Señor. My mother, she lives right down the road. One day when she went out walking her little dog, you know she gots one of those tiny furballs, I think they called Pekinese. Why couldn't she get a *real* dog—like a Chihuahua, I don't know. Anyway, this gang, they drive through the streets, keeping an eye on their territory, showing off their muscles, that sort of thing. Well my mother's dog got a little too close to the road and they hit it with the car."

"Damn. Did the dog die?"

"Not right away. It whimpered in her arms for a time while she cried and called for help."

"That's pretty cruel."

"Yeah, but those guys, you know they didn't even stop or nothing."

"Did you talk to the cops?"

"Yeah, they can't do nothing. My mom cried for a week, man. If I could…" His voice trailed like he wasn't sure how he would finish.

"Well, we roughed them up pretty good. Maybe they'll take off."

"You guys took quite a risk. It wouldn't have bothered that gang very much if they killed you."

"I get the feeling we wouldn't have had much of a chance to complain, either."

"That is true," Juan answered. "And you wouldn't have been bothered by the messy job they did, either."

"Messy?" Vic asked.

"Si Señor. These men, they are not very good aim."

Vic offered an involuntary shiver.

"Yeah," Dante said around a mouthful of burger. "We got the idea they wouldn't have stopped at one bullet each, after we looked at the spray of bullet holes across the back of our van."

"I promise you, mi amigo, they would have killed you, very much."

"Then we got away just in time."

Juan looked distractedly to the side and spotted Blitz with his tail bandaged like something from a horror movie. He frowned and studied it for a moment as if he wasn't sure what he was looking at.

"What happened to your dog, Señor Frank?"

Frank looked over at what Juan saw. Vic decided to answer.

190

"You know how dogs like to chase their tails?"

"Si, Yes," Juan answered.

"Well, our talented Blitz, here, *caught* his."

Juan shot an incredulous look at Vic. He blinked several times under his furrowed brow. Finally, he shook his head and turned back to Frank, who seemed to be the only serious businessman among them.

"I think those banditos are well connected, Señor Frank."

"What makes you say that?

"I know they have police connections. I hear a rumor they pay off the cops and some politicians, as well."

"So if we fell into the system, we'd be screwed."

"Si, si. Or much worse."

Juan's words fell like a concrete block striking Frank on the foot. He stiffened as he realized what a fix they were in. Leaving seemed inevitable. He would have rather stayed for another week and made a bigger margin of profit, just in case Vegas wasn't so favorable. But he couldn't figure a way to do that now.

"It would be best if you left town, all of you. And I don't recommend coming back anytime soon," Juan confirmed.

"Yeah, we were ready to leave, anyway," Frank lied. "We've got business elsewhere."

"I will miss you, mi amigos. Hopefully we could do some more business in the future." He held up his wad of money.

"Anything is possible, my friend," Vic suggested.

Frank thought it was a rather sad parting, despite the fact they'd known each other such a short time. But now, Vegas called and they had just over a hundred and fifty thousand pesos to dispose of.

Neon lights brightened the sky in the city that never sleeps. Frank and his boys turned off highway 515 and headed south on S. Las Vegas Blvd. Night had fallen and Frank relaxed knowing the riddle of bullet holes on the side of the van would be less visible. Customizing like that incited too many questions. They would need to dump the van and get some new transportation. If things worked out as he hoped, they'd be able to buy four or five new cars if they wanted.

Frank wondered, not for the first time, how much the electric bill ran at even one of these places. That would be like a big win once a month—every month—for the power company. He thought there might be a scam in that, but he put it off for later. Frank Mattich was no electrician. And right now they had a plan. But it didn't stop Frank from wondering about being an electrician in Las Vegas. Imagine just changing out a light bulb. He would have to charge a lot of money for even one. Some of them were quite high up. Frank couldn't remember ever seeing even one bulb burned out before. And he'd been to Vegas on many occasions.

In the meantime, Frank thought of a plan for using the slots, a method to try and keep the 'dogs' off their back. A way to avoid getting into trouble. Something simple, just a zigzag pattern through the swatch of casinos. He felt a twinge of excitement as he pulled the van into the parking lot of a small motel on the edge of the city limits where they planned to stay.

When they entered the first casino, Vic had to try the one-armed bandits right away. He'd heard Dante say the pesos worked, but he wanted to see for himself. He put a peso in the slot and pulled the handle as if he'd been practicing. Frank imagined he could see Vic in the bathroom in front of a mirror, practicing bringing his arm down. That motion would probably come in handy when they won a baseball game, as well—coupled with a resounding, *"YES!"* He probably practiced his victory dance, too. Frank felt sure he would dance like Snoopy. He chuckled at the image.

The little tiles whirred around the cylinder inside the machine, buzzing quicker than the eye could see. Then, with loud *clacks*, each window showed a single tile. When they all stopped, each one different than the other—nothing happened. Frank, Vic, and Dante hugged and jumped up and down, celebrating their success.

"Yahoo, it works," Vic finally said.

An older woman, way overweight and adding a couple dozen extra pounds with makeup, stopped near them. Her orange hair sat on top of her head, making a nest for any small creatures who didn't mind all the hairspray and perfume. She'd been walking by, but their noise attracted her attention.

"What are you all celebrating for? You boys lost. Can't you tell?"

Vic stepped forward, lumbering like a farm boy. He shrugged his shoulders and looked at the floor. He kept a stupid grin on his face. When he spoke, Frank and Dante looked at each other, wide eyed with shock by what they heard. Vic did an almost perfect imitation of *Gomer Pyle.*

"Well golly, gee, shucks, ma'am. We just like to see those little doo-jiggers go round and round. Isn't that the point?"

Frank and Dante laughed. That seemed to fit right in with the 'country boy' role.

"Stupid hayseeds," the woman said, disgruntled. She lifted her chin and walked on without looking back.

"I git the feelin' she don't like me none, Pa," Vic said, scratching his head.

"I ain't yer paw, boy. You was the milkman's. I told you," Frank replied, poking his finger into Vic's chest several times.

"Oh, yeah," Vic continued. *"I keep fergettin'."*

"Nyuck, nyuck. He was the milkman's," Dante chuckled. *"Paw, you're funnier than tits on a bull."*

193

They all looked at the woman with big, stupid grins. She glanced backward to see them and almost ran into the wall as she snubbed her nose even higher. A waitress happened by and looked quizzically at the elderly lady. When she saw Frank and the boys, she smiled and walked on past. Dante stared at the skimpy lingerie she wore as a standard casino outfit. Frank wondered how they didn't get cold. Dante appeared to be looking for buttons or snaps to get that thing off her.

Chuckling, the three men set about their plan. First, they would split up. Second, they would only work a casino for a few hours before moving to another. Third, they filled their cups with pesos and put a thin layer of *real* silver dollars on top. They kept the winnings in a separate cup. This was a common practice. Most people who go to Vegas keep their winnings separate to make it easier to count later. That way they could figure if they'd come out ahead or not.

For five days Frank and his friends collected coins, being careful not to make much of a fuss over winning. A man always had to be careful of drawing the wrong attention. They played during the day and returned to their motel room at night. "Too many people at night," Frank said to them. "More chance of running into a problem."

When they neared the end of the week, they'd managed to win the seventy-five thousand they predicted and still had nearly ten thousand pesos left. Frank's dream called to him, the taste rolled around his mouth like a breath mint. He rubbed the back of his neck and looked tiredly at his two friends.

"I suggest we finish using these pesos and get the hell out of here. I'd like to see my family again—make sure Janice is okay. We've been gone a long while."

"I say we go back to Juarez and get more," Dante said enthusiastically.

"My opinion is," Frank argued, "if we get greedy and press our luck, something bad might happen. I don't want to risk that."

"I agree with Frank," Vic inserted. "We had our mind set on seventy-five grand. We got it plus a little extra. Let's just go. We can come back in a month or two and do it again."

"Sorry, Dante," Frank said with genuine compassion. "You've been outvoted."

"What is this, a democracy?"

"Well, it could be a dictatorship if you like, buddy. But I'm the leader and I say we go. Either way, you lose."

Dante visibly sagged. When he lifted his head, he looked resigned. "I guess we leave."

"In the morning," Frank finished. "Did we get the money from the drugs we collected out of those cars in El Paso?"

"Amigo is selling it to some of his Mexican friends. I'll have it tonight," Dante said.

"Good," Frank said. "Tomorrow, it is, then. We'll have a good night's sleep, hit the casinos first thing, and be out of here by noon."

Sometimes the end comes with a whisper, sometimes with a roar. The day shone brightly, more so because they felt smarter than the people who ran the casinos. And they were sitting on a pile of money they would enjoy for months.

The casino held a larger crowd than the days before. Frank didn't think there was anything special going on, just so happened. It wasn't a holiday or a president's birthday. He chalked it up to random chance. Sometimes there were just more people than on other days. They meandered through the bustling crowd and found some slots to feed. Each went in a different direction, keeping with their plan.

Chapter 36

Frank and Vic stood nearby with a crowd of onlookers, helpless to do anything at that moment. They watched as Dante was hauled away to a back room. Frank grabbed Vic's arm and they left the casino in a hurry. No sense waiting for them to check the cameras and find out they all came together.

Dante had been caught with his pesos down. Several very large guards had taken him and Frank preferred discretion. Vic didn't like the idea of leaving and, once in the van, he began badgering Frank about his decision.

"What do you think they'll do, Frank? Do you think they'll arrest him? Maybe they'll hurt him? I hear some of these places *handle* their own problems."

"What happens in Vegas, stays in Vegas?"

"Yeah, like that. Frank, we can't just leave him to the wolves. He's our friend."

"I know."

"What do you suppose happened? How'd he get caught?"

"Dante bumped into some fat lady and spilled his pesos all over the floor."

"Wasn't he looking where he was going?" Vic asked.

"I saw him looking at a sexy waitress as she passed by. The security guard came over quickly to help him pick up his coins and noticed the pesos."

"What are we gonna do?"

"I have a hunch."

"A hunch!? Is that all we got? No plan? No one to call? Nothing but a hunch?"

"Settle down, Vic."

"I can't, Frank. That's Dante they've got in there. Our friend. We've got to do something."

"Once they realize Dante has a walkie-talkie in his pocket," Frank said, pulling out his own radio from his jacket pocket, "they'll be contacting us."

"How do you know that, Frank?"

"What business are they in?"

"What?"

"Why are they here?" Frank persisted.

"For the money?" Vic couldn't be sure of the right answer.

"That's right. They aren't in business to murder. They only want money. When they hurt someone, or worse, it's all about the money. Someone didn't pay a debt, or they were caught cheating, or something like that. All they want is their money back."

"You think that's how it'll go this time?"

"Pretty sure. They don't want trouble anymore than we do."

"I hope you're right, Frank."

"You just wait and see. When they find the radio they'll—,"

"Hey, wise guy, we have your friend."

"Right on cue," Frank said to Vic. Then into the radio, "I'm listening."

"If you want to keep him out of jail, you'd better come up with whatever you took."

"You're kidding," Frank decided on a bluff. "What are you going to do? He has no previous record. What are you going to charge him with?"

"How about theft, embezzlement, fraud?"

"What'll he get—probation? And just try and prove they were his. He collided with someone else in the casino. Maybe those coins belonged to that person."

"You have all the right answers, don't you, wise guy? Well, maybe your friend will have a sudden, freak accident."

Deciding not to risk Dante's life on a bluff, he took a bit more respect for the situation. Frank responded simply. "What do you suggest?"

"As you may have figured out, all we really want is our money back."

"I see. Then we can have our friend back?"

"We will take inventory of our machines, and evaluate what you owe us," the voice on the radio said, ominously.

"Hey, don't get crazy. We've only been here a couple days, you know."

"A man can spend a lot of money in a couple days."

"The ball is in your court."

"Yes it is."

"I'll keep the radio handy," Frank offered.

"We'll be in touch in a few hours."

"I look forward to it."

He released the button of the radio for the last time. There wouldn't be any further communication with them until they were damn good and ready.

"Do you think they'll hurt Dante?" Vic asked.

"I don't think they will do anything until the money has exchanged hands."

"Then they'll let him go?"

"I don't know."

"They might rough him up while they wait."

"They might. But of the three of us, I think he'd be the best one to get through it. Considering what he went through in Nam,

I'm surprised he keeps it together as well as he does. He will make it through this. We all will."

Chapter 37

The call came not later that day, but early the next morning. Frank barely slept a wink, Vic didn't get any. They couldn't imagine any reason why a count of the money would take so long. It should have been simple. How long would it take to calculate all the profits and losses from a few simple slot machines? Perhaps they meant to make Dante's accomplices suffer the wait, not knowing the fate of their friend.

"Are you there?"

They made no attempt at identification and no queries into the whereabouts of the friends of the man they captured. They were keeping it simple. As far as Frank was concerned, the exchange would go smoother if it stayed that way. They would only have to involve one other person. Amigo and Blitz had arrived in the middle of the night.

"I am."

"You have won a great deal of money that you shouldn't have."

"Get to the point."

"Fifty thousand."

"Fifty!? We didn't start out with that much."

"So you won well. Maybe we should check further."

"We've only been here a couple days. Twenty thousand, not one penny more."

"Once again you think you have all the answers. You're in no position to make demands of us."

"True. But I have twenty thousand dollars."

"And we have your friend."

"Listen," Frank said, gentler. He thought it best not to mention there was anyone else besides him and Dante. Vic could be the surprise, an ace in the hole. "It's *all* the money I have. I couldn't have won fifty thousand if I don't have fifty thousand. I'm willing to give you all my winnings, even what I won honestly. I will give every cent I've got. But it's only twenty-five thousand— and a little change. That's everything I have. Honest."

The painful silence coming from the radio pounded on the few remaining nerves Vic and Frank had left in their bodies. The sun had come up full and bright and Frank hoped it meant the day would go well. Vic released a deep breath he'd been holding. Sweat formed around his ears and on the back of his neck. He looked at Frank. Frank looked at him. Finally the radio spoke.

"Agreed."

"Have two guys take Dante in a limo. Don't have anyone follow. Take 15 South to 215 West. We'll meet at the McCarran International Airport."

"Why the airport?"

"It's open. Lots of people."

"Which terminal?"

"We'll call you," Frank responded, coyly.

"You're just full of demands, aren't you?"

"This is your turf. We stand to lose a lot more if this goes badly."

"How do you figure that? There's a lot of money riding on this deal."

"Yeah, right," Frank denied. "Your light bill is probably more than twenty-thousand dollars. We stand to lose the life of our friend."

"Okay, I see your point. We'll follow your instructions, as requested."

Frank and Vic watched the limo pull out of the casino's parking lot and head south. Just before the entrance to the airport, Frank picked up his radio and gave the guys in the limo a call.

"Skip the airport. Keep going on to Henderson."

"Is this some kind of game?"

"I have to make sure you aren't followed. And since letting this deal go sour will leave you with a bigger mess to clean up, I suggest you play along."

"I'll play, but not for long."

"Just head over to Burkholder Park."

Once there, they called sounding impatient. "We're here. Where are you?"

"You know the strip mall by the Community College?" Frank asked.

"Yeah, we know it."

"Good. South side. We're still watching. Don't try anything. If this goes well, you'll have your money in a few more minutes. Have your driver stay in the car and you walk Dante out into the center of the parking lot. We'll make the exchange there. After you and Dante get out of the car, have the driver park at the far side of the lot, backed in by the drug store, and wait until the exchange is over."

"That's acceptable."

The radio spoke no more.

Chapter 38

Frank pulled in to the strip mall parking lot facing the limo, as if they planned on playing chicken. He shut the engine off and he and Vic got out. They stood on either side of the van. Vic held the leash controlling Blitz. The dog danced anxiously, pulling first to one side then another, but remained tethered and controlled—more or less. The limo inched forward and stopped. The back door opened. A big man stepped out, leading Dante in cuffs. As soon as the door shut, the limo backed away about fifty yards into the parking space next to the drug store, as Frank had instructed them to do.

Vic stepped forward, maintaining reign over Blitz through sheer force. Dante and the man stepped toward them. Frank carried a bag with the money. Everything proceeded according to Frank's plan, but his sixth sense warned him they weren't going to honor the simple exchange. There would be some kind of double cross, Frank felt sure of it. He'd made provisions, just in case.

Sneaking around, completely out of sight, Amigo crept to the back of the limo and placed boards with nails under each of the back tires and snuck away like a thief in the night, although the sun sat high in the sky. Frank and Vic wore large hats and dark sunglasses to retain a little anonymity.

"I wouldn't do anything stupid," Vic said, ominously. "This dog *will* tear you to pieces."

The man looked at the dog and then back at Vic. He reached for the bag of money and Blitz pulled his lips back in a snarl. The man withdrew his hand quickly and Blitz calmed. Vic looked into the man's eyes. "Now what did I just tell you? You weren't listening. No dessert for you tonight, mister."

"Let go of Dante and we'll get out of here," Frank instructed. "Unless you'd prefer we release the dog."

The man didn't respond. From his face, Frank realized the man was pissed off, but he let go of Dante, anyway. Vic took Dante back to the van. Frank dropped the bag of money and pushed it with his foot toward the man. He turned and jumped in the van. Frank always believed in fair play. The man spoke into a radio transmitter.

"Come on! Let's go get these mother fuckers."

As they drove away, Frank and Vic heard the engine of the limo roar into life. Just as easily, they heard the popping of the back tires. They wouldn't be giving chase anytime soon.

"Don't forget to go back and get Amigo," Vic said to Frank.

"Yeah, one more block…just to be sure. You okay, Dante?"

"I'm okay, Frank. Thanks."

"I wasn't sure if they'd get rough with you or not."

"They got rough."

"They did? But you're okay, right?"

"I've lived through worse."

"I'll bet you have."

"You know, Frank, I've been thinking," Dante said.

"Already? We haven't even got back to our motel."

"You weren't planning on driving back to the Burgh, were you?"

"No. The van is worthless. I figured we'd take a plane."

"Well, I was wondering if my pretty face might be plastered all over the airports and bus stations. These guys usually have some connections."

"Well, you *are* a good looking man," Vic teased.

"Yeah, I'll be a dead man."

"No, Vic. Wait. He has a point. With all the money flying around in Vegas, it's reasonable to assume they could circulate his picture to the authorities. And the cops would back the casino owners. Too much money to be made from them. Money for everyone. Even some falling back into the pockets of those same authorities."

"Then I shouldn't go. They'll detain me, and capture you as well."

"So, what do you suggest?" Vic asked.

"I could take the van and drive Amigo back home. I'll meet you back in the Burgh in about a week."

"That sounds like a good idea, Dante," Frank answered. "You can give him the van and the dog as payment. We won't be using him again. And you can give him the rest of the pesos, too. There's only about a hundred dollars worth left."

"But what if we want to go back?" Dante insisted.

"I don't think it'll be a good idea to go back there again, anytime soon."

"Yeah, Dante," Vic added. "Give him the pesos. We won't need them."

Chapter 39

Over the years, Eddie modernized his bar. He'd added some big screen televisions for sports broadcasts, and even hired a pretty waitress named Kaitlin, a sexy twenty something with a knockout body. She drew good tips, wearing skimpy outfits. Eddie didn't have the profits coming in that Frank earned. He had to resort to anything that continued to draw in paying customers. They were becoming an endangered species in the economic downturn, and Eddie had begun to get more than a little worried.

Since taking over the bar Eddie turned down most of the ventures Frank and the boys offered him. He wanted an honest business and a life secure from the fear of legal complications. But now, the slow times forced him to consider a number of other possibilities, including 'the way of Frank', as he called it. Eddie made friends with a number of less-than-honorable men and women over time.

Neon and black lights decorated the area behind the bar, offering a unique color show reflected from the bottle labels and the clothes the bartenders wore. Being from the neighborhood, Eddie hadn't resorted to cheating his customers, and he was determined he would close before he sank to that level. The drinks weren't watered down, the prices didn't jump up, and there were no service charges for regular bar functions.

Eddie Schultz prided himself on his honesty and integrity. His father would have been proud of his efforts, had he lived. But soon enough, unless something changed quickly, the bar would be forced to close and little Eddie Schultz would have to seek employment in another way. Perhaps he could open the bar in the next town over. But, as any business man would tell you, just because it worked here in Duquesne, didn't mean it would fly anywhere else. And when the economy started to fall, the line between one town and another was often not wide enough.

Frank walked in with Vic close behind, and hardly recognized the place. He took a second look and then a third. He glanced back at Vic who seemed sure they'd taken a wrong turn. Finally Frank saw Eddie milling about behind the bar and pushed forward through the almost empty tables.

"Hey, Frank. When did you get back?"

"Just today, Eddie. Can you put on the Steeler's game? I've got a dime riding on it."

"Yeah, just a minute." Eddie reached up and turned on the set behind the bar. The sound blared out unexpectedly.

"Are you too fucking poor to afford a remote?" Vic asked.

"I forgot where I put it."

"You're looking good for a walking dead man."

"After about five or six hours of working, I find myself not walking so well anymore."

"It'll take time, Eddie. You'll heal."

"I hope it don't take too long. I'm going crazy just sitting around."

"What the hell did you do to the place, Eddie?" Vic asked.

"Look around. Things are slow. I was trying to spice it up. How about a drink?"

"Sure."

Frank noticed a newspaper on the bar to Vic's left. "Hey, pull that over here so I can see it."

Vic slid the paper over without a glance, remaining intent on the game. Suddenly Frank pounded his fist on the bar and swore.

Vic managed to tear his eyes from the television long enough to see Frank stand.

Just then, Eddie set a drink down in front of Frank and one for Vic. "What's wrong, Frank?"

"Look at these headlines. These kids are dead because of that fucking crack-shit. They're just kids."

Vic looked up from checking out the article. "Hey, Frank. You remember that 'Joey' kid we went to school with?"

"The tall one with the pimples?"

"Yeah. You remember his last name?"

"Bruda…Bruta…," Frank stumbled. "Okay, I don't remember. Why?"

"I think one of these kids might be his son."

Eddie turned the paper where he could see. "Bfruhdowczski. That sounds like the same alphabet soup."

"Vic," Frank said, determination and disgust evident in his tone. "I don't want to deal in that cocaine crap anymore. Not at all!"

"Okay, Frank. Whatever you say. We do fine with pot."

"Yeah. Pot."

Eddie looked at the two and turned, grabbing his towel from his shoulder.

"Hey," Frank called him back. "How much do I owe you?"

"For the paper?"

"For the drinks, dumbass."

"On the house, shithead."

"What the hell do you mean, on the house? We both know I've got money and your business is down. What do I owe you?"

"Just what I said. Did you go deaf or something, Frank? I don't think one drink one way or another is going to make or break my entire business. But it might be affecting your hearing. Maybe I should shut you off."

"But—,"

Just then the door banged open. Frank turned, half expecting almost anything. Standing in the door, showered in the sunlight surrounding him, was Mike Riley, followed by his brother, Donnie. Frank smiled and waved. Donnie saw him right away and tapped his brother on the arm. He pointed, Mike looked, and they both walked toward the bar. They all shook hands.

"Mike, it's really good to see you."

"Thanks, Frank. It's good to be here."

"I didn't expect to see you for a couple more months. And I certainly didn't expect to see you in Eddie's bar."

"Hey, Frank. I just got here and you already want me to be gone?"

Frank laughed. "Really, Mike. You weren't due out for a while. What did you do, escape?"

"It's called good behavior, Frank. Ever hear of it?"

"Yeah. But I didn't know *you* had"

"Funny guy. Want to crack jokes or talk business?"

Frank stood still, looking to the far wall.

"Frank?" Mike asked.

"Give me a minute, I'm thinking about it."

Both men laughed.

"Okay, business it is," Frank finally conceded. "Why don't we wander over that way? It looks like there's just a little less dust over there. Vic, wait here for me."

"Sounds like a plan," Mike said. "Donnie, that goes for you, too. Stay put."

When they got to the table, Mike jumped to the point instantly.

"I can get some beautiful green weed from Mexico."

"How much?"

"I can give it to you for eleven hundred a pound. You can probably get fifteen, maybe a little more. How does that sound?"

"Promising. Go on."

"That's about it, Frank. I like to keep it simple. How many do you think you could move in a month?"

"I have three good guys left. I figure that means we could do about ninety."

"Impressive."

"Yeah, but I don't have the hundred grand up front."

"You're good with me. I'll front you and you can owe me. That okay with you?"

"That's really generous of you, Mike. Are you sure you want to trust me like that?"

"Any reason why I shouldn't?"

"I just worry about things going wrong. What if I can't move the stuff quick enough?"

"Hey, it's your profit margin that suffers, Frank. At four hundred profit for each—times ninety—that's thirty-six grand, split between you and your guys. If you only want to make half that a month, take two months to move it. I'm good either way."

"What can I say?"

"Say yes."

"Yes. Thanks."

"You're welcome, Frank," Mike said, graciously. "I've only got one rule. We both know the RICO laws, so only you and I meet. Got it?"

"I never really did understand all that stuff. Does that beat the RICO crap?"

"Yeah, it does."

"That's great. I didn't know it was so simple."

"It can be. How about I meet you on Monday? Be here at noon."

"*High noon?*" Frank chuckled at his own joke. Mike didn't join him. "I can be here."

"I'll have the weed with me," Mike said. "So be prepared to take it."

"Got it, Mike. And thanks again."

"You bet."

They shook hands and Mike Riley walked out the front door without turning back—Donnie in tow. Somehow, this confirmed Frank's confidence in him, as if his turning back would have shown weakness. Over the next several months, Frank worked out a system where he stayed in Florida with Connie three weeks out of every month and went to Pittsburgh the other week. He passed the stuff off to Vic and Dante to distribute. Sometimes, just for some extra money, Eddie Schultz moved some as well. The sweet arrangement made them all good money.

Chapter 40

Mike Riley walked into Schutzie's Bar and found Frank sitting there enjoying some lunch. He sat down without invitation. Frank didn't mind. He quickly chewed his food to swallow and greeted his friend.

"Hey, Mike. Everything okay?"

"Yeah. I just needed to talk to you about something."

"Shoot. You want something to eat?"

"I'll pass, thanks."

"You sure? The food's pretty good here."

"Thanks, anyway."

"Okay. So what do you want to talk about?"

"I'll talk. You finish eating."

"Sounds like a plan. This stuff tastes like shit if it gets cold."

Mike chuckled. "Anyway, Donnie and I are taking our girlfriends on a vacation for a couple months."

"Hey, that's great, Mike. Wait a minute. When did Donnie get a girlfriend?"

"You remember that girl with the slight overbite that works at the Holiday House?"

"Uh…Shirley, right?"

"Yeah, that's right."

"Donnie's dating *her*? I thought he'd catch something hotter than that."

"Yeah, well, who knows about these things? He says she gives the best head." Mike shrugged. "The point is, the four of us are going to enjoy some vacation time."

"Where you going?"

"I'm not sure."

"You're not sure?" Frank asked, teasingly.

"Donnie made some arrangements, but I think we're winging most of it. Definitely tropical. I've had enough fucking cold weather to last me for a while. I don't need no nature trips to Alaska."

"I heard that. Well, I know you aren't inviting me along, so what's this got to do with me?"

"I want to give you twice your usual amount. You know, for both months."

"A hundred and eighty pounds, eh?"

"That's right. That'll give you your ninety a month for two months while we lounge around in the sun."

"I don't see a problem with that. The stuff seems to be moving pretty regularly. All I have to do is store more than usual. Now that we've got a good storage facility, we've got no problems."

"What kind of storage do you have?"

"We rented an old apartment complex. The basement works quite nicely."

"Is that safe? You're in Florida so much."

"We've got some great security and Vic and Dante don't stay in Florida, so we can handle the double load. As long as I don't have to move it any faster."

"No, you just need to keep up with the same ninety a month you've been doing."

"Not a problem, Mike. Hey, you guys have a good trip."

"I know I will. But just between you and me, if Donnie has me booked into some nature watch tour—even if it's in the tropics—

I'll string him to a tree. The only nature I want to see is my girl sunbathing in the nude."

"String him to a tree, huh? Then cover him in honey and watch the ants come, maybe?" Frank added in.

"Hey, that's not a bad idea. I'm glad I thought of it."

Both men chuckled and shook hands.

"Catch you later, Mike."

"Later, Frank."

Frank usually shared things he was doing with Schultzie. However, desperate times had changed Eddie Schultz into someone who didn't always think straight. While the Riley's were away, after he'd sold all his goods, Frank got pretty drunk—drunk enough to mention that he had two-hundred-grand of Mike Riley's money. Schultzie's eyes lit up.

"Frank, you can do me a huge favor and make a quick fifty 'G's for yourself."

"What are you talking about, Eddie?"

"I'm talking about making a hundred G's, Frank. You want in?"

"I don't like the sound of this, already." He may have been drunk but he wasn't feeling stupid.

"Come on, Frank. You know me."

"That's what I'm talking about. You haven't been in the business like me and Dante and Vic. You don't know the problems that can come up. If you're too rash and make a snap decision, you'll end up in real trouble.

"You know," Frank continued, "I got in that trouble with the Feds. It wasn't very pretty. That sort of thing can really eat away at your soul. You go through that and you come out the other side changed. Like Dante in Nam. I just don't know if you can handle that."

214

"You think I'm weak?" Eddie shouted in anger.

"I don't know if you're weak or not, buddy. But I don't want you to go through what I went through to find out. No one deserves that. I mean it."

"Please, Frank. Just hear me out."

"Eddie, you and I have been best friends for more years than I care to count. I'll listen. But I have to tell you, this isn't Monopoly money here. If you have a sound plan, maybe I'll play. If not, I'm walking. Understand?"

"Yeah. Sure, Frank."

"So, talk."

"You know any place we can get twelve kilos of primo coke?"

"I might."

"You think we can get it for two hundred grand?"

"That seems like a reasonable price. Why would I care?"

"I got a guy who will give us three hundred for those twelve kilos…if it's primo stuff. We make the sale and split the profit, fifty-fifty. That's fifty grand apiece, Frank. That would keep me in business for a long time."

"Man, you *are* crazy."

"What's wrong with it, Frank? It's easy money."

"What's wrong with it? Let me tell you what's wrong with it. There are three problems I can see, right away. The first is, you know I don't deal in that shit anymore. Ever since they started making it into crack and kids are dying, I don't want anything to do with it. You saw that news article, yourself. How could I live with myself?"

"Yeah, but—,"

"Second," Frank didn't hesitate, "I don't like fucking with Mike Riley's money like that. It just doesn't make me trustworthy. And I like being trusted. Integrity, Eddie. It's all we can keep in these times. If we don't, we're no better than the dirt on our shoes. And if he found out I was dealing coke, he'd shut me off, right quick. He hates it, too."

"Mike Riley will *never* know."

"Yeah, right. And third, coke could mean a life sentence…for both of us. Are you really willing to risk that for a measly fifty grand? Only to keep this place open a few more years and have to do it again?"

"Frank, I promise you, this will be a one shot deal."

Frank looked away.

"Listen," Eddie insisted. "I found a great location in Mount Lebanon for the new restaurant and bar. The place is beautiful. And it's such a great location, near an intersection where lots of people travel, it'll be perfect. Fifty grand puts me there, plus a little change left over. Come on, Frank. I *need* this."

"You got any idea what kind of position this will put me in? Do you know how many ways this can go bad? I'd really be risking a lot here. Our friendship means a lot, Eddie. Do you really want to strain it this much?"

"Frank, *please*. I don't know what else to do. My place is shot. My business is all but gone. I can't even sell the place and make a profit because I've already taken a second mortgage on it. I'm in so far over my head I'll have to make ten grand just to break even. I really need this, Frank."

Between the booze, the music from the juke box, and Eddie's begging, Frank's resolve faded. It would be a slick deal and some easy money. If Schultzie already *had* the connection, it would be over and done with—in the same day. Frank tried to blink away all the images of what could go wrong.

"Okay, Schultzie. I'll do it," Frank exhaled the words, antipathetically.

"Aw man, Frank. That's great. Thanks. Thanks a lot."

"Don't make me regret this, Buddy."

"I won't, Frank. Really, I won't."

Frank sighed.

Chapter 41

Fuck!

"Dante, Vic, you won't believe!"

"Frank," Dante said, softly. "Calm down. Take a deep breath and start again."

Frank stopped to breathe. He looked around Eddie's bar, now devoid of patrons. It looked like an abandoned building. A lack of customers created stale air and dust on the furniture. Frank felt a pang of regret, but not for the failing business.

"Eddie," Frank began but choked.

"He's not here, Frank," Vic informed.

"Yeah," Dante added. "We thought he was with you."

"He was." Frank's breathing remained heavy despite his efforts to calm.

"Frank, what is it?" Vic asked, sensing something deeper. "It's not like you to get excited."

"Eddie," he repeated.

"Where is Eddie? What happened to him, Frank?"

"He's…"

Dante and Vic leaned closer, waiting for the information they desired.

"He's *missing*." Deep inside Frank's worst fears tugged at him.

"Missing?" Vic sounded excited. "Is he alive?"

Frank shook his head, nearly delirious. He stared at the floor and barely noticed his friends' concern.

"Frank?"

"I think…I…didn't see any blood."

"What?" Dante shouted.

"What did you get him into, Frank?"

"I…"

"What was the deal tonight, Frank?"

"Eddie said we could make a hundred grand on twelve kilos of primo coke."

"Coke?" Vic yelled. "Coke?! You! Frank! What the hell were you thinking? Of all the things to be dealing in. You hate that stuff."

"I know," Frank sounded meek.

"That stuff kills," Dante added. "And it may have killed Eddie. What the hell are we gonna do?"

Vic crowded against Frank, anger flaring in his cheeks. He stared at Frank, who now sat in a frump. "Why the fuck did you go along with a dumb deal like that?"

"Come on, Vic. You know Frank wouldn't hurt a hair on Eddie's head if you held a gun on him."

Vic calmed slightly, backing away from Frank. "You're right, Dante. I'm sorry, Frank."

Frank still looked a bit distant, but managed a nod in Vic's direction.

"So," Dante insisted. "What do we do now?"

"I want to go look for him. But honestly, I don't know where to start." Frank shifted in his chair as if at any moment he might bolt out the door to begin his search.

"Do you have any idea who he was meeting with?"

Frank just shook his head.

Vic sat, sadly staring at Frank. Frank had become all but lethargic and Vic still twitched like he wanted to give him a slap across the head. Dante just folded his hands under his chin and stared at a spot on the floor.

Frank's ears hurt and he felt a headache coming on as he meandered through the din at Riley's Bar. He noticed Mike had improved the sound system as waves of base crashed through tables and chairs and even through Frank's body, reverberating deep inside his head. His nerves tingled with a kind of tension he was unaccustomed to. His stomach turned and his eyes kept darting to one side then the other. But straight ahead lay Mike's table and that's where Frank headed, pushing through the crowd.

Mike Riley, a big, Irish goon, sat next to his brother, Donnie. Both men had strong bones, pale skin, and flaxen hair that most women didn't generally find attractive. And Donnie had the scar on his forehead from that bicycle accident when they were all kids. Behind the Rileys stood two goons. Two more appeared out of nowhere and towered behind Frank when he reached the table, folding their muscular arms across their massive chests. Steroids surrounded him. He wished Connie could see it. This is what gangsters looked like.

Smoke thickened the air and Frank found it difficult to breathe. He struggled not to cough for fear it would look like nervousness. At the suggestion of Mike—and one of the goons behind him—Frank sat looking straight into the curious eyes of a man he called friend. Frank hoped he still had some clout here.

Pleading his case before them, Frank worked to keep his voice level and sincere. They appeared to listen intently. Well, Mike did. The rest seemed about as interested as a guy in a hair salon filled with elderly ladies. He had the distinct feeling he could have told them any story and they wouldn't have listened...or believed. The only sound they wanted to hear was the scraping of a vinyl briefcase sliding across the table. A briefcase filled with money, of course. Frank could only hope Mike Riley would be more compassionate. In the end, his life might depend on it.

"Look, Mike. I won't kid you. We got hit."

"We? You mean Eddie?"

Frank took a deep breath and stared down into his lap. A pang of sorrow stabbed at his heart. Eddie was lost. The pain held him still and he momentarily forgot where he sat. Eddie was lost. He could feel himself losing control and he struggled to maintain his composure. But Eddie was lost.

"Sorry, Frank. This isn't about what happened to Eddie. What*ever* happened to Eddie."

Frank silently nodded, trying not to sob.

"Who hit you, Frank?"

"I don't know. I never saw a face."

"No face," Donnie inserted, without any real belief.

"Look," Frank shot back with fury. "Eddie has disappeared. He may be dead. Those guys took us down."

"You don't look too injured, Frank."

"We...got separated," Frank spoke softly. "Look Mike, it was my fault. I didn't handle it right and your money's gone. And Eddie may be—," Frank choked.

"Listen to me, Frank. Listen very closely. Eddie was my friend, too. Hell, we all liked him. And I grieve with you. I really do. But this is business, you know. For all we know, Eddie is lying in the sun on a beach in Tahiti. We can't just let it go."

"I didn't think you could, Mike."

"On the other hand, you've made us a shit load of money. That's got to count for something, too."

Frank couldn't think of any reasonable response. So he sat quietly, waiting to hear his fate.

Mike glanced at Donnie, but clearly made his mind up on his own.

"This is how it's going to be. I'm going to put this on the back burner for the moment." Donnie looked at him in disbelief, obviously looking forward to breaking some bones. "But we need our money, Frank. You've got to find a way to get it back to us. A resourceful man like you should be able to come up with something."

"A resourceful man like me," Frank mumbled.

"You understand?"

"Yeah, Mike. I understand."

"Twenty-four hours, Frank. No more. If we don't have the entire two-hundred grand in our hands…"

"Yeah," Frank finished. "I get the message. I appreciate you giving me any shot at all, Mike. I know it's not the way you do business."

"Hey, Frank. You're a friend. We can be a little flexible. But you've got to give me something."

"And if I can't?"

Mike and Donnie stood as if in unison. Donnie leaned over the table, pushing his shoulders square and out. He remained wordless, but Frank understood the silent message. This would be a deal with no options, no amendments, no other chances. As close as he might have been to Mike at one time, the Irishman would surely turn his back and allow his brother to *take care* of Frank should the money not show within the time allotted.

Frank returned the silent conversation, choosing to face the man without saying anything. No sense putting his foot in his own mouth. Someone once said, 'It is better to remain silent and be thought a fool than to speak and remove all doubt'.

At this time, there was little else for Frank to do. He couldn't fight them, even with Dante and Vic. Mike left him only the one choice. Frank accepted the twenty-four hour offer and took it to heart. To him it had only one meaning.

222

A twenty-four hour head start.

Chapter 42

The Bahamas were everything you could imagine from looking at the travel brochures, only better. Tall coconut trees leaned over pristine beaches, reaching toward the crystal waters gently splashing only a few feet away. This was no California. There wouldn't be any surfer dudes here. The waves never reached anything that aggressive.

Calm waters and warm sunlight brought out beachcombers and sunbathers. Gentle, tropical breezes carried the scents of exotic fruits and the sounds of large, colorful birds. Music played all the time, wafting across the sand. Only the occasional thud of a coconut falling to the ground disturbed the serenity.

An overly happy people, Bahamians everywhere smiled and spoke in booming, open-mouthed greetings, showing inordinately large, white teeth. Their twisted drawl was a source of great amusement to many tourists, arriving daily to see more than just the palm trees and beautiful women.

Frank took it all in, smiling, infected by the friendliness of the locals. Two years had passed and he'd managed to stay on the move—one step ahead of the posse. He'd lived in Florida, Mexico, and Costa Rica, never staying in any one place for too long, never sleeping through the night. Mike Riley surely had a contract out on him. Sooner or later, one of Mike's men would catch up with him. And they would exact their account settlement. No one could live on the run forever.

A beautiful day dawned—hell—they were *all* beautiful in the Bahamas. The bar looked so indigenous. A thatch roof overhead and hand-carved wooden stools made from tree trunks offered the locals a comfortable spot to drink and the tourists something else to photograph. Three sides had no walls at all. On the fourth, the bar enclosed around back for supplies storage. Unless you were a regular, you couldn't even order a beer without an umbrella sticking out of it.

Clothes all had a signature color or print. Flowery, bright, and 'loud' declared the standard in tropical paradises like this one. Frank wore a button-up shirt, open almost to his belly, and appropriate-colored shorts to accent the beaten- up sandals on his feet. The skin there had leathered from exposure. A heavy gold-plated chain hung from his neck, more to look like a native than for any other reason. Frank had never worn a great deal of jewelry other than his wedding band. Now his tanned finger showed no traces of where it had been.

Dark sunglasses protected his eyes from the relentless yellow orb in the sky. A straw hat sat in the chair next to him. He'd managed, after some practice in front of a mirror, to mimic the Bahamian signature toothy grin, but not their dialect. Even someone who knew him well would have a difficult time recognizing him in his new persona. Tan skin, unkempt hair, and not shaving had a way of changing one's appearance. But his voice still sounded the same. So Frank learned to be rather stoic.

Sipping his drink, he glanced to his left. Coming up the short stairs, three, large men approached without averting their gaze from Frank. They all wore sunglasses and looked like hard cases. It looked like the opening shot of a movie like *Desperado*. At first glance, Frank would have been smart to sneak off. A few other people in the bar looked as though they considered running away before trouble started. Frank watched the three men approach as if in slow motion.

One of the men—a grizzled, tanned dude, the second—the kind that might be called 'smooth operator', carried a black bag, and the third—a muscular Italian guy you could tell wouldn't take any shit. He walked with a shoulder sway that reeked of bad attitude. They came up to Frank's table and stopped next to it. Looking down at him without smiling, they said nothing, as if challenging him.

Frank stood to accept the challenge, staring back.

The Italian suddenly reached out and put his arms around Frank. Frank's feet left the ground and the light faded from his eyes as the buffoon crushed him in a bear hug. A man sitting two tables over grimaced like he could feel the pain as the vertebrae of Frank's back popped forcefully into place. Frank grunted as all the breath was brutally forced from his lungs.

"Frank Mattich, you big, dumb hunky. You're a sight for sore eyes."

"Dante, you fucking ox!" Frank managed to squeeze out. "Put me down before you break my God damn ribs!"

Dante—looking larger than life, even more so because Frank hadn't seen him in so long—dropped him down unceremoniously. Then he kissed Frank on both cheeks in traditional Italian behavior and boomed out a laugh that rivaled the Bahamians' jocularity.

"It's so good to see you, man! It's been a long, fucking time."

Frank laughed weakly, gingerly examining several of his ribs. "It's good seeing you too, buddy...I think." Frank looked over at the 'smooth operator'. "And you, Vic. Thanks for coming down here to this hell hole."

Dante looked at the scantily clad, tanned women at the surrounding tables. "All the holes I see don't look like hell, Frank."

226

Vic scanned over the beaches and beautiful water. He came around the table and slapped Frank on the shoulder, smiling at him.

"What are friends for, huh? Besides, I couldn't say no to a free trip to the Bahamas. I mean, the *hell hole*." Vic laughed as he added the last.

The grizzled, heavily tanned dude sat at the table without invitation. He picked up Frank's glass and sniffed the contents. He wrinkled his nose as if the liquid within smelled putrid. Nevertheless, he lifted it to his mouth and finished the offending drink in two swallows. Frank turned and looked at him in total disbelief.

"Have a drink, Ronnie?" Sarcasm dripped from his words.

"No thanks," he burped. "I just had one."

"Yeah, I see that," Frank said in disgust. "Anyway, thanks for bringing these two bozos down. I don't know how I would have managed without them."

"No problem, Frank," he answered without the proper island accent.

"Have a seat, guys," Frank said to his friends.

Frank and Dante sat. Vic threw the bag on the floor next to the table before sitting. He reached down and patted it, sensitively—possessively.

"I brought the stuff you asked for."

"Good."

"What do you need all this for, anyway?"

"I got a deal cooking."

"So," Vic continued. "What's the deal?"

"I—," Frank began.

"Hey, I'm hungry," Dante interrupted. "Let's eat first. We can talk later, on a full belly."

Frank gave him a condescending glance. Realizing nothing would get done until Dante's ravenous appetite was satisfied, at least temporarily, Frank signaled for the waitress. He picked up one of the small menus sitting on the table and handed it to Dante.

"That's Dante for you," Vic said to no one in particular. "Always thinking with his stomach."

"Yeah," Frank added as the waitress approached and Dante stared at her, "when he's not thinking with his little head. He doesn't use the big one when he's thinking about women."

"May I help you?" She stood tall, sexy, wearing short-shorts and a midriff top, not buttoned at all, but tied off under her bodacious boobs. She wore no bra. Though she was clearly American, her tan was just about perfect, as was her body. She resembled a California girl, although her accent sounded Jersey. Her voice sang and Dante glazed over, enraptured. Again.

"Please don't ask him that," Frank whispered.

"Oh, I think you can help me, Darling," Dante said in his smoothest voice.

"You're such a *big* man," she cooed.

"You like big men, honey?"

"If they're big in the right place," she answered, looking right down into his lap. Dante smiled at her.

Frank stared in disbelief. He'd been to this bar often and never received so much as a second glance from the bitch. While he hadn't come looking for a piece of ass, she'd never even tried with him. Dante walked in and practically had her going down on him in less than a minute. The guy had real talent. Or was it magic?

"You still think you needed him?" Vic asked Frank, cocking a thumb in Dante's direction.

Frank hesitated. Then, "Yeah, I need the big, fucking dummy."

"Yeah," Vic continued. "He'll be loads of help. I'm sure we'll need a mattress tester."

228

The waitress took the orders and turned away. Dante bore holes in her ass with his stare.

"Hey, Dante. You okay?"

"I love the women down here," Dante mumbled.

"Dante! Hey! What did you say?" Frank insisted.

At the counter, the waitress turned and winked at Dante.

"I said, I *love* the women down here," he repeated.

"Hey, you still in there?"

"I'm here, Frank," Dante finally turned back to the table.

"I've got a question."

"Okay."

"Are there women anywhere that you *don't* like?"

Silence fell over the table. Dante seemed to stare into infinity. The other men waited.

"Dante?"

"Give me a minute, Frank. I'm thinking."

"Yeah, sure, buddy. Take your time."

The men all laughed.

Chapter 43

Remnants of dinner remained on their plates. Smaller shrimp meant they ate more and the peels stacked high. Hot sauce, untouched by all except Dante, had been pushed aside. Dante leaned back in his chair, rubbed his belly, and belched heartily.

Frank rested, looking at his old crew. The odd man out, the new man, Ronnie Dunn, became a close friend over in Florida. He was a real find. The best wheel man Frank ever saw, and he could handle a car or a boat with equal grace. He smuggled anything and everything all around the Gulf Coast and the Caribbean. He, like Frank, had been holed up in paradise for quite some time.

Frank gathered them together for what he hoped would be one last job. This would be his chance to even the score and get his life back—his chance to go home and be with Connie, and the girls. The smell of the dream wafted up to Frank's nose and he twitched in his seat. He could see the big house and a small business in his mind's eye. Three little faces shined up at him, eyes sparkling, hearts filled with love. A smile settled on his face.

As Frank enjoyed the warmth of friends and visions of success, the waitress came back around. She sat right down on Dante's lap without hesitation. Frank felt like he'd missed something. First they were just flirting. Now she was already on his lap. Had he missed something in between?

These guys are best crew I could ever ask for. They make me feel almost whole. There's only one thing missing. The truth is, it's just not the same without Schultzie.

Vic leaned over the table. "Hey, you okay, Frank?"

Frank focused his eyes back on the present day, leaving Eddie behind and shaking off the feeling of nostalgia that overwhelmed him like a warm blanket on a chilly night. He'd almost sunk into it, like letting yourself fall asleep when you're suffering from shock. But Vic pulled him back. His crew could protect him from anything. Even, it seemed, from himself.

"Yeah, I'm okay. Thanks. Let's get to work."

The other men sat up. Ronnie appeared more attentive. Dante scooted the waitress off his lap reluctantly. She turned and touched her nose to his. Her smile came across as intimate and sexual.

"Daddy's gotta go to work now, Baby. We'll play later, okay?"

"You promise?"

Dante stuffed a one hundred dollar bill into her gentle cleavage, touching her breasts.

"I promise. Now scoot."

He sent her off with a smack on the ass. He continued to look at her, smiling, until she'd gone completely out of sight into the kitchen. When the door closed behind her, Dante turned back to the table and became deadly serious.

"What's up, Kumba?"

Frank waved his hand at the black bag.

"Let's see what you've got, Vic."

The guys pushed back the plates and cleared the center of the table. Dante stood and passed some of the dishes to the empty table next to them. Vic lifted the bag and let it plop. He unzipped it and slid it over to Frank in one smooth motion. Frank pulled it close, spread it and looked inside. He took out a bundle of bills and ruffled through them with a greedy smile on his face.

"Nice. Real nice."

"Thanks, Frank. My guy, he's like the Michelangelo of funny money. You can't tell it from the real thing without serious testing. Hell, it even smells the same."

Frank put the wad to his nose and inhaled deeply. He closed his eyes, enjoying the almost sensual, musty odor of the bills. When he let out the breath, he allowed a gentle hum to ring off his vocal chords.

"He's an artist, that's for sure," Frank said, softly.

Frank pulled one bill from the bundle and set the rest back inside. He studied the bill closely. He held it up to look through it. Finally he grabbed a real dollar from his pocket and compared the two. He couldn't see the difference, except the one from the bag was a hundred.

He put the bill back in the wrapper inside the bag, stacking carefully, and zipped it up. No sense drawing any attention to it. Just as he looked up, he saw a smaller black man approaching. He had Rastafarian hair and lots of rings and chains. He wore oversized sunglasses and a large, knitted cap imprisoning most of his dreadlocks. As he walked, it bounced like the head of an octopus. The T-shirt he wore boasted a picture of Bob Marley, screaming out a ballad. The color clashed with his baggy pants. He dangled a cigarette from the corner of his mouth in a casual manner, as if he didn't care if he set the place on fire. He swaggered toward them.

"Here comes our contact."

Frank stood and stepped toward the guy. He welcomed the newcomer in the traditional, outstretched hand, fashion. The man shook it, smiling broadly, and came closer to the table. He dragged a chair over from the next table, under the angry stare of the couple sitting there.

"Reginald, my man."

"Frank, my good man. How very nice to see you." Reginald spoke in a most perfect British accent with impeccable grammar. The table became speechless.

"Guys," Frank introduced. "This is Reginald Wells. Reggie, meet my crew. Dante, Vic, and Ronnie," Frank swept his hand around, pointing as he spoke each name.

Each stood, gentlemanly, to shake hands and greet the man. He returned their cordiality in kind, then sat. Everyone returned to a relaxed posture. The tropical breezes swept through the open bar design and across the table, bringing further comfort.

"Frank, my friend, all is set for tonight. If you tell me you are ready, then it is on."

"Okay. Here's the deal," he spoke to the others. "Reggie introduced me to these three dudes, the Hilliard brothers."

Everyone listened intently. Frank was not one to take on anything haphazardly.

"Robert is the leader of the Hilliards. He's a lot less stuffy than you'd expect a bank manager to be."

Vic chuckled.

"His two brothers, Phillip and Desmond, are security guards."

"Jeez, what a racket," Dante said.

"Yeah. It couldn't have worked out any better for us."

"Frank," Vic interrupted.

"Yeah?"

"I don't mean to be a killjoy, but look at this place. How much fucking money can they have in their bank? I mean, really. Are we talking twenty thousand? Fifty? Why did we need so much funny money?"

"Because, my friend, the casinos here move a lot of cash in and out of that bank vault."

"How much?"

"We're talking millions of dollars, Vic. That's why the big load," Frank finished, resting his hand on the bag.

"That's a lot of cabbage in that bag, Frank."

"I spoke to Robert, myself. He told me we can do four million easily. He agreed to split fifty-fifty. That means he and his crew divide their two mill and we divide ours. I've got the figures worked out."

"Two mill?" Dante sighed.

"Has a nice ring, doesn't it?" Frank suggested.

"Man, you know it."

"And you guys get the best part, right?" Frank queried.

They all looked blankly at him.

"Come on, guys, you've got to keep up if you want to make it to 'Double Jeopardy'."

They looked at him, dubiously.

"The bank people won't be any the wiser."

"The bank people?" Vic asked.

"The bean counters in charge of making sure all the books balance."

"How does that work?" Ronnie asked.

"The funny money will filter out well before anyone catches on to us. And if they never find out, we don't even risk a parking ticket."

"And if they *do* find out?"

"If they discover a large pile of counterfeit money in their vault, so what? How did it get there? Who is responsible? It can't be that Frank What's-his-name. He never has much money and he doesn't even live on the island anymore, does he?"

"Man, that sounds like the best deal we could ever have," Dante said, grinning contently.

"Vic?" Frank asked. "What about you?"

"Yeah, I gotta admit. I can't imagine a much better deal."

"So you're in?"

"Frank, come on. You *know* I'm in. I wouldn't be any other way. We've been together way too long."

Frank smiled.

"So," Ronnie intruded, "how do we get into the bank to make the switch?"

"We go at night when the bank is closed. The brothers open up the back door for us."

"And the vault?" Ronnie continued.

"Robert has the code to get us in there."

"Sounds good," Vic put in. "Robert will be there, too?"

"Sure will."

"When do we go in?" Vic asked.

Frank glanced at his watch. "Ten o'clock."

"Tonight!?"

"Want to wait?"

"But, Frank," Vic asked, concerned. "We usually work out details before we pull a job."

"The details have been taken care of."

"But it's so soon."

"You can still back out if you like."

Vic pinched his lips into a thin line. "No, Frank," he finally said. "I don't want to back out. I'm a little surprised, that's all. But I'm in."

"Good. We've got two hours. We'll go back to Ronnie's place and move from there."

"Two hours?" Dante asked. "How about I meet you guys back here? I got a hot date."

"Two hours?" Frank objected. "What will you do with the rest of the time?"

"Yeah," Vic laughed. "Don't you usually take two minutes for that?"

"Up yours."

"Wait, Frank," Vic interjected. "He took longer on the dance floor."

"Yeah, he had to pull his fist all the way back."

"I'll catch you assholes later." Then he was gone to find the waitress.

Frank stood, mouth opened. "Some things never change."

"Once a hound, always a hound," Vic offered.

"And we thought Blitz was the dog in this outfit."

They all stood around, making ready to leave. Casually, Reginald approached Frank. He leaned in to whisper.

"Frank, may I have a word?"

"Of course, Reggie. Let's go over there."

They walked to the side.

"My sources tell me the Hilliards are planning some business with the Columbians in the next couple days. Four million dollars worth of business."

"Yeah, I heard something like that. And to think, they're only supposed to get two."

Reginald leaned back, flabbergasted. He offered Frank a most surprised look, blinking quickly, with his mouth forming an 'O'. He looked like a clown. Frank laughed at the expression.

"Did you think you were my *only* contact down here, Reggie?"

"I...I..."

"I have friends. Like you, they'll make an honest deal but they don't take to being double crossed. And they don't like it when friends get crossed, either."

"Well, in light of this information, do you think it's wise to proceed with the caper?"

"*Caper?* I like the sound of that, Reggie." He *did* like the sound of it. It reminded Frank of when they'd pulled that fast one on old man *Douche Bag* and Eddie called it a caper. Nostalgia swept past him again.

"Yeah, sure. What about making a new deal, Frank?"

"I think we're going ahead with it, my friend."

"Remember what I told you about the Hilliards. They will not hesitate to cut your throat and the throats of all your friends. In fact, they'd kill anyone who gets in their way, no matter how insignificant. They don't bargain and they don't listen to excuses. They are ruthless and have a reputation for covering, or rather, burying their tracks."

"Don't worry, Reggie."

"Don't worry?" Reggie asked, flabbergasted. "Don't worry?"

"Reg, relax," Frank said, laughing. "Nobody will be cutting any throats tonight, I promise. In fact, if I'm not mistaken, I think we're all going to have a real good time. So smile, Reg. Life is good."

"A good time? Are you crazy?"

"My wife thinks so. So does my analyst."

"Sure, funny guy. But a good time? Frank?"

Frank smiled and clapped him on the shoulder.

"Jolly good, my man." He managed to mimic Reggie's British accent.

The guys all headed out.

Chapter 44

Vic and Frank climbed into the van Ronnie had standing ready. Unlike Frank's old, white van, this smoky gray paint with tinted windows offered a bit of stealth at night. The lack of bullet holes helped keep it inconspicuous as well. Vic and Frank sat in the back with two large, black duffel bags tossed on the floor in between them. Ronnie took the driver's seat and drove back to the bar to pick up Dante. He got in with Frank and Vic, smiling like the Cheshire Cat.

As the cargo van had no actual seats in the back, the three friends sat on the floor, bouncing around as the van travelled on the poorly kept roads. They held a hand on the bags for balance. A bit of the exhaust fumes slipped in through the back doors, offering them a little cough for their trouble. It seemed like Ronnie might have been *trying* to hit every bump and pothole.

Due to a dense overhang of trees, the alley behind the bank stayed darker. Even the milky glow of the moon couldn't penetrate the nearly-solid canopy of big-leafed foliage that encroached on the building. Further out offered better light, but Frank and his crew wouldn't be wandering that far away.

"Okay," Frank said. "Let's go over it one more time. Vic and I go in with the bags. Dante, you cover the back entrance. Ronnie, stay in the van and be ready to go."

"Roger that," Ronnie said with military precision.

"Everybody got it?"

"We got it."

Dante and Ronnie picked up walkie-talkies. They began making obscene bodily function noises in them, making sure each could hear the other. Frank picked up the last radio and clipped it to his belt.

"Let's go," Frank ordered, scowling at the other two for acting childish when they needed all their concentration.

Frank grabbed his bag and pushed at the doors. The click of the door latch sounded very loud in the night air. Dante stepped out right after Vic and his alert gaze swept the area. No noises or movement caught his attention, and Dante could see nothing of interest. He remained focused, trying to burn a line of sight through the shadows.

The three moved toward the back door of the bank. Ronnie stayed in the van as instructed. Vic carried the other black bag and Dante clipped his radio to his belt so he could check his gun. He pulled the weapon out, made sure it was loaded with an active round in the chamber, then stuck it back in his coat. There it would remain hidden but still easily reached and quickly drawn.

"Dante, stand back where they can't see you. No sense giving away your presence."

"Okay, Frank." Dante stepped sideways and rested his back to the wall.

"But stay close, in case we need you."

"And don't fall asleep," Vic added.

Dante simply nodded, refusing to react to Vic's taunt. He always got quiet when they worked a job. At least he wouldn't give away their location.

"Frank," Vic said to Frank's ear. "Did you ever give any thought to what would happen if a girl walked by while he guarded us?"

"No. But thanks for giving me something else to worry about."

They knocked. After a moment, Phillip Hilliard poked his head out. He made sure the area looked clear, and then opened the door wider, motioning them in. He smiled a huge smile, showing one brilliant, gold tooth. Frank and Vic entered the bank quickly, trying to remain quiet. Phillip looked out again, taking one last glance around. He pulled on the door and it closed with a clang that sounded too much like a jail cell.

"Jesus, you think you could make any *more* noise?" Frank hissed.

The two guards smiled broadly and looked at each other.

"We're trying to be quiet, aren't we?" Vic spoke with a loud whisper.

Phillip and Desmond nodded but said nothing. They stared at Vic.

"This is Vic. Vic, this is Phillip," he pointed to gold-tooth, "and Desmond."

"It's a pleasure to—"

They looked like they were going to extend their hands in greeting, but instead they began patting Frank and Vic all over.

"Sorry, guys. We got to make sure, you know?" Phillip asked—his one gold tooth showing frequently as he spoke with his mouth wide.

"I was beginning to wonder if you guys could speak," Vic added, sarcastically.

Phillip looked inside the duffels. One of them was empty, like a black hole. The other overflowed with money, funny money. Phillip smiled, conveying his pleasure at the quality of the bills.

"Yeah," Desmond said, his accent much stronger than Phillip's. "Dis be de inside of a bank, mon."

He pointed at Frank's walkie-talkie with more than curiosity. "Wha's dat for?"

These guys were touchy, ready to slice a throat at a moment's notice. It made no sense to do anything other than cooperate. But Frank couldn't resist the urge to be sarcastic. Perhaps he'd been hanging around Vic too much.

"In case we want to order pizza." His voice flat and casual, he stared directly into Desmond's eyes.

Desmond Hilliard had a sense of humor. Frank had heard it before. But tonight he must have left it at home. He scowled at Frank and reached for his gun. Suddenly Robert Hilliard came up behind Frank through the other doorway.

"It's all right, Des."

Robert Hilliard entered from the back room. He glared at his brother and Desmond withdrew his cocked hand. Inside, Frank breathed a sigh of relief.

"Frank, my very good friend. How nice to see you again."

Robert, dressed in proper business attire, spoke like Reggie, rather than the typical island drawl. His two brothers, on the other hand, seemed less educated, probably why they wore bank guard uniforms and not business suits.

"Always a pleasure, Mister Hilliard."

"I see you've brought the money. Shall we get started?"

"I think that would be an excellent idea."

He smiled broadly, and then motioned for them to follow. He led them out of the back room, behind the teller counter. Frank and Vic followed, Phillip and Desmond brought up the rear.

Evening light shone dimly through the tinted front plate glass. The floor remained difficult to maneuver, despite the lack of obstacles left in the walk paths and the safety lighting mounted in several places on every wall. The men trod carefully. Looking out through the teller cages gave Frank a chill, reminding him of his day in jail. They turned and faced the vault.

Robert punched in the code, carefully blocking access to the keypad to prevent Frank and Vic from seeing. Frank chuckled, wondering how he'd ever get this far into the bank without their help, even if he wanted to rob the place again. The locking mechanism retracted with a clacking sound. Robert nodded to Phillip, who crossed to the front of the bank and took up a position watching the street through the large plate glass window. Robert motioned Frank and Vic into the vault.

"After you, Gentlemen."

Frank and Vic entered the vault. Robert motioned for Desmond to remain at the vault entrance. Some terrible claustrophobia—or was it a rational fear of jail cell doors closing behind him—gave Frank the feeling that Robert might try and close him and Vic in the vault, trapping them until the police arrived in the morning. Or worse, he might leave them to die of suffocation. Once Robert entered with them—Frank's fear dissipated. Of course, he remembered, why would Robert Hilliard want to trap them in there? After all, he had a date with the Columbians. And for that, he'd need the money.

"Here we are, gentlemen," Robert said, a lilt evident in his voice.

He opened a grey cabinet filled with large denomination bills. Frank sucked in a breath and stared. Vic managed to reach out and begin the task at hand.

"We must work quickly," Robert told Frank, but he noticed Robert didn't offer to help.

Frank shook off the spell of claustrophobia and fear, and took the empty bag from Vic. He handed it to Robert as Vic set the other one down. He pulled out a small, portable work light and placed it on the floor. Then he adjusted it for the best result.

"You fill that one with your cut," Frank told Robert, forcing him to help make it happen faster. "Two million. Vic and I will start putting the funny money in the vault. When this one is empty, we'll fill it back up with our share. Okay?"

"Two million," Robert repeated.

"Right. As agreed." Frank's brow furrowed.

"As agreed."

Robert started pulling bundles of cash from the vault and placing them in his duffel while Frank and Vic took identical bundles of counterfeit money from theirs and placed them on the shelves. The men worked quickly, efficiently.

When Robert stuffed the last bundle into his bag, he spoke to Frank. "Two million."

Desmond entered the vault and looked in the bag. He and Robert shared a smile.

"Good," Frank said. "We'll refill this with our share and—,"

"We got trouble," Phillip, who'd just run up, shouted. "The cops are outside."

Everyone held their breath.

"Down," Frank whispered.

The men came out of the vault and ducked down behind the teller cages. The beam of the spotlight from the cop car slowly crawled over the cage area and around the room. The men crouched nervously behind the counter as the light swung around over their heads. A few minutes passed and finally the light cut off. Then the police car slowly pulled away. The men, still squatting out of sight, exhaled.

Several minutes passed as they collected their breath. They looked at each other. When they thought enough time had passed to risk it, they began, one at a time, to poke their heads up and look. Frank turned and saw Vic crouching in the vault entrance. He laughed out loud.

"It's okay, Slick. They're gone."

"Jesus Christ, Frank. I damn-near choked on this big lump in my throat. I think it was my heart."

"They were only doing a drive by."

"I'm allergic to cops, Frank. You know that. I break out in handcuffs."

Robert laughed. An American joke he'd never heard.

"I'm serious, Frank," Vic added, offended that anyone would laugh at his fears. "I think I may have shit myself. Would you check my shorts for me?"

"No," Frank said, matter-of-factly.

"Let us finish, shall we?" Robert offered.

Chapter 45

They took their original places—Desmond taking his place at the vault door and Phillip back by the front window. Robert, Vic, and Frank re-entered the vault.

"Let's make this quick!" Frank said.

"I thought you said they were just doing a drive-by," Vic said.

"I don't like coincidences, Slick. Keep moving that money."

He and Vic hurriedly filled their bag with bundles of cash. In a few moments they were done.

"That's it. Let's go," Frank finished.

Robert closed the cabinet as Desmond grabbed the duffel. Vic reached for the work light and the other duffel. They exited the vault, feeling an increase of tension in the air. Vic only knew they were almost out with the best haul he ever hoped to see in his lifetime. Frank, knowing about the Columbian deal, expected something more. Robert closed the vault door behind them with a deafening clang.

Desmond and Robert lead the way to the back room, toward the back door and freedom. Frank and Vic followed with Phillip in back. The men stopped by the exit door. Robert turned and faced Frank, wearing a horribly macabre grin.

"Mister Hilliard," Frank began, "it's been a pleasure doing business with you. I'll just let our ride know we're coming out now."

Frank lifted the walkie-talkie toward his face, knowing if the Hilliards were going to make a move, now would be the best time for them.

"Believe me, Mister Mattich, the pleasure is *all* ours."

With an almost imperceptible nod from Robert as a signal, Phillip and Desmond brought pistols out from their jackets and pointed them at Frank and Vic.

"What the hell is this, Mister Hilliard?" Frank asked, the walkie-talkie extended only about half way up. He held still.

"My brothers and I decided to renegotiate the deal. All for us, none for you. Seems much more equitable that way."

"You son-of-a-bitch—!" Vic exclaimed as he moved forward to attack.

Frank held up a hand to stop him.

"Mister Hilliard," Frank said. "I'm somewhat disappointed in you."

"Hand over the bag, please."

Vic handed the bag over to Robert. Frank pushed a button on his walkie-talkie, no one noticed. They stood in the middle of tension so thick it suffocated them, waiting for the Hilliards to decide their fate. Robert began looking around at the ceiling and walls. Finally he looked to the bag in his hand, which had begun to beep steadily, softly.

"What is that noise?" Robert said, excitedly.

Frank replied in a very calm voice. "It's a bomb, Mister Hilliard."

He held up the walkie-talkie so all could see. Phillip and Desmond trained their weapons on him.

Frank, still calm; "Uh-oh, boys. My finger comes off the button and the bomb goes *boom*."

"He's bluffing," Phillip suggested.

"Care to take that risk?" Frank rebutted.

They stood still.

"Set the bag down very gently," Frank continued.

"If you set it off, Mattich, you'll kill yourself and your friend along with us. I don't think you're willing to do that. Are you?"

"The way I figure, Vic and I are dead men any way you look at it, Robert. The question is—are *you* willing to chance it?" Frank hesitated. "Would you gentlemen care to join us?"

Phillip remained staunch. "I think he's bluffing."

"If you don't set that bag down right now, you'll find out."

"We have them outgunned, Robert," Desmond added in.

At that particular moment, Dante glided silently in. He held a gun in each hand. He swept his arms out wide so each barrel pointed at one of the brothers. Caught off guard, Phillip and Desmond stood frozen. The guns were pointed every which way in a tableau worthy of a motion picture. In the meantime, the bomb kept beeping away inside the bag.

Robert, now sweating, looked nervously at the bag in his hand. He set it down and made a gesture that indicated he would make a dash if given the chance.

"Well, *Robert?*" Frank decided to drop the formality, under the circumstances. "This is what we Americans call a Mexican standoff."

"And how do you propose we resolve this situation?" Robert stammered.

"We take our bag, the one with the bomb, and leave. You keep your cut."

"I say we kill them and take it all, Boss," Dante said.

Frank glanced at Dante.

"I don't think so, Dante. Remember what happened the last time?"

Dante looked confused. "The last time?"

"There was so much blood. Pieces of money were painted onto the walls in the blood and body parts."

"Personally," Dante said, "I'm rather partial to the brain pieces stuck to the wall. It reminds me of Nam."

"Sorry, old friend. I think we should skip it this time. This is supposed to be a clean job. We leave too many clues in the blood. Then we have to kill all those cops when they come to get us."

"No brains?" Dante asked, disappointedly.

Frank hesitated. "Well, maybe we could kill just *one* of them, if you like."

"Wait, Mister Mattich—,"

"Shut up," Frank added.

Dante played it out to the fullest. He lowered his head and looked dejected. When he spoke, he moaned.

"I can only have one? If you had three beautiful women standing here, would you be happy with only one?"

Frank acted like he was thinking about it. He looked at the three men—they were ghosts. All their pigment had become like moonlight, grey. They stood, frozen, shaking, hoping Frank would decide in their favor.

"No," Frank said. "I wouldn't. I guess you'll have to kill them all."

"Mister Mattich, please!"

"What? What is it with you? We're talking here." Frank grabbed one of the guns and pointed it at Robert. It felt peculiar to Frank—who never carried one. "I should put one in you right now, just for being rude."

"I think we could work something out, Mister Mattich. Perhaps the deal where you take your bag with the bomb and we keep ours."

Frank stared at him then back at Dante. "I suppose we'll have to leave them *all* alive. Sorry, old friend. The cops will never

248

know we took all that money. But if you massacre these men, they'll investigate and possibly find out."

"You think the cops are that smart?"

"I think, if you leave them a trail, they might be able to stumble in the right direction. Maybe next time. Okay, big guy?" Frank dared a last glance back at Desmond and Phillip. "Maybe you'll get lucky and one of these two will be stupid and come after us. They look pretty stupid."

"You think so, Frank?" Dante asked with renewed enthusiasm. His smile returned. "Really? I can?"

"Anything's possible when you deal with idiots. And when one of them *does* follow, you can turn him into a colander."

Dante's smile spread across his face like a virus. Frank looked at Robert.

"I'm willing to forgive and forget, Mister Hilliard. What do you say?"

"Forgiveness is a virtue, Mister Mattich. Under the circumstances, I would say our original agreement seems more than fair."

Frank held up his walkie-talkie.

"Okay, nice and easy, then."

He pointed to Phillip and Desmond.

"You boys put your guns down and back away."

They both hesitated, thinking there might still be a way out of this with *all* the money. Robert motioned for them to do as they were instructed. They obeyed. Vic carefully walked over and picked up their guns.

"Mr. Hilliard, pick up the money," Frank ordered.

Robert Hilliard looked like he might still prefer to run. Frank motioned for him to make it happen and hurry it up. Finally the man bent down and, feeling around without looking, grabbed the bag that wasn't beeping.

"No, Mr. Hilliard. The *other* one."

Hilliard released the first bag. He pointed to the beeping one, questioningly, but didn't pick it up.

"What seems to be the problem, Hilliard?" Frank insisted.

Dante swung one of his guns over and leveled the barrel right between Robert Hilliard's eyes less than two inches away. Hilliard sighed, resigned.

"Pick up the bag, Mr. Hilliard," Dante said in an old 'Edward G. Robinson' gangster voice.

"Damn, Robert! What should we do?"

"Nothing," Robert answered Desmond's question. He carefully picked up the beeping bag and stood, holding it like he'd just picked up something the dog accidentally did inside the house and he hoped he could remove it without getting any on himself. "We'll take what we have and count ourselves lucky. I'm afraid I seriously underestimated our friend, Mr. Mattich."

Frank remained silent.

"What about our deal with the Columbians?

"We'll make the deal for half. Don't worry, my brothers," Robert said. "With two million in cocaine, we'll still get rich and be on top of the world."

"That's the way to keep that positive attitude, Mr. Hilliard."

"Despite what has happened, Mister Mattich, I am still grateful. Without you we would not have a chance like this."

"Outside," Frank insisted—his voice still flat and cold. "Come on, right now."

Dante spoke in a soothing voice. "You two can just wait in here," he said to Phillip and Desmond. "Your brother will be right back." Then he added just above a whisper, "Maybe."

The two Hilliard brothers looked at each other, but otherwise didn't move a muscle.

The four walked outside.

Frank, Vic, and Dante stood around the back doors of the van. They nudged Robert to throw the bag in the back. Then they got in, leaving Robert standing just outside the back doors of the van.

"Mister Hilliard," Frank added. "As I tried to say before, it was a pleasure doing business with you."

For a moment Robert Hilliard froze.

"Go back inside now, Mr. Hilliard," Frank insisted.

Hilliard began walking. He looked back at Frank to find out what he should do next.

"Go inside, you fucking looney bastard!" Vic called.

"And shut the door," Frank added.

Once inside, Robert Hilliard pulled the door behind him. Frank heard the *clack*. He banged the side of the van and yelled.

"Let's go, Ronnie!"

Ronnie pulled the van away casually, not needing to drive crazy and risk drawing attention to themselves. The rear door of the bank opened with a bang before the van barely moved three feet. Desmond cautiously looked out.

Chapter 46

"F-Frank," Dante stuttered.

"Yeah?"

"Shouldn't we get rid of that b-bomb now?"

Frank looked at him, amused.

"Oh yeah. The *bomb*," he said with emphasis on the word.

Frank opened the duffel and reached into an inside compartment. He pulled out a digital alarm clock and tossed it to Vic. Dante cringed.

"Vic," Frank suggested, "disarm the bomb."

Vic pushed the button and shut off the alarm clock. Dante took it from him and examined it. He touched several parts, searching for something volatile. No peculiar wires stuck out and inside the battery compartment—nothing but a battery. In short, he found nothing.

"Son of a bitch! You were bluffing. The whole fucking time?"

"Yep," Frank said.

Dante boomed out a Bahamian style laugh that he'd mastered in a very short time.

"You know, you should have let me take care of those guys. It pisses me off that they tried to steal from us and still got to keep their cut."

"Well, not exactly," Frank smirked.

Frank and Vic both laugh. Ronnie glanced around from the driver's seat, trying to figure out what all the laughter was about.

"Okay, what's the joke? What happened in there, Frank?" Ronnie inquired.

"The Hilliards tried to double cross us."

"Holy shit!"

"Not to worry. We, uh...*foiled* their plans."

"So how does everything sit now?"

"The Hilliards got two million," Vic said.

"That was the original plan," Ronnie confirmed.

"Yeah, but they got two million in counterfeit," Vic said with a smile.

"What?" Dante asked in disbelief.

"The original deal was for four million and that's what I asked Vic to bring. When I heard they might be up to something, I made alternate plans. I called Vic back and had him add two million more."

"You were in on this? You sneaky son-of-a-bitch. All that time you were acting like you didn't know what was going on. You should win a fucking Oscar." Dante exclaimed at Vic. Then he turned to Frank. "I can tell you had this planned right from the beginning. How did it all come about, Frank?"

Frank looked a bit sheepish, as if accepting the 'most humble' award. "While staying here in the Bahamas, Ronnie introduced me to Reggie. Ronnie clued me in on what an up-front guy he is. You know me, I'm always up for meeting new connections."

"Yeah," Dante laughed. "You're about as bad as me with the women."

"Anyway, Reggie told me about the Hilliards and their desire to get counterfeit American money and trade it for the real thing in their bank. I contacted Vic to see if he still had his friend who makes 'funny money' available, and would he be willing to do a job

253

for us. We found he was still capable but he'd been retired. Vic told him of our plan, anyway."

"Why'd you bother to do a damn fool thing like that, Vic?" Dante asked.

"I thought I could convince him to change his mind."

"And you did, I see."

"Well, for the most part," Vic admitted.

Dante frowned. "You *got* the money."

"Yeah," Vic answered. "But he'd been getting an itchy feeling like the Feds were watching him, or something. He liked the idea the money wasn't going to be distributed in the U.S. That way he didn't have to worry about it being traced back to him."

"I see," Dante said, nodding.

"He gave Vic some samples," Frank continued. "Which he brought to the Bahamas after Reggie set up a meeting with the Hilliards. Robert's eyes lit up when he saw the quality of our money. After this meeting, Vic and I sat down with Reggie and discussed our plan and any options in case the Hilliards pulled anything. Reggie wasn't totally sold on their trustworthiness, which, as you can see, his feelings were correct."

"I can see, all right. Those sons of bitches got what they deserved."

"Then," Frank continued, "I had a discussion with Vic about meeting with Mike Riley for me. I wanted him to work out a deal to take the contract off me. Mike agreed to the deal. Vic called me and we hatched our plan. Actually, we realized we might need an alternate plan when I learned from Reggie and some of my other sources that the Hilliards were going to be buying *four* million worth of coke from the Columbians. That's why we knew we needed you to come with Vic."

"But I thought you said Reggie told you at the bar after I was already here."

"That's true, Dante. I'd heard it before from other people. All in all, I'd say it worked out better financially since we ended up with twice as much money."

"But how did you manage to leave the Hilliards with counterfeit money when you were all standing right there in the bank together?"

"We had six million in one of the duffels," Vic said, smoothly.

"And the Hilliards thought there were only four in it," Frank finished. "We took four million out and put it in the vault. Two million of the real stuff went in the bag he gave Robert to fill."

"Which," Vic continued, "left two million in counterfeit still in our duffel. See?"

"Yeah, I see," Dante answered. "But what about the switch?"

"I'm getting to that," Frank answered.

"Truthfully," Vic said. "That part was a piece of cake."

"A piece of cake, huh?"

"The truth is, it was. We just needed a diversion."

Dante stared into the distance, the wheels in his head turning quickly.

"The police?"

"The police," Frank said, nodding.

"They were busy out front watching the police car cruise past," Vic said. "That's when I opened the door for you in the back. Then I just slipped back into the vault, nice as you please. The Hilliards were so scared they never even noticed me leave."

Dante's eyes brightened.

"Then I switched the bags and slipped back out. Simple."

"Actually," Frank added. "He didn't make it all the way back out. He squatted by the door and I could see fear on his face."

"You mean he got caught?" Dante asked.

"Yeah, kind of. But we turned it around, made it look like I was scared of the police," Vic explained.

"Wow, that's a riot," Dante roared. "So what happened next?"

"Well," Frank picked up, "as you can see, the Hilliards got the bag with the counterfeit money and we had the bag with the two million, real. But they thought our bag was still empty. So when we went back in the vault, we just put another two million on top. That gave us four of the real stuff in return for the four *funny* that we put in the vault. And the other two fake went to the Hilliards for all their trouble. Piece of cake, brother."

They pulled into the marina, smiling.

"That is fucking brilliant. Frank, you're a God damn genius."

"I have my moments."

"One thing, though."

"What's that, Dante?"

"It wasn't a coincidence the cops went by just at the right time, is it?" Dante threw out a guess.

Frank opened the side door of the van and Dante looked out at the black and white sedan parked next to them. Reginald stood next to it, dressed in a policeman's uniform, holding a large flashlight. From a distance he'd probably pass for an officer, but up

256

close he looked like a Tootsie Roll dressed up for Halloween. Dante saw him and couldn't resist laughing.

"Man, it's just like old times," Dante said.

They all piled out of the van and Reggie greeted them with open arms. Win or lose, no one had their throat cut. This, in itself, was good in Reggie's eyes.

"How did it go?" Reginald asked Frank.

"Are you familiar with the term, *clockwork*?"

"I thought the Hilliards were going to try something," he said.

"They did."

"Really? What happened?"

"They tried to take it all," Frank explained. "We turned it around on them and left them with two million in counterfeit. That ought to screw up their plans just a bit."

"Oh, man. I'd like to see the look on their faces when they figure it out."

Frank smiled and reached into the duffel. He pulled out several bundles of bills, a total of one hundred thousand and handed it to Reginald.

"Here you go, my friend."

"This is the real McCoy, right?" Reggie asked.

"With a bonus," Frank confirmed. "Thanks for everything. Call me and let me know what the Hilliards are up to."

"You care about them?"

"Not even a little bit. I'm just curious. I'd like to see if they actually get away with screwing over the Columbians."

"If I find out, Frank, I'll let you know."

They shook hands.

"Thank you, Frank. Good luck to you, my friend."

Reginald made his way back to the black and white sedan. The uniform didn't fit him properly and he waddled a little when he walked. Bending into the car, he hesitated a moment and looked over the roof at Frank and crew. A smile grew on his face and he just stared for a second. Finally, with a jerky wave of his hand to all of them and a knowing nod at Frank in particular, he ducked into the car and drove off.

Ronnie led the way down the docks to a large cabin cruiser. Gentle but continuous waves licked at the hull. The name 'Rumrunner' stood out on the side as if it had been painted in fluorescent paint.

"The Steel Mill Mafia rides again, gentlemen," Vic pledged.

"The Immigrant Gang," Dante added.

"And once again we survived without a scratch," Frank added.

"Well," Dante whimpered. "I did get this little one on the back of my hand from the door of the bank." He showed it to them with a pouty lip that looked completely out of place on a full-grown man.

Vic and Frank scoffed at him, waving their hands in dismissal.

"That Reggie is a stand up guy," Dante offered, thinking about someone getting hurt. "The Hilliards won't go after him, will they?"

"I don't think so. They couldn't tell who was in the cop car."

"Probably right."

"Besides," Frank added, "the Hilliard brothers will be meeting their Columbian contacts about now."

"And trying to make a deal with counterfeit money?" Dante asked.

"What are their chances?" Vic asked.

"Slim and none," Frank said, flatly.

"You think we should warn them?"

The men looked at one another and responded in unison. "Nah!"

Chapter 47

They all laughed heartily as they boarded Ronnie's boat. Bold letters on the wall by the cabin door spelled out the name of the craft, just like on the side. *Rumrunner*. The boat tilted regularly but gently from one side to the other. It felt soothing, like sitting on a rocking horse, idling the hours away.

"So, Frank. Talk to us. How did we end up after this deal?"

"Well, the original split was for *two* million, so I've had to do some recalculations."

"So, quit playing around and just tell me what my cut is, will you?"

"Half a million. Vic and I get a million each. Ronnie and the printer get half a mill. I gave Reggie 100G's. That leaves the four hundred grand I need to pay off Mike Riley.

"Half a mill," Dante swooned. "I'm going to get me a whole *bunch* of pussy when we get back."

"Yeah," Vic said to Frank, "like Mister Wonderful, over here, needs a half a mill to get laid."

"What would you know about pussy," Dante retorted. "You haven't had any even get near you since you were twelve."

"Cards, anyone?" Vic asked, changing the subject.

"Sure," Dante answered. "Go for the cards. You can't win with women so you have to beat them at the table."

"You know what they say, lucky at cards—unlucky at love."

"You guys go ahead," Frank suggested. "I'm too excited. I'll stay on deck and keep a lookout for Ronnie. Just in case, you know."

"Just in case of what?"

"In case, uh…in case he needs a look out," Frank managed.

"Frank? What's he need a look out, for?" Dante asked, concerned.

"Pirates," Frank answered.

"Yo, ho, ho, and a pirate's life for me," Vic and Dante sang in unison.

"Very funny." Frank turned and walked away.

Vic and Dante scoffed at him and turned to their game. Frank made his way up the ladder to the bridge. Behind him, Vic spoke to Dante. He could hear them, but just barely.

"You don't think he was serious, do you?"

Frank chuckled.

The '*Rumrunner*' cut through the water with precision. Frank stood by the rail looking out at the sea, as it sparkled like diamonds from the reflected moonlight. Even with the gentle chopping, the sea looked tranquil. It created a musical effect. Frank felt great. He could pay off Mike Riley after all these years and still have about a mill for him and Connie to start over. The dream sat in his hand, hopefully his at last.

But part of Frank's mind, a darkly negative part, kept reminding him that he'd been close before. His struggle seemed futile more often than not. Frank continued to watch the wake of the boat as it churned up the dark water, wondering if this time would be *the* time, the one time when the dream really came true. Ronnie interrupted Frank's train of thought.

"Frank, I've—," Ronnie began.

Frank turned quickly, wide eyed, to face Ronnie. After a moment, his eyes softened.

261

"Hey, I'm sorry, Frank. I didn't mean to startle you. You okay?"

"Yeah, Ronnie. I'm good."

"Anything I can help with?"

"No. I was just thinking about taking care of a lot of old laundry, you know?"

Ronnie shook his head no, but Frank didn't seem to notice and he wasn't forthcoming. When he did speak, he changed the subject.

"You wanted something, Ronnie?"

"Wanted?"

"You came over and began to speak. What were you saying?"

"Oh, that. It wasn't important. Just that I've only known you a few years, but it seems to me like you and your friends have led some very interesting lives."

Frank smiled enigmatically. "You could say that, Ronnie."

"I'm sure you have some good stories I wouldn't mind hearing."

"I don't think you would enjoy them. Most of it is pretty boring stuff."

"It doesn't look so boring from where I'm standing."

Frank frowned. "You sure about that?"

"Look, we have a six hour ride and I have nothing better to do than hold this damn wheel. And since I can tie it off, then I guess I'm no smarter than the rope I use to do it, eh?" At his own joke, Ronnie let out a raucous laugh.

"All right, Ronnie. You asked for it. Now, let me see." Frank trailed off, staring at the mesmerizing water with blue moonlight sparkling back from it. Ronnie said nothing further. After a minute or two of silence, except for the tiny swells slapping the hull of the boat, Frank seemed to come to a conclusion.

"We did a lot of bar hopping, back in the day. Me and Vic and Dante, we were like the Three Musketeers—inseparable. After a while, the bars started to look just like one another. There are lights and lots of people all talking shit, music too loud forcing people to shout their shit above it, and more smoke than any one person should breathe in their entire lifetime.

"Even the women started looking alike. Makeup, hair, painted lips and fingers, fake tits, exaggerated wiggle in their hips, it's a wonder any of them got lucky at all. But Dante, well, if you haven't noticed, he's another character, altogether. He adored each and every one of them, in his own way."

"What way is that?" Ronnie asked.

"He paid his respects with an aroused muscle."

Ronnie laughed, catching the joke.

"But the girls, they each seemed to appreciate it. Probably a lot of the regulars couldn't get it up anymore and anything stiff would be good enough for those girls, you know? But you know how women are."

"No, Frank," Ronnie interrupted. "How are they?"

Both men chuckled. Then Frank continued.

"All they want is a real man. Any guy with a tongue and a dick that still works and the desire to try, that's what they want. That's the guy who can make a girl happy in the sack."

"That is true, Frank. So true."

"But the real trick is getting them into that sack so you can show them what you've got. And that is where Dante has real magic. You saw it with the waitress back there. He has a talent. It's uncanny what that boy can do."

"I've seen him work," Ronnie admitted.

"Dante has ways that have never been written about or even heard of. He made stuff up as he went along. It seemed to just pop up inside his head, but for all I knew he stayed up all night thinking the shit up. And some of his pickup lines were downright hilarious. I can imagine him, standing in front of the bathroom mirror, practicing to his reflection."

Ronnie chuckled as he imagined it as well. "That's really funny, Frank. I can just see him doing that."

"Anyway, Ronnie, there were times when Vic and I didn't manage to get far *enough* away from Dante and we heard everything he did. Everything he said. It was fun watching the master at work, but it's like watching a gory movie. You have to be prepared for what you're going to witness.

"One time we were in a really upscale club in Florida. I mean, this place was top notch. All the glitz, million-dollar sound system, laser lights, fog machines, you name it, they had it. And it drew the crowds, particularly the girls. That pleased Dante no end.

"As usual, Dante insisted we go our separate ways. Vic and I were going to meet a contact and we had business anyway. But our guy was late. So we stood by the bar and had a drink, watching people dance and guys trying to hit on the girls. At first I hadn't noticed, but Dante was almost right behind us. He worked his magic. If he'd known we were right there, he might have been upset at us. Or at least moved further away."

"Why?"

"He always felt we'd screw up his game. But he didn't notice us anymore than we noticed him."

"So you were like, back-to-back?" Ronnie asked.

"Yeah, kinda. Well, to tell the truth, like I said, we weren't far enough away from Dante and after what I heard, I think I was scarred for life."

"That's crazy, Frank. What'd you hear?" Ronnie sounded ready to jump out of his skin.

"You know, I don't think Dante knows the definition of 'ugly' girl. Most of the women who approached him were

264

incredible. They began at what I call 'top notch' and went UP from there. I've never figured out how he does it. So, this girl came up to the bar right next to him, almost touching him. She wasn't Marisa Tomei, but she sure looked close."

"Who's Marisa Tomei?"

"An actress in American films. Dante thinks she's the most beautiful woman on the planet."

"I don't know her."

"Anyway," Frank continued, ignoring the fact that Ronnie didn't even know who Frank's favorite actress was. "This girl wore a solid peach-colored blouse with a sewing pattern across her tits like this." He moved his finger on his chest like crossing his heart with a big X. "Man, I gotta tell you, that blouse just held those puppies up and made them perk right out, even though she was petite.

"I don't think Dante even noticed she had a face, but I did. She looked young. When I say young, Ronnie, I mean…maybe seventeen. You'd think Dante would watch out for stuff like that. But, God damn, man, she was hot."

"Did you try and warn him?"

"Yeah, but when I got his attention he realized we were so close, *and* we were interfering. He glared at me in a way that made me feel very uncomfortable. So I backed off. Vic and I said nothing. We just, you know, enjoyed the view. Once Dante got his 'sex' on, there is no getting in the way. And he sounded so much like a used car salesman, it was laughable. But the biggest surprise was how many women actually bought his lines. Like this one did."

"Come on, Frank. You got me going now. Tell me."

"Well, they began talking, just a bit at first. Quietly, I couldn't quite hear their words over the music. Then, she must have asked him what he did for a living because the next thing I heard him say he was a designer for Playtex, and he worked with fittings—on the areas where the product needed to be improved. I could hardly believe such a stupid line. But even harder to believe was her reaction."

"Uh, Frank? I hate to seem like one of the typical island dummies, but what's *Playtex*?"

"It's a company that makes bras."

"Holy shit, man," he said, looking over the railing and down to where Dante sat playing cards with Vic. "This guy is full of it, isn't he?"

Frank laughed. "He's full of something, Ronnie. Of that I have no doubt."

"So what did she say to that?"

"She said something about how fascinating it sounded. And I tell you now, she jutted her tits out even further, like she was being defiant, you know? But Dante was so cool. He just leaned back, not looking at her tits. He took a sip of his drink and spoke to her like he really hated his job. He tried to tell her how it was just another boring job like any other nine-to-five." Frank twisted his voice and began quoting Dante. *"I have to examine a lot of breasts and bra fittings. And in the end, I only discover minor flaws. Seems like a lot of work for such a little return. But I have a good eye for what kind of bra will do the best for a woman. Any woman."*

"And the girl was completely enamored. She asked him what kind of bra he thought would be best for a girl like her. She waited and Dante looked down. I swear to God, Ronnie, he acted like he was suddenly shy. It took everything I had not to burst out laughing right there."

Ronnie was laughing. "Did he tell her what bra to wear?"

"No. He reminded her that it was all pretty boring to him. The girl looked at him with pleading eyes. *Oh, please, could you?* Frank mimicked in his best imitation of a female voice. I mean, this girl was begging him. So Dante mumbled something about having to use his hands. Then he held his hands up in front as if he was going to grab her right there in the bar. The girl had two girlfriends with her. They were standing behind her, rolling their eyes. They looked like they knew Dante was running a line of bull. But the target didn't seem to notice. Or she didn't care.

"And she acted innocent. She asked him what he meant. Maybe she was a little dense, you know?" Frank asked, pointing to his head and swirling the finger around. "But her friends kept trying to pull her away from an obvious con job. She wouldn't let them interfere with meeting a guy who could help her improve her wardrobe. To her, it would be like talking to a Hollywood agent.

"Just as he was confirming that he'd be putting his hands directly on her chest, the bartender walked by. He looked over at Dante and the girl. He just kind of rolled his eyes and smiled, you know. I'm sure he'd heard a few bullshit performances in his day, guys who would try almost anything to get into a girl's pants. And this line of bull ranked right up there with the Oscar winners. Then he laughed and walked past, into the back room."

"So what did the girl say when Dante wanted to grab her? Did they go to the back room?"

"No. She said okay and thrust them right out to the point of arching her back. I mean that girl almost pushed them right into his hands. She looked up at Dante and said, *Please?* Her two friends were completely disgusted. They shook their heads and walked away, leaving her to fend for herself with the lecherous old man. The girl looked infatuated with him. She didn't even seem to notice her friends had taken off on her. Dante's magic."

"Oh, man. She was begging him to put his hands on her?"

"Yeah, can you believe it? Dante was still trying to act like a man with morals and reservations. He hesitated, you know? I swallowed hard as I watched, trying to remain casual. I hoped he wouldn't notice me noticing him. Then Dante moved his hands to her breasts and rubbed them right there at the bar. He felt around and squeezed. After that, just to act like he was really a bra inspector, he ran his hands around the sides and under her arms, making believe he searched for problem areas.

"His eyes focused on the ceiling while he had his hands all over her. He allowed a casual 'hmmm' to escape his lips. I was still trying so hard not to laugh. Vic squirmed where he stood as if he might have been getting excited. All the while, Dante, cool as the proverbial cucumber, felt all over the girl's tits. I don't know how he kept his hands from sliding down to that cute, underage, firm ass. I know, I wanted to.

"But, in keeping with the image of a bra design technician, he maintained an air of professionalism. I was choking on a laugh trying to rise up my throat, actually gagging. Finally, Dante gave those two beautiful orbs one last squeeze and withdrew his hands. His sigh was almost inaudible. But I heard it, even over the noise of the sound system.

"When he spoke to her, he managed to sound like a professional businessman. He told her the 'Cross-Your-Heart' bra would be the best for her. He started pointing out areas where support would improve. He raised his hands back to her firm breasts, pointing at different spots, touching her at will as he spoke. After a moment of more touching, he explained further." Frank cleared his throat for another attempt at imitating Dante. "*It's true, we designed it for an older woman who might have some problems you obviously don't, but if you train them now, they can retain some of their positioning later.*"

Ronnie smiled broadly.

"What a guy, that Dante," Frank added for good measure.

"How can anyone, even a child, be stupid enough to fall for that?" Ronnie asked in complete disbelief.

"I don't know. But Dante was having a great time. I rather enjoyed it, myself. This girl, now obviously horny, seemed to be enjoying it, too. She said, '*I need to train them?*' She sounded a bit dubious, but not because she doubted what Dante claimed to be. He continued his line of bullshit.

"*Well, right now they're perfect. But later…I don't want to be insulting, but we all know what gravity does to them later on. You could ward off some of the sagging effects, or postpone them, at least.*"

"What did she say to that," Ronnie asked.

"She stepped closer to him, snuggling into his arm, pressing into him. She looked up at him with those eyes, the ones that a woman uses when she wants to get it on with you. Her voice took on a different sound, huskier, deeper. She said, *you think mine are perfect?*"

"Uh-huh," Ronnie said.

"Anyway, Dante said he didn't think he'd ever seen a more perfect pair and that she should think about modeling. Her voice rose even higher, obviously seduced by the prospect of his words. She started babbling ninety-miles-a-minute about how she'd always wanted to be a model and how she'd done some in the school newspaper and a bunch of other crap I didn't catch. Dante had her eating out of his hand. But soon, it seemed, he would have her eating out of his lap."

"Oh my God," Ronnie said, "what a horn dog."

"Well, I know it's hard to believe, but she was falling for it. He spoke like a true bullshit artist. He said he couldn't promise anything but he *did* know a few people. She sucked in a quick breath. Now her voice dropped to just above a whisper, and I could just barely hear her repeat, *you do?* I knew Dante had her. I didn't know what he planned to do with her, but she was putty in his hands, as they say. All he had to do was mold her, or rather remove

269

her pants and spread her legs. Being so young she would probably taste fresh, unused. I almost felt a touch of envy as Dante led her away, gently resting his big hand on her thin arm."

"Jesus, I think I need a cigarette," Ronnie laughed.

"Yeah," Frank responded. "I know the feeling. Anyway, Vic and I were sitting there at the bar talking about Dante. I said something about 'there he goes again', but Vic had turned away, unable to watch any more. I told Vic even though she was such a hot little number, we should have tried harder to warn Dante. I didn't want to see him get in any trouble with an underage girl. But Vic laughed at me. He reminded me that Dante never gets into trouble with girls. You know, Ronnie, I still think we could have tried a little harder to warn him. They call me a stick in the mud, but I didn't want him to get into a compromising position with a minor."

"Damn, Frank. That's funny as hell. Tell me some more. You got more?"

"Probably only a hundred or so."

"You should take this show on the road. You'd make a fortune."

"I already made one, thank you."

"Yeah, that's true. But you could write a book."

"I'm no writer, but maybe someday."

"So tell me some more stories. Did you ever catch someone else doing something wrong?"

"What do you mean, Ronnie?"

"You know, like someone else running drugs in your territory. Or did you ever see anyone get nabbed at the airport while you were there?"

"Well, not exactly. But there was this one time. We were making a lot of runs back and forth to Florida. Lots of miles on the car, you know. Well, one time at about 3 a.m., Vic and I were

270

sleeping. Dante got off I-95 for some reason or other and couldn't find his way back on. We were still in North Florida. Jacksonville—to be exact. So he woke me.

"Well, I didn't know where the hell we were either. I just woke up, how would I know? I got behind the wheel and I drove around for a while. Finally, we ended up in a residential area and it was dark as hell. Nobody moved. But we got lucky. We saw a car come to life. The engine roared and the brake lights came on. I pulled the car up behind him—blocking his exit—and lowered the passenger side window. I called out, asking if he knew how to get back on the highway.

"Well, the guy was jittery as hell and asked me to meet him at the intersection by the stop sign. I was confused. We were right there. Why not just answer our question? I asked again and got the same response. My gut started tingling but I couldn't figure anything out. Finally he insisted we meet him down by the corner where the stop sign was. He said he had to get out of there. I didn't understand but I could tell we weren't going to get anything more out of him. I drove to the corner and waited. If that guy had been selling drugs, he was being *way* too obvious, you know?

"So you might figure he'd brush us off and go the other way or something. That's what I thought. But sure enough, in a few seconds, his car pulled up next to me and I rolled down my window on the driver's side. He leaned over in his seat and called to me.

"I told him we only wanted directions and he accommodated easily enough. I thought that would be the end of it and it might have been. But Dante's big mouth never shut. He leaned toward my window and asked the guy what the hell his problem was.

"*I needed to get out of the driveway real quick. You see, my boss is an asshole, but his wife is hot. It started as a prank. I met her one afternoon in a grocery store. Well, to make a long story short, I've been banging her for months. Her husband called and is on his way home. He'll be here any minute. That's his house. He's likely to get a shot gun and ventilate my body. I'd walk away from it but damn she's so good."*

"Really?" Ronnie asked.

"I didn't know what to say to the man. So I thanked him for his directions. Then we drove off."

"Jesus, Frank. Is your whole life one big, funny story?"

"Not entirely. You remember I told you about using the kiddies' pool to add a touch of water to that Columbian pot that didn't weigh enough?"

"Yeah, you used a plant misting bottle to add enough water to make it heavier without ruining it, right?"

"That's right. I don't know if I told you before, but only Vic and I were there when we learned how to do that. Dante was probably off getting laid. But one day I forgot he didn't know and I told him to go get started and set things up and I'd be along soon enough."

"I hear a problem coming."

"Oh yeah. I walked in and Dante stood there with the pot in the pool. The mound stood almost as high as his knee. He had gone ahead and begun spraying it down, getting a head start on the process."

"That was very practical of him."

"Yeah, but he was using a garden hose."

"Holy shit."

"That's about what I said to him," Frank agreed. "I stared for a moment in shock. Then I yelled, Dante, what the fuck are you doing? He looked dazed and turned toward me. And you will never believe what his response was.

"What did he say, boss?" Ronnie asked, smiling in preparation for the laughter that he knew would be coming.

"He said, and I quote, '*I was...watering the plants.*' He had a big, stupid grin on his face and then he finally shut off the hose."

"Oh, man," Ronnie sniggered. "That's a riot. Incredible!"

"I told him he was ruining the shipment. He told me we needed to water it. I guess he didn't know what the word 'spritz' meant. He asked me if that was the name of the Olympic swimmer. I told the fucking dummy the swimmer's name was Mark *Spitz*."

"Haw! That's rich," Ronnie interrupted.

"After that I figured I'd better remind him not to spit on it, either."

"Ha!" Ronnie exclaimed.

"So I asked him why so much water. And he dared to tell me it came out of the hose that way. He suggested someone had changed the setting on the nozzle."

"Nozzle?"

"Yeah, you ever seen one of those garden hose nozzles that have a rotating head and you can get different sprays from it?"

"Oh, I know. Sure. I think my brother has one like that."

"Well I told him it didn't matter what setting it was on when we weren't supposed to be using the hose to begin with. So he asked me how he was supposed to do it. I explained about the plant misting bottle. He looked a little sheepish and said he was sorry. I figured he stayed up all night fucking some girl. With him there's always some girl."

"So what happened with the pot?" Ronnie asked.

"I didn't know if we could salvage it or not but it wasn't going to do itself. So I went to my car and grabbed the tarp I always kept in my trunk. I brought it back and spread it out on the ground. We lifted the pot by hand onto the tarp, one piece at a time, and spread it out. I remember thinking it wasn't too bad and maybe it would dry out. The summer sun shone hot and there were no clouds in the sky.

"But that wasn't the worst. Dante started talking and it would have been better if he hadn't. He said he'd been thinking. That automatically spelled trouble. I told him to please…be…quiet. He sat there. Finally, I changed my mind. He was just going to sit there and pout if I didn't hear his idea. Besides, it might be good exercise for later when I needed him to think."

"You said that?" Ronnie asked.

"You bet."

"What did he say?"

"He asked if I came over there just to bust his balls. Actually, I'd went over because I had a buyer. But the buyer had been in a hurry and couldn't wait for the dry cycle. Dante looked dejected. Then he perked up. He started talking again."

"That brings me back to what I was thinking about. I was thinking, with enough water and maybe a bunch of other ingredients, we could make some kind of…pot juice, or something. You know, they make juices out of vegetables all the time."

"I just looked at him. Honestly, Ronnie. I just couldn't believe he would even suggest something that stupid. And I really didn't know *what* to say."

"Pot juice? Damn, Frank. You gotta stop. You're killing me."

"Yeah well, I guess Dante caught my look because he turned to me and whimpered out a weak answer. *Just a thought,* he said. I sat there. I never said a word. I mean, really Ronnie, what the hell could I say? I think Dante thinks I'm still considering the idea."

"Ha! So what happened to the pot, Frank?"

"Oh, that. It was screwed up pretty bad."

"Now that's a loss, man. That is truly fucking sad."

"Yeah. But we made up for it. We made back all that money and a whole bunch more. Once we switched to the Mexican, we had a lot more money. And it didn't need to be watered."

"That's way cool, Frank."

"What's *really* cool is that we got some punk doper to buy the watered down shit, at a discount, of course."

"So you didn't even lose *all* the money. That's great. You guys have done some strange deals."

"Oh, yeah? Well listen to this. One time Dante and I were going to make a deal in the parking lot of a club and we got there early. We went inside to enjoy some of the local cuisine and refreshment. After a while, Dante went outside to wait in the car for our contact. I just had to finish my drink and pay the bill.

"While I was still on the bar stool, I noticed a few new faces sitting in the dining area. Men with suits. A lot of them. I thought I was busted again. I glanced out the big front windows and saw about eight or ten unmarked cars and I figured there might be others. As I watched, my contact arrived in the parking lot and stopped next to my car.

"Their trunk and ours were next to each other. Dante opened the one in our car and they opened theirs. Dante walked around back and met the other two guys. I strolled out next to them and helped. We passed our bags back and forth while several law enforcement types sat inside having lunch.

"After we were done, curiosity got the best of me. I walked around toward the front entrance again and looked. There, above the door, hung a huge banner. I hadn't seen it earlier, but there it hung."

"Banner?"

"Yeah, it said, *Welcome DEA Christmas Party*."

"Holy shit, Frank. You got some balls."

"Well, two, anyway."

"You mean to say they didn't notice you at all?"

"Not that I could tell. None of them came out. We certainly didn't go back in to ask. We finished our business and drove off in different directions. It was very profitable for me, and we did it right under their noses. I think I could have gone back in and danced on top of a table."

"That's a good way to get your head blown off."

"Possibly." Frank nodded his head to one side, shrugging off the concept of ever having been in any real danger. "Sometimes it's just a matter of having a cool attitude and keeping a clear head."

"What, no one ever tried to kill you?"

"Sure. Didn't I ever tell you about the time someone placed a bomb at the front door of my joint?"

"Holy shit, Frank. A bomb? You mean someone tried to blow you up?"

"I think they were just trying to blow up my place, but they didn't bother to check if I was inside or not."

"Wow. What happened? I mean, I can see you weren't killed."

"You noticed that, did you?"

"Yeah, I…Damn."

"What's wrong, Ronnie?"

"I was just thinking how much more I'd love to hear about your bomb and other stories, but I can see the Jupiter Harbor lights just over there."

"Well, Ronnie, maybe next time."

"Next time?" he smiled.

Chapter 48

Throughout his time in hiding, Frank managed to go back to Florida and visit with Connie and the girls regularly. Sometimes he'd only get an hour, other times he managed to stay for two or three days. And sometimes they got to take in a show. But no matter, he treasured those times most of all. The dream wouldn't mean very much without them.

The length of each stay depended mostly on the amount of heat Frank felt on his back. He had a sixth sense about things. The cops weren't chasing Frank anymore, so he didn't have to worry about the law. And pretty soon, Mike Riley would no longer be an issue.

This time, going home gave him the jitters. This time would be different. This time he carried his dream right there with him. As he approached, butterflies swam in his gut and he felt nauseous. He looked around at the now familiar town and maneuvered the rented car toward the motel Connie's Aunt and Uncle owned, where she lived with their daughters.

The dream, the hopes of all his life clouded his mind and he saw only where he would be very soon. He struggled with the fear it might all be stolen from him once again. It offered a sweet smell in his nose and everything looked to be the same color as money. He'd come no closer to deciding what he wanted to do with the rest of his life, but right now that didn't matter. There would be time to decide later. Perhaps he'd own a bar. But that reminded him of Eddie.

Frank forced the memory out of his head. The car didn't maneuver like one of those smaller Italian sports models, but he muscled the brute into the motel's tiny entrance expertly.

Misty eyed, trembling hands, heart pounding in his chest until it almost hurt, Frank glanced in the rear-view mirror at the bag. His life's dream sat back there, like a fare in a cab, silently waiting to arrive at the destination—his first real chance to make a secure life for his family. He felt anxious and hoped Connie would appreciate how much of his life had gone into getting here. Whether she believed it or not, he'd done everything for her, and his girls.

He hoped he could make her see.

He parked at the end farthest from the office, in front of the suite where his family had been staying for the last few years. Even though Connie had practically taken over the entire motel operation, she didn't want to appear like the caretaker. She had no official capacity and said she liked it that way. Frank laughed when she said it.

But right now he wasn't laughing. He looked at the drab, brown door in front of him as he parked. The paint had chipped and splinters were broken out from years of harsh Florida sun. The roof bent in a warped pattern. It needed repair, but still it didn't leak. A fountain, around which the driveway circled, sputtered water when it worked at all. Otherwise, the place only needed a *lot* of work.

Frank remembered when Connie first came down during the trial. It hadn't looked much better back then, but some of the paint had been brighter and less chipped. The semi-circular shape of the buildings created a courtyard, leaving some shade for tourists to enjoy. He stayed here with her for the two months of trial. He didn't know where they would live, but now they had options.

Despite the rundown look, Connie called it home, and as often as he could, so did Frank. One other car besides Connie's sat facing the building, another guest he presumed. Very few doors opened to the midday heat in July unless the maid was airing out the room. The wall-unit air conditioner could be heard from outside, straining to keep the temperature comfortable inside. Frank smiled and got out of his car.

The air smelled salty. He took off his sunglasses and squinted around at the buildings. Dilapidated as they were, the place had a real atmosphere about it that Frank enjoyed. A little outdated, but that gave it a touch of nostalgia, as if you might see some of the old movie stars lounging out by the pool, which was the only thing that didn't appear to need any repairs. And maybe you'd turn to see a fifties Cadillac Fleetwood convertible parked in the lot. Frank imagined the place flourishing back in its day.

From inside the bungalow assigned to his family, Frank heard music—the kind of music young girls played—loud and obnoxious—and he couldn't understand the words. The car wasn't here. Connie must be out running motel errands or perhaps she'd taken a short trip to the store. But Frank felt sure the girls were inside, dancing to the loud, raucous music. He couldn't help smiling as he thought about spending the day with them, and more.

Frank raised his fist to bang on the door and something moved to his right. He glanced over quickly and saw Connie approaching in haste. A smile consumed her face and he opened his arms for her to run into. She came to him and hugged him warmly. Connie rested her head against his chest without moving. Then she pulled back, but only a little.

"Hi, Frank."

"Hi, baby. How are the girls?"

"They're wonderful. Come on in, Frank."

They walked inside and the girls greeted him with joy. They all wanted to tell him something right away. School, boys, music, hobbies, and what mom did, were just some of the topics Frank managed to distinguish from their chatter. And each one wanted to be first. When the noise settled and daylight faded, Connie managed to enjoy some alone time with Frank. They sat on the couch in the living room overlooking the pool. Connie stared into his eyes with only joy in hers. The sunlight turned orange as it sagged to the horizon and beyond. The other car in the lot had already taken off, possibly for a late beach day or early supper.

"Are you here for good, Frank? Can you stay this time?"

"Almost."

"Almost?" She pulled away from him. "What does that mean, almost?"

"I have to go to Pittsburgh for a few days. But I'll be back."

"How do I know you mean that?"

"Honey, I'll be back. I'll be back for good."

"Frank, don't tease me. You mean it? Really?"

Frank just looked at her.

"Frank, you mean it this time, right? Tell me it's true."

Frank handed her the duffel bag full of money. Connie looked at it as if it might be filled with rattle snakes. She brought it close and opened the top. When she pulled the handles apart, she looked inside. She sucked in a deep breath.

"My God, Frank!"

Frank smiled.

"How much is in here?"

"Well, there's only a million, so you'll have to be frugal."

"A million? Dollars?"

"That's the usual form of currency we use, isn't it?"

"Yeah, but is it ours? Is it legit?"

"Yeah, everything's cool."

"Cool? Cool? Frank, I'm not looking for cool. Is this money legit or not?"

"It's legit, Connie. No one will ever come looking for it."

"Frank," she said softly, a note of hope in her voice.

"Yes, honey. I'm here."

"My aunt and uncle want to retire. They'll sell us the motel at a great price. We'll even have enough for a house of our own, so we won't have to live here."

"Will there be enough to do some repairs on this place?"

Connie laughed and tears came to her eyes. She glanced at the bag. "I think there will be more than enough."

"Honey, that sounds like one of the best plans I've ever heard. Tomorrow, while I go to Pittsburgh, you get the ball rolling."

"Me?"

"You can do it, honey. Take care of your aunt and uncle, find us a nice house, and when I get back, I'll get started on the repairs to this place."

"Oh, Frank," she faltered. "You mean it?"

"I mean it."

"Wait, you have to go to Pittsburgh?"

"Yes."

"But why?"

"You remember Mike Riley?"

"Riley's Pub?"

"That's right. Well, I owe him some money and I'm going to go pay him back. Then I'll be back."

"You owe it to him? You're not buying something from him?"

"It's the only debt I have left, honey. And I'll be coming back empty handed. The only thing I'm buying is a one-way ticket back here."

"Be careful, Frank," she pleaded, grabbing him and pulling him tight. Frank kissed her passionately and lifted her up. He carried her to the bedroom and closed the door with his foot. The night temperature rose.

281

Chapter 49

Mike Riley's pub hadn't changed much since the last time Frank visited. He recalled almost running out the front door and heading straight for parts far away, unknown, anywhere. The money meant nothing. But letting Mike down, breaking his trust, had eaten away at Frank for more than two years. And he'd hidden out in the tropics, not exactly the worst place, waiting for a chance to go home.

He tried to live a life. He tried to *make* a life. But the memory of Mike and the unrelenting integrity of his father forced Frank to continually question his actions. An image of his father haunted him almost every night, turning his dreams into nightmares. He questioned his own motives, and his future. Most of all, he questioned whether or not he had the right to abandon his family. In the end, his father's example won out. Not so much that he might be disappointed in Frank, but rather what kind of example Frank would, in turn, set for his own children.

Connie had been right. It turned out she was right about a lot of things. The girls needed more than Frank's money. He needed to be a father for them. Show them affection and praise them when they did well—and also to scold them when they stepped out of line. These were the tasks of a father. But most of all, he needed to be in their lives to set the example. A father was, above all else, supposed to be an example of strength and morality. He'd lost sight of that. He focused solely on the dream, the money to live the life he so wanted. He still wanted that money, but he began to see the life beside it, above it. Now he would have to try and make up for how little he'd given his girls all these years. He'd have to explore the love bonds that continued to draw him back to a simple motel in Florida.

The first step was to finish all the old business. To get a fresh start he needed a clean slate. He could not leave anything hanging over his head. That meant seeing Mike Riley. It didn't appear Mike had been putting any more money into his place. Perhaps he thought the area was dying out. Or maybe, after Frank disappointed him so much, he chose not to trust anyone else. Maybe he just wanted to leave for warmer climates.

Frank wanted to retire. He had spoken with Vic before him and Dante came to the Bahamas. He'd needed Vic to do him one special favor. He'd needed Vic's help setting up the meet with Mike Riley. Without Vic, walking cold into Riley's place like this would have been even more frightening. It could mean a death sentence.

When Vic told him Mike was willing to make a deal, Frank smiled wider than he had in a very long time. The end lay in sight and he felt the dream within him, like a trusted companion and bodyguard.

But now, in Mike's place, he didn't feel like smiling. A sinking feeling crowded his stomach. He wanted to get this business over and get back to Connie and the girls. The dream consoled him and gave him strength. Mike was a good guy and Frank wanted to settle his debt. But now his home life beckoned. The dream beckoned. To answer that call was what he wanted—all he had left.

Or so he thought.

"Frank, I'm glad you came back." Mike stood up next to a table near the bar. One burly body guard type stood behind him. Mike extended his hand. The body guard glared at Frank and crossed his arms over his massive chest.

"Mike, it's really good to be back." Frank took the offered hand and shook it.

Mike motioned for Frank to sit. They both sat down.

"How's Donnie?" Frank asked.

"He's serving two years for possession. And if I ever find out who set him up, I'll fucking kill them."

"Donnie's in jail? I'm really sorry to hear that, Mike," Frank replied, genuinely. "I didn't know."

"Yeah, I'm sorry too. Donnie gets a bit wacko now and then, but this just isn't right."

"I know."

"He's my kid brother."

"And family means a lot," Frank agreed.

"Yeah. That's right," Mike said.

Frank put the briefcase on the table and slid it across to Mike. "And that brings me to this."

Mike opened it, eyed all the money, and then handed it to the body guard. The burly man took the case to a nearby table. He began counting, quite efficiently from what Frank could see. To Frank, the man didn't look all that smart. For all Frank knew, the way things went these days, he probably had a degree…or two.

"I want you to know it wasn't personal, Frank. I always liked you. I think you know that."

"I understand, Mike. I really do. Business is business, that's all."

"Yeah, business." Mike Riley seemed a bit sad, like a father who had been forced to punish a child for doing something wrong.

"But you gotta know, Mike, it was the same for me," Frank returned.

"Huh?"

"I took off because I couldn't come up with the money right then. But it wasn't personal. I didn't *want* to stiff you. And I came back with the money as soon as I could get it for you."

"I see that."

"So," Frank said, trying to be patient. "How's business?"

"Not doing so well. The economy around here is shot since the mills closed. A lot of people managed to hang on for a while. But sooner or later, they were all bound to die or drift away. Without the mills, there was no way to breathe life back into the community."

"That's too bad. I always loved this neighborhood. But you've managed to stay open."

"Barely. I've had to pump money from my other ventures into this place to keep it alive."

"That must be costly."

"It is. But people still come in from time to time. It's all good."

"What about you and me, Mike?" Frank asked sincerely. "Are we good now?"

Mike looked over to his body guard. The guy managed to move his head up and down without a neck. He closed the briefcase and took it into the back room. Despite his muscles, the man walked more like a business man than a body builder. Mike turned back to Frank.

"Yes, Frank. We're good."

"I'm so glad that's over. It's been hanging over my head far too long."

"I'm glad, too, Frank. This has been a thorn in both our sides. Now we can rest."

"Now I can join my family."

"You know, Frank, you really had it going on here. It used to be a sweet deal."

"That's true. Life was good."

"Well, it wouldn't take much for you to get back into the swing. I wouldn't be in too much of a hurry to *front* you any big shipments, exactly, but we could still make a profit together. You were good at what you did."

"I don't think so, Mike. I'm just not there anymore, you know? Thanks anyway."

"Yeah," Mike sighed. "I got the feeling something was different about you when you first walked in."

"I'd like to think that's a good thing."

Mike shrugged one shoulder. Frank smiled. Four hundred thousand was a small price to pay for his integrity, even if Mike Riley didn't appreciate it.

"Oh, hey. Frank, wait a minute. I have something you might find interesting."

"No deal, Mike."

"No, not that. Listen, this has really been bothering me. A Pittsburgh Connection friend of mine said Snake Barron paid them off on a two hundred thousand dollar debt about two weeks after Schultzie disappeared."

Frank said nothing.

"Don't you find that to be a rather large coincidence?"

"Yeah," Frank said, hardly able to form the words through the mixed thoughts in his head. "Quite a coincidence." He turned, still thinking.

"Hey, Frank. If you ever want some work, just remember who to call. I could always use a good man."

Frank turned back to face him. "Listen, Mike, it's like I said, I'm retiring. I've got a dream of my own I want to pursue."

"You sure about this, my friend?" Mike gave it one last try.

"Thanks, Mike. I really mean that. I'm glad you can still call me friend. That means a   lot. As for the deal, thanks, but no thanks. I just can't do it."

They shook hands and Frank walked out the front door of Mike Riley's bar a lot slower this time, possibly for the last time. Frank felt a pang of sorrow. Much of his old life, like his childhood, had gone for good.

Chapter 50

Schultzie's bar, now owned by Zack, sat devoid of all life. Save Zack. Frank stopped just inside and allowed his eyes to adjust to the change in lighting. The jukebox throbbed a melancholy beat. Zack stood by one of the back tables making believe it needed to be wiped off.

"How you doing, Zack?"

"I'm doing good, Frank," Zack lied. "You?"

"A lot better these days."

"Glad to hear it."

"Dante told me to meet him here," Frank said. "You know anything about that?"

"He's in the back with Vic." Zack waved his hand in the general direction of the back room. "Want something to drink?"

"No thanks, Zack. I'm cutting back." Frank patted his own stomach. "The old gut doesn't handle the stuff like it used to."

Zack shrugged. "Okay, Frank." He went back to taking the varnish off the table top.

Inside the back room, Dante and Vic chatted around an old card table. To the left, Frank noticed the movement of someone else in the room with them. Frank recognized him as a member of the old *Steel Mill Mafia*.

"You remember Kemo, Frank?" Dante introduced him.

Kemo stepped forward and shook Frank's hand. Frank remembered the big Indian because he stood out in a crowd.

288

"How could I forget an A-one guy like Kemo? You look good," Frank said, smiling.

"Thanks, man. It's good to see you again," Kemo said, smiling right back.

"Thanks," Frank said politely, while he wondered why they were having this meeting.

"I guess you're wondering why we're meeting here, Frank," Dante said.

Frank briefly wondered if Dante could read his mind, then dismissed the idea. The curiosity must have shown on his face. They all sat down. Frank looked around the table and knew something was brewing. He had a feeling they were planning a deal. He knew he didn't want anything to do with it and yet, something told him to wait and listen.

"Frank," Kemo began, "my sister's married to Snake Barron. His name is appropriate because he's one sneaky, rotten, underhanded, mean bastard."

"Don't beat around the bush, Kemo, tell me what you *really* think," Frank inserted.

Kemo looked startled. "Come on, Frank. He beats my sister. He treats her like shit, even in public. He says things about her behind her back. She's not even treated as well as a dog. I can't imagine what else he might be doing to her."

"Why doesn't she leave him?"

"Aw, she can't do that, Frank. The guy's a powder keg. If she sneezes when he's trying to watch television, he slaps her. She don't know what'll happen if she really stands up to him."

"She could leave while he's gone, like at work."

"He's quite resourceful. If he finds her, she's as good as dead."

"Okay, she's in a bad situation. What's all this got to do with me?" Frank asked, casually.

289

"During one of Snake's tirades, while he was beating her, he told her he would do to her what he and his buddy did to Schultzie."

"Snake told you this?"

"No, man. I don't talk to that asshole. My sister told me."

"That's pretty thin, Kemo."

"I know, but she says he mentioned it a couple times."

"Oh?"

"He told her about luring him to a warehouse. Frank, he said they killed Schultzie and dumped his body at the junkyard." Kemo pumped up his large body like he might explode. "Schultzie was a good guy, Frank. He never hurt anyone, did he? I used to come to his bar sometimes after work. Everybody liked him."

"Clearly not everybody." Frank felt anger welling inside.

"This guy's an asshole, Frank. He not only killed Schultzie, but he's boasting about it."

Fury flared in Frank's eyes. He jumped up and banged his fist against the table top repeatedly. He hurt inside. *Schultzie!*

"That motherfucker is a dead man," Frank growled through clenched teeth. A drop of blood splattered on the table where one of Frank's knuckles had split.

"I know how you feel, Frank. But you can't go off half cocked and get to him. Calm down and listen to me for a minute, will ya?" Kemo said.

"Calm down!?"

"Come on, Frank," Dante said, standing up. "Just hear him out. What can it hurt?"

Frank breathed heavily. Almost snorting like a bull. He looked over at Dante and back at Kemo. He didn't relax, but he took a deep breath.

"Listen, Frank. If you're going after Snake you need a plan. He's not easy to get at."

"Why?"

290

"Somehow he got an old Secret Service car. Frank, it's bullet proof."

"Bigger guns," Frank stated, distractedly.

"Also, I gotta tell you," Kemo continued. "I think he's protected by the government."

"Why do you say that?" Vic asked.

"I don't know this for sure, but I'm pretty convinced he snitches for them."

"How do you know?"

"Guys come to the junkyard."

"Guys," Frank repeated. "So what?"

"You know. *Guys*. Those government types, they all look like government types. It's like *The Untouchables*. They all gotta dress the same and have the same fucking hair cut. Even the same cheap goddam sunglasses so you can't see their shifty eyes."

"Okay," Frank admitted. "So, guys come there. Like I said, so what?"

"Well, I've heard them through the heating duct. Sometimes it gets muffled, but a lot of times I can hear."

"Tell him what you've heard, Kemo," Dante insisted. "Tell him what you told us before."

Frank perked up.

"I heard him give the names of guys—guys I didn't know. But later I'd see them in the paper or on the news. They'd been busted."

"Coincidence?"

"Every one, Frank?" Kemo asked, shaking his head from side to side. "Every fucking one?"

"Anyone we know?"

"Nobody I know."

"Do you, by any chance, remember any names?" Vic asked.

"Sure, a couple. Let me see, there was Joe Martin, Don Riley, uh…, oh yeah, Pete Wilson. Maybe a few others if I think about it for a while."

Frank grew very excited as he heard Kemo's roll call. "That's Mike Riley's brother and some of his pals." He turned and added, almost under his breath, "That son of a bitch took out Schultzie."

"Look Frank, I came to you because you're smart. You guys know how to do things."

"We do."

"I want this guy out of my sister's life. I don't care what it takes. I don't want to see her treated like that anymore."

"We're not divorce attorneys."

"Come on, Frank. Don't bust my balls. I'm not interested in divorce. Can you do something about this asshole or not?"

"Do you think it would be okay if we stop by and see the junkyard for ourselves?"

Kemo rolled his eyes up, thinking. "Snake and his little 'buddy guard', Igor, are leaving for a week. They're going to Vegas. You think they'd invite me? Not on your life," he answered his own question. "I'm just shit stuck to their shoes."

"When do they leave?" Frank asked.

"They're taking off Sunday morning."

"Will anyone else be there?"

"Just me," Kemo answered with a big grin creasing his usually stoic face.

"Me and these two big dummies will swing over there around noon and have a look around. Will that be okay with you?"

"That's okay with me, Frank. Anyway you want it."

Vic and Dante nodded their heads intently. The bank hadn't been the last job, after all. And Dante, for one, seemed really happy about it.

Chapter 51

Frank looked around the junkyard. Something about them captured the imagination of an artist. They have a feel, a certain panache, like a man who's been bred with money. If you took all the junk cars and all the evidence of junk away from the place and left only a dirt field, it would still *feel* like a junkyard.

Frank always thought the thirty-foot stacks of crushed derelicts retained a regal status, fitting of the icons of a bygone era, before the gas crunch. Names came to Frank's mind, the names of legends—*kings* in their own right. Magnates, Lords, and Nobles, we stood in awe of them and possessed them with pride. Names like Cadillac, Lincoln, Ford, and Chrysler—these were the great historic figures, revered by many men, and returning much in kind.

The automobile empowered its owner. It could whisk them away to faraway places only dreamed of otherwise. It saved lives, bringing injured people to the hospital faster than its four-legged forefather. It became the true testament of status and affluence in the working class.

Stacked high in yards like this one, despite being wrecked beyond any repair, somehow they'd been returned to their previous social stature. It gave them one last, magnanimous purpose before they were melted down—to offer privacy for activities best left private. They skulked over drug deals, assaults, and even murders. There was no life left in them, but still a usefulness that could be measured—and could be bought for a price. In this way they still represented affluent status.

Towering rows created a maze. Once at the center, Frank brought the car to a stop. Kemo stood there waiting for them, squinting against the midday sun. He waved.

Frank unfolded himself out of the car, followed by Vic and Dante. The office stood straight in front of them, behind Kemo. To the right, Frank noticed a gigantic cylinder, big enough to fit six cars, sitting next to a hole that looked like it had been dug for a purpose—to bury that cylinder. Behind it, the mound of dirt that had been removed stood taller than the car stacks.

To his left, Frank saw the rusted corpse of a school bus, its yellow faded to grey except where rust had taken over and turned it brick red. Windows broken, tires removed, the hulk took away from the class of the other cars, like rednecks moving into a ritzy neighborhood.

"If Eddie's body *is* here, got any idea where it might be?"

Kemo shook his head. "There's no telling, Frank. And Snake certainly isn't going to show us."

Frank squatted down almost on one knee. He sifted a handful of dirt through his fingers, letting it fall in gentle wisps. He studied it as if it could tell him something. He whispered under his breath, "This is where Eddie is."

"Did you say something, Frank?" Dante asked.

Frank stood. He surveyed the area with glazed eyes. Dante watched him closely. Had he really come here thinking there'd be a marker where poor Schultzie laid? In between gusts of wind whistling through the twisted metal, the silence of death hung over the whole place. Frank turned in a circle hoping his sixth sense would kick in.

"What the hell is all this stuff, Kemo?" Dante asked.

Kemo smiled like he was the tour guide for a jungle safari. He enjoyed the yard and took great pride in knowing all about it. He took a couple steps toward the cylinder and the hole. Waving his hand, he described it all with great reverence.

"Eight years ago, this was a storage area for school buses," he pointed back at the bus, waving the other hand and looking like a Catholic priest offering benediction, and then returned to the cylinder. "This is a storage tank for gas. There are two more over there. They were used to fill the buses."

"No wonder I've never seen a school bus at a gas station," Vic exclaimed.

"When the school bus company went out of business," Kemo went on, "Snake got this place for a song. He turned it into a junkyard. Great men have great dreams, right?"

"Yeah, sometimes," Frank said, thoughtfully.

"Anyway," Kemo continued, "a few years ago the EPA started making waves all over the country. About six months ago, they finally got around to our little neck of the woods. They discovered the tanks and ordered Snake to have them removed."

"What for?"

"I heard it has something to do with leakage. The gas residue seeps out and gets into the water table." He made a gesture of helplessness. "I didn't even know gas *had* residue. It all sounds like a money thing to me."

"Hey, Kemo," Dante called. "Didn't you hear? Everything's about money."

"Kemo, what's that over there?" Frank asked, pointing in a different direction.

"That? Oh, that's one of those cranes with the magnet to pick up the junk cars. Haven't you ever seen one on TV?"

"Yeah, but they're usually a lot bigger than that one. It looks like a kid's toy. Does it have Tonka stamped on the side?"

"That's all it takes to get the cars around. They're pretty strong."

295

Frank looked around for a while. Vic and Dante stood near Kemo, shrugging their shoulders. Kemo turned and looked at the two men.

"What's he looking for?" Kemo asked in a whisper.

Vic and Dante looked at Kemo, then at each other, and shrugged again. After a minute, Frank returned and headed for the car.

"Vic, Dante, let's get out of here."

The three men walked to the car. Kemo brought up the rear but worked his way out front to speak to Frank.

"You got an idea what you gonna do, Frank?"

"I'll let you know, Kemo. When is Snake due back?"

"Say, six, or maybe seven, Saturday night. I'm sure he'll come right here since he don't trust me."

"Thanks, Kemo. I'll talk to you soon."

They drove off quietly, but Vic could hardly contain his curiosity.

"What's the plan, Frank?"

Frank stared out the window, unable to focus on any one thing, lost in deep thought.

"Come on, Frank," Vic said. "What's going on? None of us want to do something stupid. We finally scored the big one from the bank job. All that money won't do us much good if we're in prison, you know."

"Or dead," Dante added.

Frank remained introspective.

"Can you, at least, tell me we're not going to jail for the rest of our lives over this?" Dante asked. "We get to spend all that money, don't we?"

"I need to make a phone call. Stop somewhere in town, would you? Find a pay phone for me."

"Okay, Frank. Who are you going to call?"

Silence.

"Frank?"

Chapter 52

Vic and Dante sat in the car while Frank used the pay phone.

"Yeah, it's me," Frank said.

Silence. Finally, *"Go ahead."*

"You want some payback?"

Chapter 53

Saturday night. The junkyard looked like a party for misshapen shadows. Igor chauffeured the Secret Service car toward the office, Snake lounged in the rear. Only a few yards from the building, their headlights shone on the side of the shanty structure. Between the car and the dilapidated office stood Mike Riley and two of his lieutenants, who had emerged from the car stacks and taken up position to block the approaching vehicle.

The car came to a stop about three yards from where the men stood. Igor left the lights on and the motor running. Snake, sitting in back like a visiting dignitary, rolled his window down only three-quarters of an inch. Keeping behind the protection of high tech bullet proofing—Snake talked like a man without fear.

"What the fuck is this? Who are you?" Snake demanded.

Igor didn't wait for an answer. He shifted the car to reverse and put all his weight on the pedal. The car chewed at the loose dirt but came to an abrupt stop when Igor saw two trucks pull in behind and block the exit.

"Shit!" Igor exclaimed with an accent so broken, most people couldn't recognize its origin.

Snake pushed his lips to the crack in the window and poked the barrel of his gun out next to his face. He no longer saw a need to feign ignorance about the identity of the men in front of him. This time he addressed Mike directly.

"What the hell do you want, Riley?"

"So, now you know me?"

"I know you. What do you want?"

"I just want to talk, Snake."

"You came all the way out here on a Saturday night with a couple of your boys just to talk?"

"That's right, just to talk. Why don't you step out?"

"What do you want to talk about?"

"Some guy named Donnie."

"I don't know anyone named Donnie!"

"Sure you do. You had him arrested."

"You don't know what the fuck you're talking about, Riley. I'm not a snitch."

"I beg to differ," Mike yelled, pointing one gloved finger. "I *know* you're a fucking snitch. You see, Donnie Riley is my brother."

Snake's eyes grew wide as he realized his mistake.

"Can we make a deal?" he whined. "Maybe I can make it up to you."

"What's my brother's life worth, Snake?"

"Maybe I could help your brother when he gets out."

"Help him, how?"

"I could help set him up in business or something."

"No, we're going to need something different. You see, I could have set him up in business myself, if he'd wanted me to. Try again."

"Hey, I don't think I have enough money to influence a guy like you, Mike."

"Don't try to flatter me, Snake."

"I'm not."

"I'll tell you what," Mike said, finally. "Why don't you sign the yard over to your wife, give her a fair divorce, and then get out of Pennsylvania and never come back. I'll accept that as payment."

"What the fuck are you talking about?"

300

"I want you outta here."

"I live here, Mike. Just like you."

"Not any more, Snake. One way or another, you're out."

Igor jumped into the backseat. A multitude of weapons were arranged in a compartment behind the front seat for easy access. Igor grabbed an Uzi and lowered the other window about an inch and stuck the nozzle out.

"Fuck you, assholes!" Snake cried. "Come and get us."

Mike and the two men with him jumped for cover as the bullets began to fly toward them. Hiding behind junk metal, they returned fire. Mike Riley's men in the trucks behind the limo got out and began shooting at the car, as well. The car showed no signs of distress.

The deafening noise rang out for several minutes. Snake and Igor hoped for a lucky shot. Mike and his men hoped the bullet-proofing wasn't as stable as had been advertised in the original sales pitch. Neither made any headway.

But a new noise added to the din, a noise distinctive from the others. Snake and Igor looked around, feverishly, but saw nothing. Mike and his men continued their shooting, keeping Snake and Igor pinned down.

Kemo sat in the crane and manipulated the magnet over the car. Then he turned it on. Currents of electrons created an irresistible attraction between the roof and the magnet. They made hard contact. Snake reached for the door. In his haste, or perhaps on purpose, Kemo had dropped the magnet with a little too much force and the roof bent down just a bit, jamming the doors shut. Snake and Igor were trapped.

Kemo, experienced in using the crane, lifted the car and expertly swung it around at whim—headlight beams shining into the night like spotlights on Hollywood Boulevard. Kemo's smile could be seen gleaming even in the semi-darkness. Mike and his men slowly emerged from their protective cover to watch the show. In the air, with Snake and Igor struggling, the car shook like two people parked on Lover's Lane even after Kemo stopped swinging the crane. Mike's men laughed.

"What the hell are you two doing up there?" one of them called.

"Fuck you, Riley. Let us down!"

"Is that what you two girls are doing?" another man called. "Fucking?"

"I'll fucking kill you. Let us down!"

A moment of silence seemed to make Snake even angrier. "Riley!"

Mike looked over at Kemo, still sitting in the crane seat. He yelled so his voice would carry over the engine.

"You heard the man. Let them down," Mike said, smiling.

Kemo shifted the lever to switch off the electromagnetic field generator and the car came away from the magnet with a crunching sound. All the way down, Snake and Igor screamed like two teenage girls. The car crashed to a stop at the bottom of the large hole. The noise it made as it hit the ground was loud enough to cause Mike's men to hold their hands over their ears. The wheels broke off, the doors flew open, most of the glass shattered, and the hood bounced up. The trunk, miraculously, stayed closed. It didn't matter.

Mike Riley stepped forward to look at the car that now appeared to be so small in the deep pit. At least now it belonged in the junkyard. Mike's men came up and stood behind him. They still smiled. Kemo came running over from the crane cab. He looked at them, then at Mike, and then into the hole. Mike nodded at a ladder laying against the building, and Kemo set it into the hole. Mike and Kemo both climbed down to take a closer look. The rest of the men stayed up on level ground.

"Shoot the rotten bastard, Mike," Kemo snarled.

Mike looked down and saw Snake still moving around, only now he moved like a broken worm. Blood covered him almost everywhere. His leg twisted at an angle that seemed impossible for an unbroken limb. His arms didn't seem to be functioning very well. He coughed and spat out blood. Sometimes when he squirmed just right, you could see the resemblance to his namesake.

"Fuck you," Snake blubbered.

He managed to get his head off the ground and look back into the car. Mike and Kemo followed his gaze. Igor still sat in the back seat. A twisted shard of metal from the side panel had bent around and pierced him through the largest portion of his chest. He had probably struggled for a few seconds, grasping at the life that escaped his broken body. His shirt was black with blood. The Uzi lay on the seat next to his left hand. Suddenly Snake didn't feel so tough.

"Please, Mike. Give me a break."

"Looks like you've already got one," one of Mike's men said, pointing down at Snake's leg.

"Come on, Mike. I'll pay you anything."

"Anything?" Kemo said with sarcasm.

"Anything!"

"Maybe you should have taken my offer."

"I told you I'm willing to pay, Mike. I'm not willing to leave."

"Fuck him, Mike. Just shoot the miserable bastard. He fucking hurts my sister. Let's make sure he don't do that no more."

"Fuck you, Kemo. I won't hit your sister anymore. I'll hit you!"

"Mike?" Kemo asked.

"Would you like to tell me about the two hundred G's in coke you paid to the Pittsburgh Connection?"

"That's bullshit. I don't deal with those people. They're crazy."

"Not as crazy as you. So," Mike sounded intimate, friendly. "Why don't you tell me about the accident."

"Accident?"

"The one that ended with Eddie dying."

"I never hurt Eddie. Why would I? He was a nice guy."

"Wrong answer," Mike spit, lifting his gun to point at Snake's head.

"No! Wait! All right. You're right, it was an accident. But I didn't do it. Igor did. You know how punchy he could be. Eddie moved toward him and Igor just reacted, you know?"

"Then you covered it up and buried his body out here somewhere."

"Well, I didn't want to make more enemies in one day."

"Where's he buried, Snake?"

Snake brightened, smiling. "I could show you."

Mike Riley looked up at the stars, now clearly visible. A thin cloud cover had hung around the area most of the day and gave no sign of breaking off. But now the night sky showed clear and looked beautiful. A bit of a chill sank in, but that was pretty common in Pittsburgh.

"Nah."

"Can we just shoot this asshole now?" Kemo asked.

"I'm not going to shoot him," Mike answered, turning.

"Oh, thank you, Mike. Thank you. I owe you."

Mike glanced back at the snake in the dirt. His face showed no expression. Kemo looked confused. The plan was to eliminate Snake.

"Giving him a second chance wasn't part of the plan, Mike," Kemo spat.

"Come on, Kemo."

"What are we going to do?" Kemo asked, curiously.

"We're going to clean up our mess, that's what."

Mike led Kemo out of the hole, then called to his man sitting in the bulldozer on the other side of the dirt mound.

"Hey, Kenny, fill in this awful looking hole. Kemo doesn't want his sister's new junkyard looking like this!"

"NO! NO! Mike! You can't do this! Please! Please!!!"

Mike walked to the back of the pit, ignoring the weakening screams. Kemo smiled broadly, happy for his sister. Mike could hear the driver rev the engine a couple times and then the pitch changed as he put it in gear.

From their angle, Mike and Kemo couldn't see the dozer, but when the dirt mound began to crumble, it was almost over. Snake continued to plead from the bottom of the hole. He tried to crawl out but the soft dirt and his broken bones made it impossible without help. No one alive would help Snake.

At the other end of the hole, the dirt began to fall in. It poured up over the far side of the car and fell over the roof to the side where Mike and Kemo stood. Snake's shouts became desperate sobbing.

"Oh, please, Mike. Don't do this. Please."

The dirt fell ever closer, finally falling onto Snake's feet and legs. His words turned into wild screams of mortal terror. The bulldozer motor roared with indifference, like the dark lord of the underworld ignoring the pleas of the damned saying they didn't deserve to be there.

The dozer backed off to get another bite of the rich, brown earth near the bottom of the pile that had once stood there. Mike held up one finger to the dozer driver, holding him back. The dozer stopped and the motor settled into a calm idle. Mike squatted down at the edge of the hole and ran his finger through the soft dirt.

"I don't know what you're making all that noise for, Snake. You said you'd pay anything but you didn't want to leave."

"But Mike, this isn't right. We could work something out. Maybe I could take a very long vacation or something."

"No. Even if you did honor the agreement, which I doubt, you'd come back. Your kind always does."

"But, Mike. Give me a chance," Snake pleaded.

"I already did. You wouldn't give me what I asked for, so I'm taking it. Your wife is divorced, she owns the yard, and you've left for good. Donnie will be happy and maybe Eddie can rest in peace, too." Mike ran his hand along the edge one more time and shook his head. "You know something, Snake? This is a fitting end for a guy like you who's always lived so close to the ground."

Mike stood and stuck his finger up again but this time he twirled it around. The dozer engine revved as if it could talk, saying it was ready. Snake tried screaming over it but could barely be heard. When the dozer came back toward Mike this time, it fully covered the last of the hole and Snake's screams became muffled. They continued for several minutes before becoming extinguished by the lack of oxygen.

Mike smiled, gently.

"Mike," Kemo said, weakly. "Remind me never to piss you off."

He turned to Kemo. A kind of satisfaction lit up his face—both their faces. Mike looked around the yard and turned to Kemo.

"I have another brother, Kemo. Did you know that?"

"No, I didn't."

"Yeah, he went legit. He owns a concrete business on the other side of Monroeville."

"Really?"

"Yeah. I'll send him over tomorrow. I think this place would look good with a nice, newly cemented lot. Would your sister like that?"

A knowing smile spread across Kemo's face. "I think she'd like that a lot."

About a hundred yards away, up on a hill, out of sight, Frank, Vic, and Dante sat in a car, watching the events transpire. When the weight had fallen on the limo, another weight, a symbolic weight, was lifted from the car they sat in. Poetic balance, one might call it. Frank didn't feel like a poet. He felt sick. And he still felt empty without Eddie. But the book had been closed on that part of his life and he felt a sense of satisfaction as well.

As if by coincidence, Frank smiled at the same time Kemo did.

"Rest in peace, Schultzie. You were a good friend." Frank's voice faded off. He added one more thing almost as a whisper. "Our *best* friend."

Vic and Dante responded in unison.

"Amen."

"Let's get the hell out of here," Frank softly moaned.

Chapter 54

He passed the Florida border without incident, a line no one could see—a border that created a separation from one state to the other. To the human eye, nothing changed. Frank drove without hesitation, he carried no drugs and there was no other reason to be concerned, other than the fact he travelled a few miles per hour *over* the speed limit.

The warm Florida air burst in through his open window, flapping his shirt sleeve. Just before the first of the Jacksonville exits on I-95 South, the highway crossed over the Nassau River. Early morning traffic was thin and Frank managed to pull the car over and walk out on the bridge. For a moment he stood and watched the lazy water trickle by. He took his little book of contacts and considered his actions for only a moment. Then he tossed the book into the water and watched it sink out of sight, swaying side to side.

Back in the car, he realized his lifelong dream awaited him up ahead and urgency drove his foot. Still he managed to keep it around the speed limit. He cranked up the radio and sang along, not caring a bit if he was on key.

The girls had grown by leaps and bounds over the last few years. He hardly knew them anymore. The separation from Connie hurt. He couldn't tell what she wanted anymore—although he hoped to God it was him. She'd liked the money and travelling, but even so, Frank felt a chill—a distance—in the air most of the time when he'd visited.

But now, that was all over. The time had come to turn up the heat and warm them both. But it was also time to clean up his act and become a businessman—go legit. The kind of life he'd led was best left to younger, more reckless men. Frank just wanted to go home.

Daydreaming brought him to Jupiter much quicker than he'd realized. A sigh of relief escaped his lips as the familiar streets presented themselves in front of him. The briny smell of salt air mixed with a variety of fruit trees fragranced the breezes. Palms swayed, waving at him, welcoming him, coaxing him to hurry. She waited for him.

A frightening idea struck Frank as hard as a fist. Could he be a good father? He turned his car south, heading toward the motel, and came to a decision. He didn't know how to be a good one. His own father had denied him affection. He hadn't spent the time nurturing his girls, or giving them guidance and insight. And he hadn't shared the stories of their heritage, to carry on the family origins.

A father's job took a lot of time and Frank looked forward to the challenge—to being a part of their lives. The girls would enjoy hearing about where their family came from and stories about his own mother and father, their grandparents. Although Frank's father came to America at a young age, Frank knew some stories of the land of their origins. He would pass them on to his children.

But could he be a *father* now? It takes more than stories to be a father. A lot of the teachings of a father should begin when they're babies. Could he make up for lost time? Would they even accept him back in their lives?

He turned into the now familiar courtyard of the motel and quickly scanned the parking area. Several cars sat in front of different bungalows. Frank thought it was a good sign that more cars were there. Business, a business he should be owner of by now, was picking up. Frank smiled.

He got out of the car and his motor ticked as the heat came off it. The sound reminded him of the night he lost his best friend. The pangs of pain returned and he struggled to bury them deeper. This would be a day to rejoice, a day to celebrate. He refused to allow sad tidings to mar this moment.

Connie's car, in the next slot, had a thin coat of dust from not being used for a day or two. Again Frank smiled. His wife was such a home body, a wonderful woman. From now on, he vowed, life would be great—for all of them. He banged on the door.

The door opened and Tina, the eldest and well into her teens, almost a young lady, looked up into his face. She took in a deep breath. Her arms came away from the door and she brought them out front to grab him. He admired her shorter, more mature haircut.

"Daddy!"

Frank hugged the girl, feeling nothing but joy as tears fell from his eyes. Suddenly two more faces joined them, greeting him, all hugging at the same time, tackling him like football players. Janice and Sara giggled as they pushed their father. Frank fell over, laughing, hugging. From a distance he heard Connie's voice calling to them.

"What's wrong, girls?"

When she made it to the front and saw them all a-kilter on the couch, she sobbed, spasms wracking her chest and shoulders. She leaned against the door jam. Frank managed to push the girls off him and stood facing his lovely wife. She regained some control and just looked into his eyes.

"What's wrong, honey?"

"I thought…"

Frank touched her arm, but waited for her to finish her sentence.

"When we talked before, I got the feeling you were leaving. For good, as in—not ever coming back."

"Why would you think such a thing?"

"You breezed in, handed me a bunch of money to set me up for the rest of my life, and disappeared. What should I think?"

"I told you. I only had to pay Mike Riley back what I owed him."

"It took a while, Frank. And if you were coming back, *you* would be here to take care of the rest of my life. That's still what we need. And then you were gone so quickly, like you were afraid."

"Afraid? Me? Afraid of what?" Frank gently scoffed.

"Afraid that if you stayed too long you wouldn't be able to get away."

"I think that may be true," he answered, pulling her close.

"You think?"

"I'm afraid it might be."

"Be afraid," she joked. "Be *very* afraid." And she held him tighter, like she would never let him go.

Chapter 55

"Hey, Dante. What brings you here?" Dick Stinner said, shock raising his voice a pitch or two. Dick stepped inside the building Snake had used as an office for his junkyard.

"I came to see Kemo."

"Ah."

"And you," Dante said in a lower voice.

"Me?"

"Yeah. I figured you'd be around here sooner or later."

"It's not exactly a secret that Snake and I were doing business. Have been for quite a while now."

"I know. There is something, though, that *has* been kept a secret. Isn't there?"

"What do you mean?"

"Not many people know you were the one who set Eddie up that night in the warehouse.

"What the fuck are you talking about?"

"You went into his bar a lot."

"Most of us guys at the mill went in there. Or we went to Frank's joint. Hell, some nights we did both. So what of it?"

"I worked in the mill, too, Dick. Remember? I have friends there. You were heard."

"Heard saying what?"

"Making the arrangements for Eddie's meet."

"Well, you don't know the whole story. You probably just heard it wrong. It's true I told Eddie about the deal. But I was just trying to help him. He needed money and I had connections. All he had to do was get the stuff. He said he could. I swear I didn't know it would go down the way it did."

"Yeah, you keep talking, shithead. You forget—we already know he met with Snake Barron in that warehouse."

"N-No way. I-I knew a guy who wanted to buy some coke. He had the money. T-That's the truth, D-Dante."

"And by some huge coincidence Snake paid off a two-hundred thousand dollar debt two weeks later? How the hell do you explain that, dickhead?"

"Uh. He, uh, it was that deal where we took the semi filled with Moly."

"I remember hearing about that scheme around the mill. You almost had a good idea there, Dick. The problem is, when Snake paid off his debt, the mill had already been closed."

"Oh yeah. Sorry. I forgot. I meant the other semi."

"The *other* semi?"

"Yeah, you remember. The semi filled with new television sets. Snake and I hijacked it. You must have read about it in the paper."

"As a matter of fact, I did."

Dick relaxed a bit. He sat down in the heavy metal desk chair and breathed a sigh of relief. The first hint of a cocky smile twitched on Dick's mouth. At Dante's next words, any remnants of a smile fell completely off his face.

"It happened six months after Eddie disappeared," Dante accused.

"Hey, Dante. I—!"

"Don't even bother, Dick. I've already spoken with Kemo, here. I know about a lot of your dealings with Snake."

Dick looked over at Kemo. Dirty daggers shot from his eyes, but Kemo remained unscathed. As they sat there, a new look washed over Dick's face. He wasn't scared. He wasn't friendly. Malevolence twisted him into an ugly man with bitter highlights and angry tones.

"So, you like to talk, Kemo? Maybe I should help you out with that."

"What do you mean?" Kemo asked without fear.

"I could cut an extra mouth into your neck so you can talk to more than one person at the same time." Dick smiled deviously, cruelly.

"You know, Eddie was a friend. You hurt him. Then you want to hurt another friend—Frank. You even asked me to help you. How low do you think I am?"

"Right now I'd say just about dirt level."

"You hurt my friends, so I hurt you," Kemo stated.

"What the hell did you want to hurt Frank for, anyway?" Dante asked.

Dick turned back toward Dante. "After Frank fucked me over at the mill, I wanted to get him back. He took my stuff and didn't pay me for it. That's like stealing. Whatever happened to honor among thieves?"

"The money we got for that load Frank 'stole' from you? We were making that much every week, dumbass. That is, until *you* came along and screwed it up."

"Why the fuck didn't Frank come and kill Snake himself?"

Dante sat back and stared. "Snake is dead? When did *that* happen?"

"Two nights ago. Don't tell me you didn't know. Some guys were here to meet Snake. There was a gunfight. Snake got killed."

"And where's his little henchman?"

Suddenly Dick realized he was babbling, spilling all kinds of information. "I don't know."

"You were here?" Dante asked.

"I-I, well…no. But I heard."

"Heard what? Gun shots? All the way in town?"

"Fine!" Dick's temper flared. "I was here. I saw the whole thing. I can identify who did it, how they did it, and *where* they did it."

"You know who did it?"

"I saw his face. I heard his name when Snake spoke to him."

"So why not go to the police?"

Dick sat quietly, fuming over having been twisted into admitting so much.

"You didn't talk to the cops because you were into something with him."

"Come on, Dante. You're no angel. You know how the business works."

"True, I'm no angel. But women worship me," Dante teased.

"Damn," Dick said almost under his breath. "If Frank had only killed Snake, everything would have been perfect."

"Excuse me?" Dante asked. "You wanted to set Frank up for murder? Was that your petty plan?

Dick didn't say anything.

"Why did you want Snake dead, anyway?" Kemo asked. "He made you lots of money."

"Yeah, he did."

"So?" Dante insisted.

"Well, he liked to slap his wife around. Sometimes it was more than a slap."

"What business is that of yours?"

"I like her. Pretty, when she wasn't all bruised up. I met with her a couple times when Snake wasn't home, you know?"

"You've been messing around with my sister?" Kemo stepped forward, menacingly, but Dante held him back with a raised hand.

"Your sister?" Dick seemed genuinely shocked.

"Snake Barron married my sister. Didn't you know?"

"I—guess I didn't."

"So, you were fucking Kemo's sister," Dante said, shaking his head. "You are such a low life."

"No! It wasn't like that."

"You weren't fucking her?"

"No. Well...I mean...it's not like that."

"Oh? What is it like, then?" Dante continued his cross examination.

"You know. I went there and we..." His voice trailed off as he searched for the right words. "I treated her like a lady."

"Then you fucked her."

"She was willing."

Kemo, speechless, stepped forward again, looking like he might just explode all over Dick.

"Any reason I should hold Kemo back from ripping your head clean off?" Dante asked.

"Look, she deserved better than that jerk."

"Well, I'll go along with that. But what makes you think you're any better?"

"Hey! I treated her nice."

"So why did you continue to work with Snake?"

"I needed the money. Frank sure wasn't going to help me out."

"What the hell did you need so much money for, dickhead?" Kemo asked through clenched teeth.

"I can answer that, Kemo," Dante said. "Dick has a little problem."

316

"He does?"

"I do?"

"Dick can't stay away from the track and the tables." Then he turned to Dick. "You have a little gambling problem. Don't you, Dicky boy?"

"My sister doesn't like gambling," Kemo stated.

"How would you know?" Dick asked Dante, ignoring Kemo.

"I have an acquaintance in Vegas. You've lost big time out there, haven't you?"

"You went to Vegas? You went with Snake? He never took me," Kemo interjected.

"That's why you needed the Moly," Dante continued. "Isn't it? You needed money to support your habit."

"Fuck you."

"You know what's really fucked up, Dick?" Dante asked.

"What, smart ass?"

"I didn't catch on before, but the night you took all those cans…"

"What about it?"

"It was the night after you lost big time at Frank's tables. I remember you made such a ruckus. But I didn't make the connection at the time."

"I lost big *all* the time at Frank's tables. He probably had them rigged."

"Is that what you tell them in Vegas?"

"I win sometimes in Vegas."

"You lost out there, too," Dante said in short words, almost losing his temper. He took a couple deep breaths. "So you needed something else. Our deal with the Moly must have seemed heaven sent."

"And you guys screwed it up for me."

317

"*We* did? As I recall, asshole, *you* were the one who tried to carry out too many cans."

"Yeah, and now I'm going to carry you out," Dick said, reaching inside his jacket.

The gun came out of its holster and swung toward Dante. The barrel drew a bead straight at Dante's head. Dante didn't move. He'd faced off with guns before, this was no different. But he thought Dick might be just *antsy* enough to 'accidentally' pull the trigger if Dante moved around too much.

Dante stared him down. The air grew thick. Dante leaned closer, getting near the gun barrel. He said nothing but his lips parted as if he might whisper something. When his head was just about to touch the barrel, he stopped. Suddenly he backed off and spoke as if the gun didn't exist.

"I want to tell you a story about something I learned while I was in Viet Nam." Dante leaned back in his chair, relaxed. "It's not a very long story, really. But did you know I was taken captive by the North Vietnamese and held in a P.O.W. camp? I saw men tortured in ways you'd never begin to imagine. Most of the techniques I wouldn't have the stomach to apply to someone, myself. But some were less…evil. Like, one time I saw them tie a young man down to a chair with wires attached. And when they switched on the juice, he danced like it was disco night, all over again.

"After a few seconds of jolt, he became very pliable and cooperative. I learned a lot about electricity from the North Vietnamese. I know you only need a regular wall socket to get enough juice. I know how much it'll take to kill you. I know how much I can give you and you'll still recover." Dante leaned forward. He got real close, very near Dick's gun. He spoke softer. "I know just how much to give you so you'll never have children.

318

"But let me tell you what I learned to be most important. I got in the habit of checking a chair before I sat in it. I'd take a quick look to see if there were any wires attached to it."

Dick didn't have a clue what Dante was talking about. He looked down slowly. There, at the bottom of the front, right leg, he saw it. An electrical wire—stripped on the end and attached with black electrical tape. His head jolted up as he realized, all too late, that he was sitting on a trap. Suddenly Dick began to twitch, spasmodically. He danced in the chair like a man who just won the lottery. The gun fell from his hand.

Dante stood up and walked around to stand near the twitching man. He leaned his butt against the desktop edge and crossed his ankles. After a moment, he nodded at Kemo. The Indian flipped a switch on the wall and the twitching man went limp. Dante leaned forward and lifted Dick's head by his chin. He looked into the bulging eyes and tried to see what was going on with the asshole inside. Then he leaned back.

Dick didn't see Dante nod at Kemo again. Kemo flipped the switch and the pain returned to Dick's body. He made one solid spasm almost out of the chair and his teeth clenched in a death grimace. His eyes rolled back in his head and drool leaked out of the corner of his mouth. The sound he made resembled a small motor boat motor or a dirt bike engine.

Dante knew the agony Dick was suffering. He took sympathy and nodded back at Kemo. The pain stopped. Dante leaned back against the desk and crossed his arms in front of his chest. Kemo looked disappointed, like he would have preferred to leave the switch on and go have lunch.

"You see," Dante continued, "it's just a matter of running wires to the chair and plugging them in to a socket with a switch. Lots of places have switched plugs. Did you know that, Dick?"

319

The man didn't seem very interested in anything at that moment. His head wobbled around like a newborn who couldn't quite hold it up yet. And even though the electricity had been turned off for the moment, several parts of Dick still twitched out of control. His fingers looked like they were playing a piano concerto. One knee jittered like a man bouncing a baby. And his eyes quivered.

"I'd like to tell you some other stories from Viet Nam," Dante began again. "Would you like to hear them?"

Dick groaned something unintelligible.

"I didn't quite catch that," Dante said, leaning forward and lifting the man's head again.

Dick's muffled response wasn't even clear enough to hazard a guess. Nevertheless Dante continued, "I'll take that as a yes."

"You see, the North Vietnamese are quite clever when it comes to causing pain. This I know from firsthand experience. One of the more interesting tortures involved a pair of pliers. A man stood in the compound, naked, tied to a tree. The leader approached him and grabbed one of the prisoner's testicles with those pliers. He squeezed until it popped like he'd squished a grape. The man would scream in agony. I heard one of those soft pops, almost sounded like a tomato bursting when you hurl it at a wall."

Dante turned slightly and lifted something off the desk. When he turned back, Dick's eyes were as huge as paper plates. In Dante's hands rested a twenty-inch pair of channel-lock pliers.

"Remember that night, Dick? I told you if you ever crossed us again, what I'd do to you?" Dante slapped the jaws shut a couple times. It produced the desired effect. Kemo smiled broadly—very happy.

"Would you like to hear that sound, Dick?" Dante spoke like a young boy with a Playboy collection he wanted to show a friend. "The sound of bursting tomatoes? It's the most amazing thing."

Kemo shook his head enthusiastically. Still unable to control his spasms, Dick barely shook his head, no. His mouth seemed glued shut. He looked like he was trying to cross his legs to protect himself, but the knee just wouldn't go up high enough to get over. He really looked pissed off, but he was in no condition to offer up any resistance.

Dante knew how incapacitating that felt. A man grew up learning to fix things and solve problems. He even learned to walk away from some fights for the sake of integrity. But being completely out of control took away his manhood. It took away his ability to choose. And Dante knew about losing your manhood, too.

Again Dante took pity, remembering those times when his own manhood had been threatened. By this time Dick was little more than a pile of flesh, but he would recover. Dante thought about how durable the human body could be. In Nam he'd seen men endure a great deal of pain and live to tell about it. To describe these ordeals, one would think no human could survive. And yet, many did. Many P.O.W.s came home and, to the best of Dante's knowledge, lived generally normal lives. So this piece of shit would make it as well.

Dante reached over onto the desk where Dick's gun had fallen out of his hand during the first electrical jolt. It was a nice little pea shooter. Dante removed the clip, leaving one in the pipe. He threw the clip in one pocket and stuffed the gun into another.

"Kemo, let's help this poor bastard up onto his feet. Shall we?"

Kemo and Dante managed to get him up, although he didn't look too steady. He bore most of his weight himself, while Dante and Kemo helped him maintain his balance. They walked out of the little office trailer and into the junk yard where Snake Barron was buried. The sun aggravated Dick's sore eyes and he did his best to shield them with a hand.

The two bigger men led the simpering Dick through the tall stacks, taking several turns. Dick felt lost. His dazed mind couldn't comprehend direction and they'd taken too many twists to remember. He'd lost track. Finally, they came upon a hole.

Dick looked at it in sheer terror, struggling against the other two, trying to back away. He obviously remembered what happened with Snake and another hole in the junk yard. Kemo held him fast while Dante stepped around in front and faced him. Dick struggled to look around Dante as if the hole itself menaced. It's smaller size and almost vertical walls gave it a grave-like appearance.

"Hey, Dick," Dante said. "It's okay. There's no reason to be scared anymore. You can relax now."

Dick managed to moan something. Then Dante stood to the side and kicked the man in the ass so hard he fell forward, losing his balance. The hole was at least two feet past Dick's arm reach to the top. Actually, when he and Kemo dug it, Dante measured ten feet from top to bottom.

"Hey, Dick," Dante called. Kemo stood right behind him with his arms crossed and somehow looked even more like an American Indian. "I'm going to give you something we never had in Nam. A choice." Dante tossed Dick's gun to the ground at the bottom of the hole.

Dick looked at it without understanding. Then he looked back up at Dante, quizzically.

"I know what you're thinking. You could shoot us and escape. Well, forget it. Even if you *could* shoot us, you wouldn't be able to get out of this hole by yourself. And no one is likely to happen by for at least a week. That's when Mike Riley's brother is coming to pour concrete over the entire place. It should look beautiful, don't you think?"

Fear furrowed Dick's brow.

"Oh, didn't you know? Mike's brother is in the concrete business. He came by and said he'd be back, but he's very busy right now and it'll be about a week."

Dick bent down and hefted the gun.

"And one more thing. About shooting us? You probably can't aim well with all that electricity running through your body. Plus, you only have one bullet. You can't get both of us." Dante turned his head and glanced back at Kemo, who stood smiling. "Sorry."

Dick managed an unintelligible scream. He floundered around the bottom of the hole, trying to get out, trying to move. The electricity still misfiring through his body wouldn't allow his muscles to work properly.

"Listen, asshole," Dante said. "Maybe you killed Eddie and maybe you didn't. I don't know. Snake, or even Igor, may have pulled that trigger." Dante still spoke in a calm voice, "But you led him to that warehouse. You set up a deal between Snake and Eddie and you probably *knew* what Snake had planned. And then you were going to whack me and Vic and Frank out of some stupid quest for revenge? For something *you* did wrong? But, hey, do you know what the worst part of all this is? You did it all to support your fucking gambling habit. It wasn't even for a worthy cause. A man's life was taken so you could piss away another shitload of money. You make me sick, man."

In a fit of rage and fear, Dick brought the gun up and pointed it at Dante. Dante stayed completely still, not even blinking. He stood at the edge of the hole and just waved a finger back and forth at him.

"Anh-anh-anh. You only have one, remember? Since you'll probably never get back out of this hole, you might want to save it for a last resort." Dante used his finger, pointing at his own temple like a gun, to indicate what he meant. "Of course, a frightened little man—like yourself—might want to go ahead and use it right away. Save yourself all that needless suffering."

Dick looked up at the two men, speechless.

"It's okay, Dick. We'll wait."

Finally, Dick found his voice. "I'll kill you for this!"

"You couldn't kill an insect if it ran under your shoe, ass-wipe."

"I would have killed you all. I wanted to kill Frank. You and that other asshole would have followed."

"It's good to have aspirations, Dick. Everybody should want to accomplish things in their lives. But you should have had loftier goals."

A moment of silence passed between them.

"Look, Dante," Dick said, calming a little. "Maybe we could work something out, make some kind of deal."

"What the hell have *you* got to offer? You can't even keep up with your losses at the track. What are you going to give me, your debts?"

"I have connections, Dante. I can get things. Just tell me what you want."

"If you could really get anything, you wouldn't have ended up in so much trouble with your gambling. And you certainly wouldn't be in *this* position," Dante pointed at the hole.

"Sure, you're right. But I can get other things. You remember that blonde actress in that movie you liked so much? How would you like to bang her? I know her. I could introduce you. A big, strapping guy like you could bed her easily."

"You don't fucking know her, asshole."

"Yeah, I do. Really. There was this 'high-roller' party at one of the Vegas casinos last spring. I managed to get in. I lost my shirt, but I got her number."

"You lost your shirt? I think you lost your fucking mind."

"Just tell me what you want, Dante."

"Okay, I'll tell you *exactly* what I want. Can you give me Eddie's life back?"

"Come on, man. Surely there's something I can do for you. Something besides *that*."

"Well, I like money. But then again, you've managed to piss all yours away. That's why your home was foreclosed. Isn't it?"

"You think you know it all, don't you?" Dick huffed. "Well, you know what? Fuck you, man. Just *fuck* you, royally!" He danced and jumped as he shouted, pointing haphazardly with the gun. He waved it around in the air like he'd forgotten it was still in his hand.

Dante squatted down and examined the wall of the hole with his hand. He looked back down at Dick standing helplessly at the bottom. "No," he said softly, danger evident in his tightly coiled words. "I think it's more like, 'fuck *you*'." Dante took in a deep breath and stood. "You know, Dick," he looked around as he spoke, "after this place is paved it'll be worth a hell of a lot more money. Just imagine, you'll be part of something with some real value. Probably for the first and last time in your miserable life."

During Dante's rhetoric, Kemo moved off without being noticed. Suddenly the motor of the dozer sprang noisily to life. All the color left Dick's face instantly. He knew the sound and what it meant.

"Please, Dante."

"I heard that Snake begged at the end, too. What a piece of shit. You assholes wouldn't have lasted two fucking minutes in Nam."

The dirt began falling in on the man and he whimpered like a baby. "Dante?"

"Hey, Dick. Is there anybody you'd like me to notify?"

325

"Yeah, the police, asshole."

Dante brushed off his comment with a simple gesture. "Just thought I'd ask. You know, in case there were any family members who would like to celebrate your passing."

"Fuck you, asshole."

"Damn, I'm getting fucked so much here. I hope I don't get pregnant."

"Fucking jerk."

"Will you still respect me in the morning?" Dante swished his hand in a humorous gesture. Dick didn't find it amusing.

"I want you to do me a last favor, Dick," Dante called over the dozer motor.

"And what's that?"

"I want you to hold your hands up like in one of those old western movies." Dante raised his arms straight up to demonstrate.

By now the dirt had almost completely filled in the bottom of the hole. Although he struggled to get on top of it, Dick's electricity-filled muscles and twitching nerves just wouldn't let him get an edge. In another minute, the hole was nearly filled in. He hadn't raised his hands.

Barely two feet from the top, Kemo shut the dozer down and walked around by Dante. They both looked down into what was left of the hole. Dick had managed to get over a little of the dirt. His head remained above and he'd kept his hands barely visible, although the dirt came up to his chin. He squirmed, but the dark, rich earth around him would not give. Small noises escaped him as he struggled to breathe against the pressure around his chest.

With some difficulty he managed to get his head turned enough to eye Dante. Standing at the edge of the hole, Dante looked like the picture of serenity. He didn't smile, but his face relaxed and his eyes shone. Of course, Dick still had the gun, but Dante didn't concern himself with that.

"I bet you're wondering," Dante droned, "how long it'll take you to die after we fill in the rest of the hole. This close to the surface, you'll probably still be able to breathe. So you'll have to die of starvation.

"That could take ten days, or even two weeks. The concrete will be here before that. They'll pour that shit right over you without even knowing you're there. Then again," Dante said, hesitantly. "Let's not forget how the human body works. Thirst will overtake you long before hunger. Three days, you'll probably last. Three days and then you'll be gone for good."

Even though the heavy dirt restricted his movements, Dante saw Dick shudder—presumably with fear. Dante looked at Kemo—who stood smiling as if this were a day at the beach—and said, "Three days."

"So," Dante said, turning his attention back to the man in the hole. "You want to tell me why you set Eddie up?"

"I wanted to hurt Frank," Dick squeaked.

"Oh, I assure you, you did. But why did you have to hurt Eddie?"

"That piece of shit wouldn't get rid of some stuff for me one time when I asked him."

"Eddie ran an honest business."

"Eddie had people in and out all the time. He could have made the right connection."

"You talked to the wrong guy, Dick. You should have been talking to Frank."

Dick laughed maniacally. Dante figured the ordeal was over. He pointed straight up and looked at Kemo. Then he swirled his finger in a small circle. The gesture looked oddly like the one Mike Riley had made when he wanted Kenny to finish burying Snake and Igor. Dick's eyes rolled over toward the dozer.

"Let's put him out of our misery, shall we, Kemo?"

327

"We shall." Kemo smiled as he walked over and put his foot up on the dozer's track.

Before Kemo could get fully into the seat, a shot rang out. Kemo ran back over to see if Dante was still okay. But the Italian stood at the edge of the hole with his mouth agape. He didn't move.

Kemo looked into the hole and saw the remains of what used to be Dick Stinner. Blood from his head rolled through the dirt, settling into a puddle near Dick's left shoulder. The silence felt heavy.

"Jeez, Dante. I thought you said you weren't going to kill him," Kemo hissed.

"I didn't."

"Okay, sure. But you said we were just going to get him to leave town."

"That's right. All I wanted to do was scare him. I didn't think he had the guts to actually pull the trigger."

The two men stood motionless, watching the dirt fill with blood. Dante shrugged his shoulders and looked at Kemo. The Indian smiled and turned toward Dante.

"You going to tell Frank it's over?" Kemo asked out of genuine concern.

"Frank and Vic already think it's over. There's no need to bother them with anything further. They've both started new lives."

"Really?"

"Yeah. Vic is going back to Vegas. He met a really nice girl out there. I didn't know you could find a genuine nice girl in Vegas. I think she may have busted his cherry."

"His what?" Kemo asked.

"Cherry, you know. She took his virginity. In all the years I've known him, I've never seen him get with a girl."

"Never?"

"Not that I recall. Anyway, he has his money from our last job and he's going to invest in a small cabaret out there—small acts, laid back place for the locals to hang. He said he might even call it *Schultzie's*."

"That sounds nice. Maybe, when I go to Vegas, I'll visit him."

Dante chuckled. "I bet he'd like that."

"What about Frank?" Kemo inquired further. "Where did *he* go?"

"Ah yes. Frank went back to Florida to be with his wife and three girls."

"That's really nice. He's gonna be happy there."

"I certainly hope so. I just can't imagine Frank Mattich settling down. Not completely."

"Maybe he'll surprise you."

"It won't be the first time Frank managed to surprise me," Dante said as they walked back toward the trailer. "I like to think I managed to surprise him once or twice as well." He slapped Kemo on the back and pulled him close to his side. "Now don't forget to fill in that hole," he advised.

"I won't," Kemo laughed. "But hey, what about you, Dante? Haven't you got any plans?"

Dante thought for a moment. "Maybe I'll go buy a bag of coke. I hear there's a new waitress at the diner in Duquesne."

Chapter 56

Tommy Garcia and his friend, Denny Glick, two Florida State University students, arrived on Andros Island at Kamalame Cay to celebrate summer break. Tommy arranged for them to get to the Bahamas for a little treasure hunt. Just a ride on a fishing boat for a few hours and they stepped onto the sands of a new world, or more correctly, a very old world. The soft, white crystals collected on their shoes as they ran ashore. The music captured their attention almost immediately and they ended up dancing the afternoon away with a couple local girls.

Fortunately, Tommy had also made arrangements for some lodgings. But all too soon morning burst into color, and sunshine burned into every crevice. No shadow survived its ruthlessness. The boys rose from a restless-but-short night as the sun seared through thin eye lid walls. Anticipation had stolen their real reason for lying down. Despite the lack of sleep, they were eager to begin the hunt before them. Tommy gathered their scuba gear and Denny struggled with his pants.

A small boat, willing to carry them out for a pittance, chugged through the water in search of the coordinates Tommy had provided. The captain, a stout man with a pock-marked face, stared at them. He didn't look like he cared two shits about a couple kids looking for a good time hunting treasure. Denny was sure he only cared about whether or not they came across with the money when they were supposed to. The two deck hands sailing with the captain laughed heartily at the college boys and their white skin.

330

"What you doin' out here, mon?" one asked with an accent Denny found humorous.

"We want to do some diving."

"What you be diving for?"

The boys looked at each other, quickly. Then they turned toward the deck hand.

"S-Souvenirs," Tommy stammered.

"Ah," he finished, turning toward his friend. "Dey be looking to bring home some rocks, mon." Both men began to laugh raucously.

"Maybe dey be lookin' for treasure, mon."

"Perhaps dere be some garbage down dere, for dem to take home."

"Yah, mon. Very valuable."

"Hey, I just came out from de crapper. Maybe dey like to take home sometin' *real* valuable."

Tommy and Denny did their best to ignore the two Bahamian comedians.

"Maybe de 'little white boys' have a treasure map." Much more laughter.

"That will lead them to our garbage, mon!"

"Or my crap, mon!" They could barely speak anymore as laughter bubbled out every time their mouths opened.

They arrived at the spot about forty minutes later. Denny thought it was the longest forty minutes of his life. The captain came on deck and told them where they were. He ordered a dinghy set afloat for them. Inside it contained a diver's buoy and a canteen of fresh water. He spoke to them briefly before casting them off.

"This is de spot, young gentlemen. Weebee back dis way in about tree hours. You bee ready." Then he pointed at the spot in the water. "Right heah."

331

"Not over there?" Tommy pointed a few yards away. His sarcasm went unnoticed by the big Bahamian.

"Tree hours."

"This is what we're paying him for?" Denny said.

"Don't worry about it," Tommy reassured.

"Bullshit." Then he spoke directly to the captain. "What if we don't want to pay you?"

"Den I still leave you heah. But you get no dinghy."

All three Bahamians laughed loudly.

"Ha!" one of the sailors exclaimed, pointing at Tommy's crotch. "Maybe dey already have no dinghy."

"Maybe dats what dey came looking for," the other one added, falling away to laughter once again.

Tommy shot them a condescending look. After handing the money to the captain, the boys got in the dinghy and the larger boat sped away, rocking them drastically for a few moments. They hung on for dear life. After the motored boat pulled far enough away, the smaller craft settled into something calmer, almost serene. A couple fishing poles would have made the picture complete.

But they had another purpose. The boys made last minute adjustments to their masks and fell backwards into the water. Each one splashed through the surface and began to breathe through the mouthpiece. The forced air made them a little dizzy at first. As soon as it cleared they descended into the clear blue-green waters of the Atlantic. Brightly colored fish swam in small schools next to them, passing close by—nonchalantly. The slightly cooler temperatures of the water gave them a chill, but it soon settled into an excitement for whatever mysteries, and hopefully, treasures lay below.

Sunlight pierced deep and blue prevailed all around. Nevertheless, each turned on their flashlight and saw nothing worth investigating. But determination drove them to swim out, searching

332

for their ultimate goal. After almost an hour with no results, Denny saw the shadow of wreckage a few yards away, near the reef. He signaled Tommy.

Both swam to the object. Submerged in about a hundred feet of water and lodged under a reef ledge, sat a boat—a twenty-five or thirty foot cabin cruiser. It had been there for a number of years. Barnacles clung to the hull, all the paint and markings had peeled away, and assorted fish and crabs wandered in and out of the broken windows. A meatless skeleton sat at the helm, smiling morbidly back at them, a hand raised in dark greeting. The boys made their way back to the hatch so they could enter the craft.

Something shiny caught Denny's eye, something on the other side of the ship's body. As Tommy wormed his way inside, Denny swam over the top toward whatever had caught his eye. What he found made his heart skip a beat. He signaled Tommy but the motion couldn't be seen. Tommy didn't come.

Denny stared at the three objects floating just above the bottom. They looked like large, helium balloons. Concrete anchors tethered three men but the gasses in their bloated bodies struggled to reach the surface. The men, probably there for a couple weeks, stared back with fixed eyes, searching, even at this late stage, for salvation. One wore a suit but the other two had on guard uniforms. Denny couldn't tell anything from the corroded badges. The middle one wore a huge, demented smile. His gold tooth shone in the light breaking through from the surface.

www.ingramcontent.com/pod-product-compliance
Lightning Source LLC
Chambersburg PA
CBHW062025170626
46813CB00001B/292

* 9 7 8 0 9 8 4 6 8 2 7 3 7 *